DEAD BEFOR

Rafferty & Llewellyn British Mystery Series

Geraldine Evans

Dedication

This paperback novel is dedicated to Saundra Wright, the lovely lady who is rapidly becoming one of my most enthusiastic readers.

Blurb

Freshly-promoted British Detective Joe Rafferty has 4 ambition; To prove to his new boss that he has the ability to lead a murder investigation.

But, right from the start, things go wrong. To say the case of 'The Faceless Lady' is a challenge is putting it mildly. Not only is Rafferty's main suspect for the murder a man who brings out his prejudices to the full. He can't even rely on his family for support—as usual, they bring their own challenges for a hard-pressed detective.

And he discovers the adage that trouble comes in threes is all too true. Even his new partner is a high-moral-ground kind of guy; not the best match for Rafferty. Or his family.

With his boss and the media scrutinising his every move, Rafferty is under pressure. And as the days pass the pressure mounts. He's in danger of the wheels coming off of his inquiry and proving his boss right about his competence. He desperately needs a break in the case.

So when his cousin seems to hold the key to the crime, Rafferty clutches at it. But lingering doubts remain—can he really believe the cousin who's proved himself an idiot in the past?

If he's wrong, he not only lets a murderer escape justice, but he will get a black mark against his career that his boss will make sure follows him forever.

Reviews

'This often-comic tale sharpens the appetite for more.'
PUBLISHERS WEEKLY

'Evans' humour seriously added to my enjoyment of her book. This, her first, as well as the rest in the series, are well written with standout central characters and clever plots.' AUNT AGATHA'S BOOKSHOP, ANN ARBOUR, USA

'Classic crime. I was definitely hooked into this story and needed to know who had committed the crime and why. It was very well written and flowed nicely from scene to scene.' ALEXIS LENO, AUTHOR OF SHIFTING FATE, A FANTASY NOVEL

'Don't miss this gem! Geraldine Evans is a great writer, because of the distinctive voice of her characters. The book was well-thought-out, and the best part was the laughter spewing out of me, because of this author's great sense of humour.' Reader Reviewer

'Great series! Thoroughly enjoyed.' Reader Review

'Evans has a winner in the Rafferty & Llewellyn series.' Reader Review

'Great storyline.' Reader Review

'Loved the twist in the tale.' Reader Review

'A police procedural with hidden depths.' Reader Review

'Likeable pair of detectives.' Reader Review

'Intriguing. Well-written.' Reader Review

Dead Before Morning

Rafferty & Llewellyn British Mystery Series

Geraldine Evans

Copyright Page
Dead Before Morning
Geraldine Evans

Published by Solo Books
This paperback edition published 2019
ISBN: 978-1-9997216-0-2

©Copyright 1993 (hardback), 2011 (digital), and 2019
(paperback)

Discover other books by Geraldine Evans at:
geraldineevansbooks.com

Cover art by: covershotscreations/Nicole

Chapter One

This novel is written in British English and uses this language version's spelling and slang. You will find a list of these at the end of this book for any with which you are unfamiliar.

'Is it yourself?'

Detective Inspector Joseph Aloysius Rafferty winced as his mother's voice threatened to pierce his eardrum. And, although briefly tempted to plead not guilty, he had to agree that yes, it was himself.

Surely, he demanded plaintively of his reflection in the hall mirror, a hangover, a murder, and his mother all in one morning were more than any man should be expected to cope with? Especially at six thirty and after less than four hours sleep.

This was his first murder case as Senior Investigating Officer, and he was keen to do well. Of course the sadistic fates immediately put the kibosh on that by ensuring he had celebrated his promotion not wisely, but too well the night before. To say he was feeling fragile was an understatement. The last thing he needed was his Ma putting on her best wheedling voice, and he hurried to get his excuses in before she got into her stride. 'I can't stop, Ma. Sergeant Llewellyn will be picking me up any minute.'

'I won't keep you then, son, but I didn't know who else to turn to, and what with the wedding and all...'

Rafferty frowned, and stared at his rapidly cooling mug of tea. News of the murder had already taken its toll on his hung-over wits, but the word "wedding" on his Ma's tongue was even more worrying, and he struggled to get his brain into gear. 'What wedding?'

'I know Jack's only a distant cousin,' she remarked briskly, 'but surely you haven't forgotten that he's over from Dublin to marry my niece, Deirdre?'

That wedding. Rafferty scowled. How could he have forgotten that Jailhouse Jack, the world's most incompetent criminal, was preparing to plight his troth and pass his genes on to the next generation? What a wonderful addition to a policeman's close family the bridegroom would be. Thank God the happy couple would be going back to Ireland straight after the wedding, and surely even Jack could stay out of trouble for the few weeks he'd be—

'He's in a spot of bother, Joseph.' After shattering his hopes, his mother didn't pause for either of them to catch their breath but went on to explain that his troublesome cousin was being held at the Harcombe nick on suspicion of lifting a lorry load of whisky. 'I know what you're going to say,' she continued, before he could get a word in, 'but this time I'm convinced he didn't do it.'

That would be a first, Rafferty thought, thankful that between them, the Irish Sea, and a three-times removed cousinship, usually kept Jack from embarrassing him.

'It would be a shame if he got put away right before the wedding. Can you go and see him and sort it out, son? I wouldn't ask, only I've had Deirdre here half the night, crying her eyes out. She's scared she'll have to cancel the wedding.'

Rafferty scowled. Better for her – and him – if she did. Jack was already causing aggravation, so God knew what trouble he'd cause if they managed to make it to the altar. As if he didn't have enough on his plate with his first murder investigation as SIO without being expected to sort out Jack's little problem. Especially as one of his old enemies was in charge at Harcombe, and as soon as he set foot in that nick and revealed his mission of mercy, the shit would hit the fan.

His relatives were the limit, especially as some of them felt that if they must have a copper in the family, he might at least have the decency to be a bent one. Rafferty consoled himself with the thought that he hadn't made a firm date with the looming fates. Jack could cool his heels for a bit, and then maybe Deirdre would have come to her senses.

After all, he now remembered, the wedding was still two weeks off. He had plenty of time.

His Ma must have read his mind, with that uncanny ability of mothers everywhere, because she commented tartly, 'It's not everyone that avoids matrimony like you, Joseph.'

He ground his teeth, frustrated that she should still be harping on that. Unfortunately, the hoped-for remarriage of her braw boy was ever close to his mother's heart. Rafferty broke in quickly before she got into her stride. 'I haven't the time for that, Ma,' he told her firmly.

He glanced out of the window of his Essex flat and shivered. The day was bleak, the mist off the North Sea was thick, and he could barely see the shoreline. For once he was pleased to see his Sergeant drive onto the forecourt.

But the pleasure didn't last long. About as long as it took for Llewellyn to move the car closer, and Rafferty was able to see his new sergeant's thinly-handsome face. Llewellyn consulted his watch, and then gazed up at Rafferty's window, with a suffering-bravely-borne expression.

Rafferty scowled again.

Llewellyn had transferred from Gwynedd in Wales, and Superintendent Bradley, after interviewing him, seemed to think Llewellyn was the ideal foil for him. He'd only been in Essex a short while, but already he was getting on his nerves. All right, he was nifty with the computer, but his pernickety personality invited put downs.

Added to Llewellyn, the fact that the new Super had decided he didn't like Rafferty's face made him reluctant to get out of bed in the morning. Rafferty didn't know why their new super had taken a dislike to him, but after a month of putting up with Bradley's snide comments every time he had to report to him, the feeling was mutual. It was fortunate that his promotion had come through before Bradley was confirmed in post, because it was evident, that if Bradley had his way, he'd be bumped down a rank, not up one.

Rafferty sighed. It was turning into one of those days, and he hadn't even left the flat yet.

For once he managed to interrupt his Ma in full flow, and said firmly, 'I really must be off. Llewellyn's here.'

He paused, wishing he didn't have to tell her, but he'd never hear the end of it if she had to find out from the papers.

Taking a deep breath, he said quickly, 'There's been a murder.'

He allowed sufficient time for her to give an echo of the "M" word, before continuing. 'Yes. It's rather a nasty one. A young girl.'

According to Bill Beard, the desk sergeant, the girl had been brutally battered, her face left in such a state that it would have looked more at home on a butcher's slab. 'She was found at that private psychiatric hospital here in Elmhurst and—'

His Ma's swift intake of breath echoed down the line. 'It'll be one of them dangerous cyclepaths escaped. They're always doing it. The people in charge of these places should be locked up. You stay well away, son,' she advised firmly. 'Let that superintendent sort it out.'

Rafferty gave a hollow laugh. 'I *am* a policeman, Ma. And I'll be in charge of this one. They promoted me, remember?'

Still smarting from his superior sergeant's last correction of his own imperfect use of the English language, Rafferty said, 'And it's psychopath, not cyclepath. Not that he necessarily is one,' he added hastily. 'Just because the girl was found in a psychiatric hospital, doesn't mean one of the patients did it, you know.'

'Doesn't mean to say they didn't, either,' she retorted. She tutted worriedly. 'Sly as a fox, some of them. You watch your step son.'

He intended to. 'I've got to go.' No doubt the rest of the team would already be there working hard and calling him rude names in his absence. 'About Jack, Ma, stop worrying. I'll see to it.'

He knew he'd never hear the end of that, either, if he didn't. But at least she'd dropped the matchmaking mama role. For the moment. He lifted the mug to his lips.

'Thanks son.' Pride edged some of the worry out of her voice as she added, 'I'll tell Deirdre that "My son, The Police

Inspector's got it in hand, and Jack's as good as free".'

Rafferty practically choked on his tea. He wished he shared his Ma's confidence that springing the prospective bridegroom would be as easy as catching him usually was.

'Well, I won't make you late for your murder. Look after yourself, Joseph, and don't take any nonsense from any of them high and mighty doctors at that hospital. Arrest the lot of them if you have to.'

He almost laughed out loud at this blasphemy from the normally doctor-venerating Kitty Rafferty. It was only his throbbing head that stopped him. Instead, he dryly commented, 'I'll bear it in mind, Ma. Good-bye.'

***

The constable beckoned the car forward, and as the heavy hospital gates thudded together behind them, Llewellyn's dark eyes took on a mystic light as he remarked ominously, 'There'll be trouble over this one. Mark my words.' Having delivered this cheering prognostication, he said no more.

Rafferty, determined that the Welshman's black prophecy wouldn't undermine his confidence, did his best to ignore him.

He was helped in this by his first sight of the house. He came from a long line of builders and house renovators, and its classical Georgian elegance — which the well-tended grounds framed so perfectly — brought Rafferty a few precious moments of delight in a day unlikely to contain many pleasures.

The handsome, seven-bay house was built of pale Caen stone, a popular import in such a stone-impoverished part of the country. The projecting central section was crowned by a graceful pediment, and the ground floor, raised above the semi-basement, was reached by stone steps. Slender pillars flanked the canopied front door and they were flanked in turn by single windows with two more on either side of the recessed sections of the house. Perfection.

Just then, the sun came out from behind the early morning cloud, and he stared, as all thirteen of the large sash windows seemed to wink at him, like all-seeing eyes, as though mocking his ability to discover what they had witnessed in the night; a sight undoubtedly shared by the secretive, half-closed dormer eyes of the attic floor.

The optical illusion fanned the flames of the superstition that Llewellyn had already successfully kindled.

Rafferty switched his gaze determinedly ahead as his Welsh prophet of doom drew up behind the earlier arrivals.

'Dr Dally's here,' Llewellyn remarked unnecessarily with a sidelong glance at Rafferty. 'He must be nearly finished by now.'

'We all know quick and speedy doesn't always win the race, Sergeant,' Rafferty retorted, stung by the dig. 'Not that Sam Dally's either when it comes to letting us have some results.'

Pausing only to put on their protective gear and give their names to young PC Smales, Rafferty reflected that it was a pity the girl had chosen a mental hospital in which to get herself murdered; on his first serious case since his promotion too. Now he wondered anxiously if the spiteful fates were about to enjoy some fun and games at his expense. It wouldn't be the first time.

As they walked round the shrouding screen, Dr Dally raised a shaggy grey eyebrow teasingly. 'Late again, Rafferty?'

Dally's jocular greeting merely earned another scowl. But as Rafferty got his first view of the corpse, he had to swallow hard, again regretting the previous night's celebratory alcohol intake at his promotion. The girl was lying on her back and someone had certainly made mincemeat of her. What might once have been a pretty face was now a soggy mess – her teeth were gone, her eyes were gone, her nose was gone – all smashed to a bloody pulp.

It looked as if someone had taken a sledge-hammer to her. 'The press will have a field day with this one,' he remarked grimly.

Considering it was April, the previous night had been quite balmy, yet, surely, he was only imagining the sickly scent of corruption? Behind him, Llewellyn remarked in funereal tones, *"'So will we all decay. The past is the only dead thing that smells sweet.'"*

Rafferty gave him a jaundiced look. 'Thank you, Dylan Thomas.'

'Edward Thomas, actually, sir,' Llewellyn corrected, and launched into a mini lecture, apparently believing that it was his duty to lighten the darkness of his boss's ignorance. 'Killed in action in World War One. Then there's R.S. Thomas, the Welsh vicar. He—'

'All right, all right,' Rafferty broke in, irritated as usual by Llewellyn's display of erudition, sure he did it out of some deep, mischievous desire to get under his skin. 'A murder scene is hardly the place to launch into a history lesson.'

His puce complexion regained some of its usually fresh colour as he put Llewellyn in his place, but it drained away again as he gazed at the dead girl.

Poor bitch, he thought. Whoever, whatever she was, she surely hadn't deserved such an end.

Curiously, the naked body didn't have a mark on it. Weird. And as his eyes travelled over the slim cadaver, he wondered at the unfathomable ways of women. Why would a natural blonde dye her hair black?

Without looking at him, Rafferty tersely told Llewellyn, 'The first priority is going to be to find out who she was. Tell Fraser I want her prints processed urgently.' He hoped to God they were on file. If they weren't, it could be a nightmare trying to identify her. He raised his gaze to Dally, and asked, 'What can you tell me, Sam?'

'Little enough, Rafferty, little enough.' Sam's plump body rocked back on its heels, and behind his spectacles, his eyes lit up with relish as he watched Rafferty's face.

'You look a bit green, my boy.' He fumbled beneath his coveralls, and with difficulty, extracted a small silver flask.

'Have a medicinal nip. Doctor's orders,' he added firmly as Rafferty hesitated.

Forgetting his scruples, and ignoring Llewellyn's disapproval, Rafferty reached gratefully for his medicine and took a swig. 'Should be on prescription.' He grinned as the alcohol hit the spot. 'Irish?'

Sam Dally snorted. 'It's only the best that the Highlands can offer. I can see it's wasted on you.'

He took the flask back and had a quick nip himself. 'Ah. That's better. Just what the doctor ordered.'

Rafferty brightened, pleased to know he had company in his suffering. Especially when that company was in the rotund shape of the tonic-toting Dally. 'Heavy night?'

Sam nodded. 'Doctors' do at *The George*,' he explained. 'Annual event. Wouldn't miss it. Our erstwhile chairman's wife, Lady Evelyn Melville-Briggs organises it, so it couldn't fail to go like clockwork. Shame she didn't seem to enjoy it. Not surprising she was so quiet, of course. Her old man was in a towering rage when they arrived.' He snorted. 'Some hoo-ha about the door-man. I didn't stop to listen to it.'

He put the flask back in his pocket and became briskly professional. 'Been dead at least seven hours. Rigor mortis has started to set in around the head and neck. The blow to the back of the head is probably what killed her.'

Rafferty raised his eyebrows. He could have come to that conclusion for himself. Even with the body lying on its back, he could see the skull was badly caved in, making a mess of bone and brain. Pensively, he asked, 'Could a woman have done it, do you think?'

Sam nodded. 'Wouldn't need as much strength as you'd think; only stealth to creep up on her, and then determination to keep whacking, like Lizzie Borden.'

Rafferty felt queasy. Carefully avoiding another sight of the corpse, he raised his gaze, hoping to distract himself.

At the edge of the trees, he caught sight of a well-dressed man, pacing with barely contained impatience. He nodded carefully in his direction. 'Who's that?'

Sam followed the direction of Rafferty's gaze, and, in an echo of Llewellyn, he remarked, 'That's Trouble, Rafferty. Trouble with a capital T.'

Dally rubbed his hands together with relish as he glanced sideways at Rafferty. 'That's the owner. Consultant Psychiatrist

Dr Anthony Melville-Briggs. But you'll find plain "Sir" will do. Husband to the Lady Evelyn etc, etc. I wouldn't like to be in your shoes when he finds out that not only a lowly inspector's in charge of the case, but he's inexperienced, to boot.' He gave Rafferty a sly look. 'Perhaps you should listen to your Mammy and get married again. Old Tony certainly shows what marriage can do for a man.'

Rafferty's lip curled. Sam Dally, compassionate Doctor of Medicine, could always be relied upon to hit a man below the belt.

One marriage had been enough; his relief that Angie's death had brought an end to their mutual unhappiness still caused him guilt. And despite his mother's continued attempts to get him married off for a second time, Rafferty resisted.

Still, he mused, at least it gave her less time for her other little hobby, and unlike that, her matchmaking didn't carry with it the risk of a jail sentence for the pair of them. 'Got any more unwanted advice?'

Sam shook his head. 'Why cast more pearls before swine, laddie?' he asked sweetly. He glanced again at Melville-Briggs, and a mischievous smile lit up his face as he set about removing the restorative effects of the whisky. 'I was at medical school with him, and he barely had a bean before he married Lady Evelyn. You could see he was determined to go places even in those days.' Sam Dally took off his glasses and gave them a brisk polish before continuing in a mock throwaway manner,

which didn't fool Rafferty for a second.

'Well in with the Chief Constable, so I understand. Me, I don't mix in such exalted circles.'

The last tattered fragments of Rafferty's good-humour vanished. As his brain throbbed against his skull, he studied the Chief Constable's best friend, even as Sam Dally studied *him*.

Dr. Melville-Briggs had that look of sleek self-satisfaction that only a man with the good fortune to marry money acquires. He was in his early fifties, Rafferty guessed, but had kept himself in shape. With white hair swept back, he could have been taken for a Shakespearean actor awaiting the plaudits of the crowd.

Rafferty hoped he didn't intend to indulge in any histrionics this morning, but after what Sam had said, he wasn't optimistic.

Dr. Melville-Briggs's cheeks wore an unlovely hectic flush probably caused by a combination of temper and shock, and Rafferty came to the depressing conclusion that the doctor was taking the crime as some kind of personal affront. But then he was rich and successful, and probably imagined his select establishment would, by its very exclusivity, be shielded from the sordid world outside his gates.

He reflected that it must have come as an unpleasant surprise to find that his little kingdom wasn't quite as inviolate as he had imagined.

Hoping he wasn't about to reap the whirlwind of this disappointment, Rafferty saluted Sam, took off his protectives once he'd got beyond the tape, and pulled his suit jacket roughly straight. He took a deep breath before he headed towards the other doctor as he prepared to give Melville-Briggs his second shock of the day.

Chapter Two

With Llewellyn dogging his heels, Rafferty made his way over to Melville-Briggs and introduced himself. Bloodshot blue eyes surveyed him without enthusiasm.

Rafferty remembered what Sam Dally had said about the doctors' do the previous night and realised that here was another casualty of the morning-after-the-night-before syndrome. Melville-Briggs had probably anticipated a day off after the night's excesses. So had Rafferty. He was just about to commiserate, when the doctor forestalled him.

'The constable on the gate said the CID was on their way.' A faint frown marred the smooth perfection of Melville-Briggs's brow. 'I take it the Chief Inspector will be along shortly?'

Rafferty recalled what else Dally had said. That Melville-Briggs was a friend of the Chief Constable, and he knew he had to step warily.

Although the doctor's voice was as fruity as a greengrocer's stall and polished to an almost glossy perfection, stress had brought out a hint of his Birmingham origin. And Rafferty guessed that the Brummie-boy-made-good would demand the best as if he had been born to it, rather than marrying it.

His shoulders slumped as he realised just why Bradley had allocated the case to him.

Today wasn't a good day to be a working-class cop called Rafferty, with a superintendent intent on using him as his whipping boy. Talk about heads you lose, and tails you lose as well.

Expecting fireworks, Rafferty took a deep breath before he explained. 'I'm afraid the Chief Inspector won't be coming, Sir. We're a bit short-staffed at the moment.'

Melville-Briggs gave a confident little laugh. 'I think you'll find you're mistaken about that, Rafferty.' A professional smile briefly dazzled. 'Obviously the station doesn't realise who I am. The Chief Constable's a personal friend of mine, and once I've telephoned him, he'll be glad to oblige me.'

Presumably satisfied that Rafferty now realised his star quality, Melville-Briggs patted him on the back in a consoling manner as he dismissed his hard-won skills. 'Don't take it personally, Rafferty. But this is a very select establishment. A certain diplomacy is called for if my patients aren't to be upset. I'm sure you understand?'

He understood all right. What it didn't need, Melville-Briggs was implying, was some heavy-footed oaf like himself. But it was very tactfully put.

He hoped the doctor would be as sensitive to his feelings in a second or two.

'There's been no mistake, Sir. There really is no one else available.' Taking another deep breathe, he added, 'And the Chief Constable's on holiday. Trekking in the Himalayas, I believe.'

'Trekking in the Himalayas—?' Melville-Briggs's lips pursed, but they opened sufficiently to murmur, 'I see,' in clipped tones, as he gave Rafferty's off-the-rack suit a swift, assessing glance.

Rafferty got the impression that neither his shiny new rank, nor his shiny new suit, cut much ice with the doctor. And as he glanced down, he admitted ruefully, that the breakfast egg that had left its previously unnoticed visiting card on his tie was unlikely to inspire confidence. He sighed faintly—he wouldn't mind so much about his stained tie letting him down, but he'd only eaten a couple of mouthfuls before his stomach started to protest.

The doctor concealed his disappointment well; Rafferty had to give him that. Melville-Briggs fingered his jaw thoughtfully and smiled again; a smile of singular charm that immediately put Rafferty on his guard.

'Now. How can I put this? It's a trifle delicate, and I wouldn't want you to think me insensitive.' He studied Rafferty's face intently.

Rafferty felt like a lab-rat under this scrutiny. Not to mention having a sense of déjà vu as to where this conversation was going. Melville-Briggs had evidently assessed his character much as he had assessed his suit. He seemed happy with his conclusions.

'It is important that this distressing matter is cleared up as quickly as possible. The publicity...'

He winced as if in genuine pain, before he put his hand inside his beautifully cut pearl-grey suit, and murmured, 'Perhaps a donation to the Police Benevolent Fund will ease things along a little, hmm?'

Although the doctor's attempted bribery was discreet, Rafferty was under no illusion that bribery was what it amounted to.

What did the man expect him to do? Fit up a likely criminal with the murder? Or did he imagine the crime could be swept under the carpet like last week's dust and conveniently forgotten?

Rafferty gave a grim little smile and wished he could forget the doctor's high-placed friend. 'The police are always grateful for such generosity, Sir, but perhaps it would be best if you sent a cheque direct to the Fund? We don't want anyone getting the wrong idea, do we?'

The doctor withdrew his hand from his pocket. 'Of course not,' he agreed smoothly. 'Excellent idea. I can't imagine why I didn't think of it.'

Balked of an early solution to the crime, Melville-Briggs's voice lost a little of its silken charm. 'You know, Rafferty, I've been thinking, and I'm convinced that there was an ulterior motive for this crime. Someone wants to ruin my reputation and that of my hospital.'

'You've evidence of this?'

''No evidence as such,' he admitted without a blush. 'But a man in my position makes enemies. Why else would anyone dump a corpse here? It's obvious when you think about it.'

Rafferty blinked. It wasn't obvious to him. 'Was there any particular reason for you to think that, Sir?' he asked woodenly. Anxious not to cock-up this early in the investigation, he found a spurt of energy to curse the malignant fates that had landed him with the case.

'Ask yourself, who has most to lose by this murder? I have, of course,' he answered his own rhetorical question. 'This crime was intended to cause me maximum loss, inconvenience and embarrassment.'

Rafferty was tempted to remark that the victim had suffered a greater loss. Fortunately, his pounding head made him reluctant to clash swords, so he managed to resist the temptation. 'I'll do my best to minimise your inconvenience, Sir,' he promised dryly. 'Now, have you any idea who the dead girl might be?'

Melville-Briggs shook his head. 'None.'

'Are any of your staff missing, for instance?'

'No. I've already checked. And the current patients are all accounted for, too.' He frowned. 'It's rather a mystery who she could be, as visitors can't gain access to the grounds without signing in at the lodge—fire regulations, you know.'

Rafferty had hoped the girl's identity would be easily established, but now that hope vanished, he became as brisk as his hangover allowed. 'We'll need an official statement from everyone here, Sir, and as you're anxious for us to get this crime speedily solved, perhaps I can ask you to start the ball rolling?'

'Certainly. You'll find my statement's very straightforward. If you'd like to take this down, Sergeant?'

Llewellyn whipped out his notebook.

'Between the hours of 8.00 p.m. and 2.00 a.m. on 11/12 April, I was at a medical dinner at *The George* in Hamborne. No doubt the door-man will remember us arriving.'

Bemused, Rafferty could only stare at him. Who did he think he was? God or visiting royalty?

'I was accompanied by my wife, Lady Evelyn, and I didn't leave the hotel during the entire time.' He directed his next remark to Llewellyn, who, in his smart-suited, shiny-shoed way, seemed to meet with Melville-Briggs' approval.

'If you will get that typed up, Sergeant, I'll sign it.'

'Certainly, Sir,' Llewellyn agreed with an air of brisk efficiency that Rafferty recognised. His new sergeant was nothing if not efficient. But did he have to be so obviously competent, today of all days?

Rafferty restrained the involuntary lip curl, and said, 'We'll need to see your wife, of course. Just a formality,' he added with an attempt at diplomacy as the doctor frowned. 'Will it be convenient if we call at your home at, say, 5.00 o'clock this afternoon?'

'I'm afraid you'll have to make your own arrangements with my wife, Rafferty. I shall be in the flat here this evening.'

He fixed Rafferty with a firm eye. 'I trust you'll make every effort to catch the perpetrator. If the case lingers on it could be—unpleasant.'

He didn't specify for whom—he didn't need to as the question that followed reminded Rafferty where any retribution would fall.

'When's the Chief Constable due back, by the way?'

'Not for another fortnight, Sir.' Thank God. Before his sleeping brain knew what was happening, he heard a voice that sounded remarkably like his own, say, 'But I'm sure we'll have this case wrapped up before he returns from leave.'

'I'm glad to hear it, Rafferty.'

Rafferty's stomach growled its dismay. That was the sort of thing that happened when you'd apparently left your brain snoring and came out without waking it up. As soon as the words were out of his mouth he regretted them, but naturally the cavalry of common-sense arrived too late to do any good. With a sinking feeling, he hoped he'd be able to live up to his incautious boast.

There was the faintest suggestion of respect in the doctor's eyes though, and it restored a little of Rafferty's shaky confidence. Earlier he'd noticed a wooden door set in the wall a few yards from the body. It was locked, but its nearness to the corpse piqued his curiosity. 'Just as a matter on interest, Sir, who would have keys to that side door in the perimeter wall?'

Melville-Briggs appeared ill-at-ease at this simple question, and it was a few seconds before he admitted, 'Apart from myself, no-one.'

Rafferty guessed the doctor realised that should his alibi not check out, possession of that key raised him to the unenviable status of chief suspect. But worrying about how that admission would affect the investigation would have to wait till tomorrow. Today, it was as much as he could do to go through the motions. If he just managed to get through this first day he'd make sure he felt half-human tomorrow, then he could recommence the investigation in earnest.

'The staff all use the main gate. I insist upon them clocking in and out every day.'

Rafferty, still smarting from the doctor's cavalier dismissal of his detecting abilities, thought him the type who would be sure to extract his pound of flesh from the wage-slaves.

'All the keys are kept at the lodge,' the doctor went on, 'and the staff must sign for them. Then, at the end of the shift, they hand them back to the lodge-porter. The key to the side-gate isn't on the general rings.'

Once again, there was that faint unease. Rafferty made no comment. He would allow Melville-Briggs's well-polished skin to sweat a little. It would do him good. If anyone else did have a key to that door the gateman would be able to tell them.

'As I said, Sir, I'll need to speak to the staff and patients as well. Could a room be made available?'

'I'll speak to my secretary,' Melville-Briggs agreed briefly. 'I'm sure we'll be able to come up with something suitable.' He fixed Rafferty with a determined eye, and added, 'though I must insist that my patients are disturbed as little as possible. Frankly, I fail to see any reason to question them at all.'

Rafferty thought it likely that Melville-Briggs's concern was less for his highly-strung patients, and more for the possible loss of revenue from his patients' wealthy and easily-alarmed relatives.

'I'm afraid it is necessary, sir.' His voice was firm as he added, 'This was a particularly brutal murder, and before I charge anyone, I need to be sure we have a water-tight case.

The patients may have seen something that would put the identity of the murderer beyond doubt. Perhaps one of them—' Rafferty broke off abruptly as he realised the suggestion that one of the doctor's precious patients might have done the deed was unlikely to go down well.

Melville-Briggs' small eyes narrowed, as though he had followed Rafferty's thought processes and didn't like their conclusion.

His voice was sharp as he said, 'Assuming the girl died sometime last night, they'd all have been in bed and sedated, with nurses in constant attendance.' The doctor eyed him coldly. 'Anyway, the patients sleep in the bedroom block and their windows overlook the rose-garden, not the gate.'

Rafferty rallied. 'Even so, we still need to take their statements and eliminate them from our enquiries, Sir. They may have seen someone suspicious hanging about earlier yesterday.'

No matter how rough he felt, Rafferty knew he needed to cover as many angles as possible today. Especially as Superintendent Bradley would be his usual critical self when he made his report at the end of the day. Rafferty intended to give him as little ammunition as possible.

Melville-Briggs gave in ungraciously. 'Oh, very well.'

'We'll be very discreet, Sir,' Rafferty soothed.

After a second glance at Rafferty's suit and loud pink tie with its contrasting splodge of yellow yolk, Melville-Briggs didn't look convinced, and, after a pained glance at Rafferty's unruly auburn hair, he closed his eyes briefly. 'Now, if you'll excuse me, I must get back to my patients.'

Rafferty wasn't sure if he'd imagined the, *'While I've still got some left,'* tagged on to the end of the doctor's reply. With a curt nod, Melville-Briggs made for the house.

Rafferty sighed, and scratched absently at the egg stain on his tie.

He was beginning to understand why Bradley had handed the case to him. It was a poisoned chalice. Bradley expected him to fail. Such investigations inevitably brought unpleasant complications. And Melville-Briggs was just the first of these complications. Just because, so far, he'd been reasonably accommodating, didn't mean it would last.

'Dally was right,' he remarked grimly to Llewellyn, as he watched the doctor's retreating back. He even walked rich. 'Gentleman Jim's going to be trouble. Did you notice the charm beginning to wear thin?'

'He just needs a little careful handling, Sir,' remarked Llewellyn quietly. 'As the Bible says, "*A soft answer turneth away wrath,*"' adding, as Rafferty stared at him, momentarily speechless, 'Proverbs 15, verse—'

'Yes, yes, all right!' Rafferty snapped, not altogether surprised at the discovery that Llewellyn had the number of the proverb off pat. 'I had my fill of bible-thumpers at school without you starting.

'Anyway,' he added flatly, 'I'm here to solve a murder, not massage Melville-Briggs's inflated ego.' But he was a friend of the Chief Constable he reminded himself with a grimace.

Llewellyn had a point, though he didn't intend to give his sergeant the satisfaction of knowing his remark had touched a raw spot. 'So, you catch more flies with honey than you do with vinegar,' he said sardonically. 'I'll bear it in mind.'

But he was conscious that he'd have to do more than that. It went against the grain, but he knew if he didn't want him to start a loud and angry buzzing, Melville Briggs was one ugly bluebottle he would be wise to coat in as much honey as he could muster.

***

Dr Dally had finished his examination, and the body was ready to be taken to the mortuary. Rafferty stood and watched as the shrouded corpse was placed in the back of the mortuary van. So lost was he in silent, contemplation, that he jumped, as from behind him, there came a cackle of maniacal laughter.

He turned, and found himself eyeball to eyeball with a man in pyjamas, presumably one of Dr. Melville-Briggs's precious patients. The man's pupils were wildly dilated, and his curly dark hair and long beard gave him the air of being straight out of the Bible's Old Testament.

His first words did nothing to contradict this impression. 'So the whore has gone, then?'

Rafferty, all senses suddenly alert, found himself nodding. 'Did you know her?'

The idiocy of his question was apparent as soon as the words escaped. Melville-Briggs had probably been correct when he'd said the patients would have been quiet and sedated at the time of the murder. And if that was so, how could this one even guess at her identity, especially as her features had been rendered unrecognisable, even by her own mother?

But surprisingly, the man didn't seem to think his question in any way odd. 'Of course I knew her. Doesn't every man recognise that foul, naked wanton, the Whore of Babylon?'

As the mortuary vehicle came around the far side of the house and continued up the drive, he raised a wiry, pyjama-clad arm and pointed. 'Jezebel has gone now. The devil will find a place for her in hell. So shall end all fornicators.' He lowered his condemning arm and began to pound his bunched-up fist into the palm of his other hand.

Rafferty noticed that the man's fingers were stained with a red substance that looked like blood. With a little chill, he wondered whether Melville-Briggs might have been wrong.

Was it possible this poor, sick creature had somehow evaded the nursing staff and gained entrance to the grounds?

His confidence immediately plummeted, and he again regretted his proud boast. Because having an outsider commit the murder would be awful enough, from the doctor's point of view, but to have one of his patients proved the guilty party would be very bad for business. Very bad indeed. He would probably prefer the case not to be solved at all.

If one of the patients was the murderer, it was evident he would have a fight on his hands. And Rafferty suspected that Melville-Briggs was the kind of man who would fight dirty.

Chapter Three

Llewellyn broke into his reverie. 'I had a word with Constable Hanks. Seems the body was found this morning by one of the gate porters.' He consulted his notes. 'Name of Gilbert. Apparently, he was just coming on duty by the side gate.'

'He had a key to that gate, did he?' Llewellyn nodded. 'You're sure, man?'

Llewellyn looked down his long nose at Rafferty's sharp tone and cheap suit, and replied coolly, 'Quite sure, sir. Gilbert's at the gate-lodge now should you wish to question him about it yourself.'

Too late, Rafferty recalled that his superior Welsh sergeant had been educated at a fee-paying private establishment and had then gone on to Cambridge University to read English, Classics and Philosophy. His notebook certainly testified that he held a degree in the correct use of the English language, which was more that Rafferty did. He had left school at sixteen after an indifferent education, which probably explained why his sergeant looked hacked off that he should question its accuracy.

After swallowing a bubble of amusement, Rafferty found himself wondering again why Llewellyn had decided to join the police. He hadn't even come in on the special entry scheme for graduates that offered accelerated promotion. That got his grudging respect.

But, like so many university types whom he encountered on the force, Rafferty considered the Welshman had little "nose" for things, and he thought smugly of his own extremely sensitive nasal member. 'So,' he remarked finally, when the atmosphere had reached the Arctic shade of cool. 'The chief suspect now has company. Pity.'

Dr Melville-Briggs was either a liar or a fool who didn't know what went on in his own hospital. Or did he expect his orders to be obeyed without question? Surely, Rafferty asked himself, a psychiatrist, of all people, knew that rules were made to be broken? If Gilbert, the gate-porter, had a key to the side gate it was likely that others had too.

Ignoring his head that thumped with every step, Rafferty made off briskly towards the gate lodge, determined he'd walk efficiently if he couldn't manage the rest just yet. Hampered by his still bruised dignity, Llewellyn followed more slowly.

***

Gilbert, the gate-porter, was a sharp-featured little man, who gave the appearance of having a grudge against the world. He sat, nursing a pint mug of tea, looking very sorry for himself. The mug was inscribed with the legend "work is a four-letter word," and Rafferty got the impression that it stated a large part of Gilbert's limited philosophy of life.

'Yes,' the porter admitted, with a show of reluctance when Rafferty began to question him, 'I found the body. Gruesome it was.' His eyes swivelled sideways at Rafferty and he whined self-pityingly, 'By rights somebody should take me 'ome. Ain't right to expect a man to carry on working after seeing such a sight.' He took a gulp of his tea. 'Ain't right,' he repeated glumly, as though he felt he was being unfairly deprived of a legitimate day off.

'I'm sure Dr. Melville-Briggs will let you go just as soon as you've answered a few questions.' Rafferty's lack of belief in Dr. Melville-Briggs's compassion for his fellow-man was evidently shared by Gilbert, whose face became even glummer.

'Him?' He snorted. 'Not likely. There's more chance of me getting the sack than sympathy from him.'

Despite the aura of gloom that clung to him, Rafferty got the distinct impression that Gilbert was enjoying himself in a perverse way. He was star for the day. Tonight he would probably hold court in the local pub and expect to be bought free drinks all night as he told and re-told his grisly tale.

Rafferty thought Gilbert and Llewellyn should get on well together; they both seemed to get pleasure from looking on the black side. Though the clearly Cockney Gilbert's murder of the English language would surely hinder any deeper acquaintance for Llewellyn, that grammatical Puritan.

'Have you any idea who the victim might be, Mr. Gilbert?'

Gilbert shook his head. Although Melville-Briggs had told him no-one from the hospital was missing, Rafferty wanted to double check. 'Are there any girls with long dark hair amongst the staff or patients?'

'There's one or two, but they're away at the seaside. Lucky so-and-so's.' His face resembled a depressed bloodhound. 'Wish I was.'

Rafferty gave him a few seconds to wallow, then he raised the depression stakes. 'I believe you have a key to the side gate. Is that right?'

Gilbert looked sharply at him. 'Who told you that?'

'Never mind that. Do you, or don't you?'

Gilbert looked shifty, as though he was about to deny it. But he must have realised the futility of such a denial, because he nodded once, briefly. Then, with the air of one who – if he had to take the road to hell – wanted to make sure that it was on the coach during the staff outing, added, 'Mind, I'm not the only one. I like to oblige people when I can. Do 'em good turns like.'

Gilbert was a most unlikely do-gooder, thought Rafferty, eyeing him without enthusiasm. Fiddling the tea-money and stocking his freezer from the hospital kitchens would be more his line. Scared that possession of the key would incriminate him, was Gilbert confessing to the lesser sin of providing half the staff of the hospital with illicit keys?

Rafferty groaned softly, but he needed to be clear on the point. If so, it immediately threw the list of suspects wide open. 'I understood from Dr. Melville-Briggs that no-one but him had a key to that gate and that all the staff had to use the main entrance.'

Gilbert snorted again. It seemed to be his favourite mode of expression. 'Supposed to. Only this morning I was a bit late, like, and thought I'd sneak in. Jack would 'ave covered for me and clocked me in as usual.' He sighed heavily. 'Now I s'pose when his lordship finds out, I'll be for the 'igh-jump.' His voice rose indignantly. What did she want to go and get herself murdered 'ere for? On the very morning I was late, too. It ain't fair.'

The wretched victim seemed to have discommoded everybody. Rafferty probed a little deeper. 'Jack's the night lodge porter?'

Gilbert nodded again.

'Did he see anything?'

Gilbert grinned with sour amusement. 'Old Jack? No. Didn't know nothin' about it till I told 'im. Likes to get 'is 'ead down of a night, does Jack. No chance of that on the day shift, worse luck.'

Rafferty rubbed his gritty eyes. He could do with a bit of shut-eye himself. He blinked and forced himself to concentrate. 'How many of the staff have keys to that side gate?'

Gilbert's grin faded. 'Most of em,' he replied gloomily. 'I suppose you'll want a list?'

Rafferty agreed that it would be helpful.

With several mutterings and mumblings, Gilbert provided it. As he wrote, he continued his explanation. 'I go through the pantomime of locking the rest of the keys up in this cupboard 'ere.' He indicated the metal key cupboard that hung on the wall.

'But it's only to keep old smarmy-pants happy, 'cos they all keep the keys to the side gate. They usually 'ang around the staffroom for drinks before they start, and I bring the general keys over in bulk then, before ol' Tony shows up. I do the same in reverse before they leave, so they can use the side gate without having the bother of dropping the general keys in at the lodge. I'd let 'em keep the keys if it was up to me, less trouble all round, but you can never tell when 'is lordship might decide to check up. He can be right sneaky like that.'

Rafferty wondered whether Melville-Briggs would be pleased to discover the reluctant admiration behind the complaint of his gate-porter.

Suspecting he knew the answer to that, Rafferty began to feel less hungover as he put his next question. 'But I thought they had to sign in and out as well as hand over the keys?'

Gilbert's eyes slid away, and Rafferty gave a faint nod as he was proved right. So Gilbert supplied a certain skill as a forger along with his other services. Enterprising bloke. 'Never mind. Go on,' he prompted.

Gilbert seemed relieved that Rafferty was obliging enough to gloss over his little difficulty, and now he became confiding. 'Like I said, most of us come and go as we please through the side gate. It's handier like, for the bus.'

After a pause for another gulp of tea, Gilbert took the opportunity to get on to a safe topic. 'Lady Evelyn's okay, but him…'

Apparently, aware his monologue was about to descend involuntarily to more airing of grievances, Gilbert scowled and curtailed that conversation, presumably unwilling to risk its finding its way back to the doctor.

Instead, he launched into a brief rundown of the current situation. 'This whole place is hers, you know, even if he acts like Lord of the Manor, he owns none of it.'

This comment seemed to give Gilbert great satisfaction, for he rubbed his hands together and sniggered. 'Anyhow, her and her brother were the last of the line and the name would have died out, see?' He sniggered again. 'Though if you saw her precious son, you'd think she might have saved herself the trouble.' His hand waved graphically. 'I can't see her gettin' an 'eir out of 'im!'

'Oh? Is he...?' His flapping wrist was every bit as graphic as Gilbert's had been.

'Supposed not to be—he's gettin' married after all. But whenever e's been 'ere on the cadge from his old man he's looked as limp as a week-old lettuce to me. I 'eard as how he's got himself a fancy car-renovation business in London, paid for by his ma, complete with muscular mechanic. I reckon he's only marrying that horse-faced Lady Huntingdon's daughter to keep in with his mum.'

Gilbert gave a malevolent grin. 'Probably rather shack up with that mechanic, Harry. Mind, if you saw the bride, you might agree wiv 'im. She was 'ere at Christmas with some big-shots ol' Tony was showing round, and you'd think she'd been sucking on a lemon from the sour puss of 'er.'

Gilbert was well into his stride now and had perked up considerably. ''Lady E lets him use all this you know.' He waved his arms to take in the beautiful house and grounds and all that went with it. 'My old woman 'elps out at the 'all when they 'ave big Do's, and not much gets past 'er. You'd be surprised at what people let slip after all them fancy wines. Rivetin' some of it,' he added with satisfaction.

Rafferty made no comment, though from Gilbert's complacent expression, he suspected that he used the information his wife picked up at these Do's at the Hall to extract a little blackmail money from the well-to-do diners.

Gilbert continued his confidences, thankfully oblivious to the note-taking Llewellyn behind him. 'Her brother had let the whole estate go to wrack and ruin. She 'ad it all tarted up when she inherited from him. No expense spared, so I 'eard. She organised the whole show. Even acted as the doc's secretary while he got 'imself established. Very capable woman is Lady Evelyn, no airs to 'er—not like 'im. She even encouraged 'im to be one of them 'ead shrinkers.

'Mind you, she's right, there's money in it. All them neurotic women he treats—very profitable, I reckon, though few of them seem to ever get cured. Why wave good-bye to the goose that lays the golden egg? Think he's a god they do.' The porter's thin lips curled. 'Mind, I don't reckon her ladyship would agree wiv 'em.'

'Oh?' Rafferty's ears pricked up at this hint of further gossip. 'Why's that?'

'My old woman reckons they don't get on. He's got a flat on the top floor 'ere, and he often stays the night. That's why he finds the side gate so convenient.'

He tapped his nose. 'Very cosy that flat is, too, for 'im and his assorted lady friends. Regular procession of them there is.'

Lucky old Tony thought Rafferty. Not only a rich wife to buy him success, it seemed she put up with his bits on the side as well. 'She must be a very understanding woman,' he remarked.

'I don't know about that. But she's one of the old school—the put up and shut up sort. Believes in duty, the stiff upper lip and all that. Mind, I don't 'old that against 'er. It's the way she were brought up, and at least you know where you are wiv 'er. Not like 'im.' Gilbert's face lost the complacency. Belatedly, he seemed to realise he had been a trifle indiscreet, and now he looked anxiously at Rafferty. 'ere, you won't tell 'im I've told you all this will you?'

'Think of me as a priest, Gilbert,' Rafferty reassured him. 'I hear everything but repeat nothing.'

Rafferty's reassurance didn't seem to comfort Gilbert at all. If anything, he looked more hang-dog than on their arrival, as though he found the possibility of a cop keeping a confidence less likely than one of Grub Street's finest doing so.

His face set, Gilbert turned, gave a grimace when he noticed Llewellyn's notebook, slouched over to the kettle and turned it on, resolutely keeping his back turned.

Rafferty let a brief grin escape. He had clearly got all the porter was going to confide for the moment. So he borrowed Gilbert's phone to organise the house to house, the search for the murder weapon, and the victim's clothes. Then he headed to the house, conscious of Llewellyn walking a pace or two behind like a lesser wife.

As Rafferty strode up the long drive, he prayed that the victim had a record, because, if she hadn't, it was likely to be a long case. And after his incautious boast to Melville-Briggs, he didn't fancy having to break the news to him if he should turn out to be wrong. He was as likely to get the same short shrift on the sympathy front as Gilbert.

Still, at least Melville-Briggs should have found them a room. Presumably he had worked out by now that parading his patients past the gutter press for their interviews at the police station was unlikely to improve his profits or his reputation.

Chapter Four

Melville-Briggs was half-way down the stairs when they entered the house. And, like the arrogant Lord that Gilbert the porter had likened him to, he paused and waited for them to come to him.

Rafferty paid this grand-standing no attention at all. It was designed to intimidate. Superintendent Bradley went in for similar poses. He resolutely ignored them all.

Instead, he let his gaze float over the house's interior, which was a delight to the eye.

There was none of the usual institutionalised scrimping here, Rafferty noted, as he started up the stairs. The carpet was thick and luxurious; the stairs magnificent; the open strings of the tread-ends were decorated with scrolls and the treads carried turned banisters with graceful refined curves. Of solid oak, like the paneled walls, they hugged the side of the house as they rose to meet the first floor.

Rafferty tore his thoughts aware from the beauty of the house, and finally acknowledged the doctor as he reluctantly relieved him of the role of chief suspect. 'I've just been talking to Gilbert, the gate-porter, Sir, and it seems that most of the staff here have keys to that side gate. Naturally, that widens the entire scope of the case.' He added the last piece of information in an excuse-building exercise should the investigation drag on, even though he had his doubts that such an excuse would cut him much slack with the doctor.

Melville-Briggs's eyes narrowed and the look in them boded ill for the unfortunate Gilbert. He subjected Rafferty to a thoughtful scrutiny, before commenting, 'Well, if this case is to be solved, you'll want to get on, I'm sure.' He led the way briskly up the stairs.

Rafferty addressed his backside. 'Have you managed to find us a room, Sir?'

Melville-Briggs nodded. 'I've spoken to my secretary and we've sorted out something suitable.'

Suitable for what? Rafferty mused. His lowly rank? Was it to be the attic or the basement? As he followed Melville-Briggs's broad and expensively tailored beam up the stairs, he hoped it wasn't the attic. The thought of all those stairs was enough to bring on his smoker's cough.

Ex-smoker's cough came the stern voice of conscience. There was to be no backsliding this time. He was determined on it.

'I'll need a full list of the staff, Sir.' One of the first things to do would be to get their movements checked out.

Apparently, the great man didn't soil his hands with clerical work. Melville-Briggs didn't pause in his regal ascent, but waved his arm, and said irritably, 'I think you might save such requests for my secretary, Mrs. Galvin. She's perfectly capable of dealing with such matters.'

They reached the landing that ran around three sides of the hall. Melville-Briggs paused, and glanced speculatively at the two policemen. 'You know, Rafferty,' he began. 'I've been thinking.'

Rafferty waited to hear the results of these deliberations. He hoped he wasn't to be treated to another lecture on the importance of the hospital and its residents. But as Melville-Briggs went on, he discovered he'd wronged the man.

'You remember I mentioned I thought someone had a powerful motive for leaving the body of that poor girl on my premises?'

Rafferty nodded warily and waited.

'I've given it some more thought and realise that it's my duty to give you the name of the man I suspect.'

This unexpectedly helpful attitude increased Rafferty's wariness. Was the doctor trying to settle some old score by his allegation? He didn't doubt he was capable of it. Most people had ulterior motives for what they did, and they all came out of the woodwork in a murder investigation.

You're just an old cynic, Rafferty, he told himself. Perhaps the doctor was simply improving with acquaintance. It seemed unlikely, but the thought was encouraged by the fact that for the first time, Melville-Briggs had mentioned the unfortunate victim with every appearance of compassion. Up till now, it had been only himself and extensions of the same – his hospital, his patients, his patients' relatives – that had merited his consideration. 'Yes, Sir?' he said encouragingly. 'Go on.'

'This is strictly confidential, of course, but I suspect a man called Dr Nathanial Whittaker.'

Melville-Briggs seemed to expect Rafferty to know who he was talking about without further explanation. When he explained that he didn't, the doctor tutted a few times, then told him tersely, 'He's the owner of the Holbrook Clinic a few miles away.'

'Have you any reason to think he might wish you harm, Sir?'

'He threatened me only last night. In front of witnesses, too. Rather a coincidence, don't you think?'

Rafferty remained silently non-committal, and Melville-Briggs went on in the manner of a man with a deeply-felt grievance which he felt wasn't being given sufficient consideration.

'Shows what was on his mind, to my way of thinking. I believe his lack of success has unbalanced him. It does that to some men and, of course, his entire life's been a disappointment. No wonder his wife left him. You might find it interesting to look him up in the Hospital Yearbook and send for some of his literature. You'll be able to see just how unimpressive his place is. Bitterness and failure can do sad things to a man's morals, Rafferty. In your line, you should know that. You must encounter such people all the time.'

'But surely he wouldn't go as far as murder just to damage you, Sir,' Rafferty said quietly. There again, it might sound a crazy motive for murder, but it wasn't the craziest he'd heard. And Melville-Briggs would make enemies with the greatest of ease. Hadn't he taken an instant dislike to the man himself?

'But what about the patient's relatives?' Rafferty asked reasonably. 'Even a doctor can't just lose a body without questions being asked.'

'I grant you, any patient such a doctor might lose would never be an important patient. Good lord, no,' he added, as though the bemused Rafferty had just accused him of something quite shocking.

'Not that Whittaker attracts that type of patient. Drop-outs and dregs are more his line, you'll find, the sort who wouldn't be missed, and Whittaker takes a lot of National Health patients. He smiled sardonically. 'He has to. Few private patients would be foolish enough to go to that mismanaged clinic of his. His patients tend to come and go as they please.'

He paused, then added with what he clearly thought was a winning argument. 'Why should anyone think it odd if the occasional one vanishes? Such people discharge themselves all the time without bothering to go through the official formalities. Sometimes they die—from an accident, or an overdose, or an accumulation of the abuse to which they've subjected their bodies. Sometimes they just give up and turn their faces to the wall.'

A murder victim that hadn't even been murdered. It was a bizarre suggestion. Rafferty's gaze met that of his sergeant. Bizarre, but not impossible. 'Would he have access to a key, though, Doctor?'

Melville-Briggs sniffed. 'As it appears that Gilbert handed them out like Smarties, it's not beyond the realms of possibility, Rafferty. Or, one hopes,' he added tartly, 'beyond the ability of the police to find out.'

Chapter Five

Melville-Briggs opened a door on the first floor that overlooked the drive, and said to the woman behind the desk, 'These are the investigating policemen, Mrs. Galvin.' He didn't bother to provide their names. 'I believe I mentioned that they require a room?'

She acknowledged this with a nod, and then glanced at Rafferty. 'I imagine you require details of our staff, their duties, hours of work, etc?'

Rafferty nodded encouragingly. Her voice was pleasant; low and musical. She was perhaps in her early thirties. An attractive, delicate-featured woman, there wasn't a strand of dark hair out of place in the ruthlessly neat French pleat, and Rafferty wondered what hidden depths such an outwardly controlled appearance might be concealing.

There seemed to be an air of constraint between her and the doctor. Intrigued, Rafferty glanced speculatively at them both. But Melville-Briggs, having made his wishes known, wasted no more of his valuable time. He went out, shutting the paneled door firmly behind him, as much as to say, "Don't bother me with minor details".

Mrs Galvin smiled enigmatically, before she turned away and became firmly business-like. Extracting two thin files from the filing cabinet, she handed them to Rafferty, and explained. 'The green file lists all the staff on duty this week, and the buff file covers the full complement of staff, from the medical staff through to the cleaners. Though, of course, most of the nursing staff are currently away on escort duties. We usually take our patients away for their short spring holiday about this time, so there's only a skeleton staff and a few patients here.'

Rafferty brightened. That was the first glimmer of good news he'd heard all morning. 'And they're all accounted for?' Mrs. Galvin nodded. 'You'll understand that we need to establish the victim's identity as speedily as possible.' With faint hope of getting a positive response, he asked, 'Have you any idea who she might be? What she might have been doing in the grounds?'

'I'm afraid not. I finish work at five thirty, so have no idea who might frequent the premises after that time.'

There had been a certain distaste in her voice. Rafferty wondered if some of the night staff smuggled in a girlfriend to help the lonely night shift hours pass. He hoped so, and if some of the other staff proved as confiding as the hospital porter, it should make establishing the victim's identity easier.

He bestowed one of his more winning smiles on Mrs Galvin. 'Can you tell me what sort of patients you treat here?'

'We accept a variety of cases, but we specialise in drug-dependency, and most of our patients come into that category.'

'How long do most of them stay?'

'We tend to take in the really hopeless cases, I'm afraid, those that have been assessed and treated unsuccessfully elsewhere, and whose psychoses are long-established. You could say we provide a permanent and secure home for the sadder elements of society.'

Few empty beds then, Rafferty mused. Very profitable.

'They lack for nothing,' Mrs. Galvin went on, as though anxious to remove the cynicism Rafferty suspected might be lurking in his blue eyes. 'Perhaps you don't realise that in the grounds we have an extensive range of facilities to keep them happy and occupied? For instance, we have an indoor heated swimming-pool, a Jacuzzi, a gymnasium for our younger clients, and of course we encourage them to develop an interest in gardening—it's a very soothing occupation for disturbed minds, we've discovered.'

As well as making a small saving on gardeners' wages. Convenient.

'Do you handle really violent cases at all?' asked Llewellyn, getting to the heart of the matter.

'Occasionally,' she admitted cautiously. 'But the patients are carefully supervised at all times. There is no possible—'

'I'm sure they are,' Rafferty interrupted soothingly. He remembered the patient he had encountered in the grounds, and asked, 'Could you let me have a list of the in-patients?'

Her manner became brisk. 'Not without Dr. Melville-Briggs's authority, I'm afraid. Most of our patients come from very distinguished families and we have to be discreet.'

Rafferty didn't press the point. They could always apply for a court order to release the files if it should prove necessary.

After giving him a searching glance from steady grey eyes, she added, 'You'll find the staff lists clearly marked to show those on sick leave or holiday leave, those on escort duty and so on. All the symbols are explained at the base.'

'You keep a tidy filing cabinet, Mrs. Galvin,' Rafferty complimented. 'Really first class.' He thought ruefully of his own untidy and neglected paper work. When this case was over, he resolved, he really must tackle it.

Her grey eyes held a hint of amusement as she remarked, 'It's my job, Inspector; I hope I'm reasonably efficient at it.' She handed over another document with the comment, 'This is a plan of the hospital and its grounds. You might find it helpful.'

Rafferty nodded. 'Would you have a Hospital Yearbook? Dr. Melville-Briggs thought we might find it useful.'

'Really? I can't imagine why, but yes, of course, I have a copy.' She reached over to the book rack on her desk and passed it to him. 'It's this year's.'

'I'm obliged to you. I'll let you have it back as soon as possible.'

She nodded and walked briskly to the door. 'If you'll follow me, I'll show you the room you can use.'

She led them along the corridor, and to Rafferty's relief, down the stairs, rather than up to the attic. She opened a door at the far end of the hall, and they descended another short flight of steps. These had no fancy scroll work and were plain and serviceable—clearly those used by the servants in an earlier era.

After negotiating several dusty corridors and interconnecting empty rooms, Mrs. Galvin at last led them to their temporary office.

The room allotted to them was in a rather mouldy smelling semi-basement at the back of the house. Rafferty turned on the light. The naked bulb illuminated a cheerless little box, empty but for half-a-dozen rickety-looking chairs, and a battered table upon which countless schoolboy hands had carved their initials. He guessed that Melville-Briggs had chosen the room as punishment for not falling in with his wishes over the attempted bribe.

Two telephones rested on the table and he picked one up to check that it was working.

'That one has an outside line,' Mrs Galvin told him. 'The grey one is for internal calls. I'll supply you with a list of the various extensions.'

He nodded his thanks before glancing up. There was a small window high up in the wall, but all it illuminated were the cobwebs festooned around it. Rafferty gave a wry smile and murmured, 'Be it ever so humble...'

Mrs. Galvin looked embarrassed. 'Perhaps I could try to arrange something a little more...a little larger.'

Rafferty surmised that her boss was unlikely to take kindly to the idea, especially if, as he suspected, his slanderous accusation against a fellow medical man proved so much hogwash.

'Don't trouble yourself, Mrs. Galvin,' he said magnanimously. After all, he mused, he might get the attic next time. He tried his smile again, and this time there was a definite softening in the dark grey eyes. 'This will do us very well, won't it, Sergeant?'

Llewellyn looked around the room with a marked lack of enthusiasm. 'I'm sure it will serve our purpose, Sir.'

His dour tones gave the impression that, once installed in the room, they intended to wield truncheons with vigour, and Rafferty winced. He half-expected the Welshman to enquire if it was sound-proofed. But perhaps he was being unduly sensitive, as Mrs. Galvin didn't seem to read any more into the remark.

'If you need anything else, please ask me. I'd rather you didn't trouble Dr Melville-Briggs.'

Her sentiment echoed Rafferty's. Until they had identified the victim, the less he saw of that gentleman, the better. Gallantly, he escorted her to the door. 'Thanks for your help, and I promise I'll try not to trouble the doctor more than strictly necessary. I'm sure he's a very busy man.'

A slight flush tinged her delicately-boned cheeks. 'Oh yes. I think you could say he keeps himself fully occupied.'

Rafferty thought he detected a certain irony in her tone, but at his sharp glance her voice immediately softened.

'He has much with which to concern himself. The patients can be very demanding, and he has to think constantly of their welfare.'

He'd have to if he wanted them to keep laying their golden eggs, was Rafferty's immediate reaction. 'Dedicated type then, is he?' he enquired mildly.

'Dedicated? Oh, yes, I think you could say that. Hence the flat he keeps for his own use here. Lady Evelyn doesn't encourage him to bring his work home.'

Particularly not the blondes, brunettes and redheads, that Gilbert had more than hinted at. Rafferty broke into a burst of laughter at the thought but managed to turn it into a coughing fit.

He waited till Mrs. Galvin had departed before he let the laughter out. He winked at Llewellyn, and said,. 'I see what she means about Tony's "work". Perhaps our faceless lady will turn out to be one of them.'

Chapter Six

They worked their way through the files that Mrs. Galvin had given them and soon had several impressive looking lists. After careful checking, it was confirmed that no-one from the hospital was missing. All the staff and patients currently away on holiday at the Dorset coast had been accounted for. Which meant that the victim had come from outside.

It was curious, because Rafferty had earlier dispatched Constable Hanks to question Jack, the night gate-porter before letting him home. And Jack had been adamant that not only had no unknown visitors been signed in the previous evening, but that everyone he had signed in had been signed out again. As Gilbert had told them, Jack hadn't seen or heard anything; as far as he was concerned, it had been a quiet night. It pointed to the dead girl being very much an unofficial visitor as he had suspected.

Rafferty looked at the clock. 'Right. It's time to go a calling.' He bundled the files together and handed them to Llewellyn. They'd fixed an appointment for five o'clock with Lady Melville-Briggs. 'Perhaps Lady Evelyn will be kind enough to drop the great Narcissus in it?' he said hopefully. 'Wouldn't that be nice?'

As expected, Llewellyn immediately contradicted him.

'Unlikely, sir. Besides, there must be plenty of other witnesses to confirm Dr. Melville-Briggs's alibi.'

'Well, I can hope,' Rafferty retorted, adding caustically, 'Get a move on. We don't want to be late twice in one day.'

***

Elmhurst Hall was the only property down a quiet country lane and was well-concealed from prying eyes. Rafferty had made Llewellyn stop off at the public library to borrow a book on local history on their way to see Lady Evelyn, and the hall featured prominently. He was looking forward to seeing it.

The high, wrought-iron gates were open, and Llewellyn turned the car into the drive. The building was mainly early Tudor, but Rafferty's part-trained builder's eye recognised that the great hall was medieval. The old stained-glass glowed with an unearthly light, well set off by the simple black and white timber-framed walls and he stared blissfully, absorbing it all.

The man-servant who opened the door must have been warned to expect them, for after checking their names, he led them through an inner high arched door, which to Rafferty's delight, led to the original hall. It was magnificent and as he looked round him a lump formed in his throat.

The roof timbers soared fully fifty feet above the floor and looked as though they had been crafted by a giant's hand. Enormous king-posts rested on collar-beams, which, in turn, rested on moulded braces, all coated with the rich patina of centuries. His gaze took in old battle banners, swords and shields hanging from the wall, enormous serving dishes and a vast oak table, which must easily hold thirty people. Barely aware that he had stopped to stare, it was only when Llewellyn cleared his throat that he remembered why he was here.

The butler opened another door and introduced them. Lady Evelyn rose from her chair and came to greet them. 'Inspector. Won't you and your Sergeant come and sit by the fire? These large rooms grow a little chilly at this time of day.'

Rafferty was glad to sit at the vast hearth and warm himself. Llewellyn settled himself and his notebook at a short, discreet distance.

Lady Evelyn sat opposite Rafferty on the other side of the hearth. 'You'll both take coffee with me? It's all ready.'

Rafferty nodded his thanks, and while she served him, he studied her. He guessed her to be around the late forties. She was tall, and although the fine skin and grey-flecked auburn hair were her only real claims to beauty, she had an indefinable quality that no cosmetic could provide. He wondered what she had seen in old Tony. Her grey, worsted skirt and high-necked white blouse were plain, the blouse adorned only with a discreet gold brooch on which there was some Latin inscription, the meaning of which Llewellyn would, no doubt, take great delight in explaining to him later.

Taking his cup, he settled back comfortably as she served Llewellyn. It was a restful room, and if the chair upon which he sat lacked cushioned modernity, its straight back and high curved arms offered repose. Even Llewellyn seemed to have relaxed, Rafferty noticed, with amusement, and looked as contented as the melancholic composition of his features would allow.

Rafferty glanced curiously around the room, at the well-worn, but presumably expensive rugs, at the many paintings of fierce-looking earlier Melvilles, each neatly labelled, the photographs that adorned the desk top and mantelpiece. He was reluctant to introduce the unpleasant topic of murder into such peace, but, he reminded himself, as he was here as a policeman and not an invited guest, he'd better get on with it.

Putting, his cup down, he began. 'As I believe my Sergeant explained on the phone, we're taking statements from everyone in any way connected with your husband's hospital, Lady Evelyn. In most cases, it's just going to be a formality, of course, but we need to eliminate as many people as possible from our enquiries.'

She nodded. 'Naturally, I'll help in any way I can.' Her eyes shadowed. 'A most distressing business. I understand her face...' Lady Evelyn paled and stumbled to a halt. It was a few moments before she was able to go on. 'Forgive me. It's all been rather a shock.' She gave a moue of distaste. 'My husband rang me earlier and revealed some of the more unpleasant details. Her poor family—have you been able to identify her yet?'

Rafferty shook his head. 'Of course, it's early days. You've no idea who she might be, I suppose?' he asked hopefully.

Lady Evelyn shook her head. 'I rarely visit my husband's sanatorium these days, Inspector. Even the staff are mostly strangers to me now.' She gave a faint smile. 'A consequence of a busy life, I'm afraid. At one time, I used to know them all.'

'I see. I understand you and your husband were at a medical dinner at *The George* in Hamborne last night?'

'That's right. It's held every year.'

'It went on till 2.00 a.m. I understand?'

'Yes.' With a tinge of irony, she added, 'I found it a rather long night, but as the proceeds were in aid of the local nursery and I'm on the committee, I felt obliged to attend.' She smiled self-mockingly. 'A case of noblesse oblige, as they say.'

Rafferty nodded understandingly. How often had he felt obliged to do what he would rather not? His wife, Angie, had made any number of scenes whilst he had been studying for his sergeant's exams. Too often, for the sake of peace, he had abandoned his studies to escort her to some function or other, and they hadn't even offered the consolation of supporting a worthy cause. That was why he had failed his exams the first time. She had hated the police force and its anti-social hours of duty. "Duty, duty, it's always duty," she had often screamed at him. "What about me—my needs? Don't they count?"

A log crashed in the grate and brought Rafferty back with a start. He found he had relaxed once more and forced himself to sit more erect in the chair. 'Were you both present at *The George* for the entire night? Your husband—'

'Anthony?' She stared at him. 'Surely you don't suspect my husband?'

'No, no,' he reassured her. No more than anyone else, anyway, though certainly no less, either. 'As I said, it's probably only a formality, so if you can assure me that you were both there all evening we won't trouble you any further.'

Lady Evelyn fingered her gold pin and gave him a bleak little smile. 'This is rather unfortunate. We weren't together the entire evening, you see, Inspector. Once the meal was over I saw little of him, so I'm afraid I can't give him an – alibi – I suppose the term is. As you can imagine, on these occasions the medical fraternity talk shop and their partners tend to be left to their own devices.' She spoke lightly as though it were a matter of little moment.

But Rafferty had been in enough similar situations in his own marriage, and knew what it was like to be ignored, left on the side-lines while one's partner joined more congenial companions.

Almost as though in defence against his silent and unasked for sympathy, Lady Evelyn brightened. 'I'm sure it will be a simple matter to prove he was there the entire night. There were enough people present, and as Anthony seemed to know most of them, someone's sure to be able to confirm what he says.'

'How did you get to The George that night, Ma'am?' asked Llewellyn. 'I understand you have a chauffeur?'

'Yes. But, as it happens, it was his long weekend off and I'd stupidly forgotten to ask him to change it—so annoying. And by the time I did remember, he'd already left. Normally, of course, for such a function, we would use the Bentley and Anthony was rather put out when we were reduced to my car.'

'But surely you could still have used the Bentley?'

'I'm afraid not, Sergeant. The Bentley is a manual and I only drive automatics. When we discovered that Anderson, our chauffeur, had left for the weekend, we both knew that I would have to drive.' She smiled faintly. 'There are usually excellent wines at dinner and on such occasions my husband likes to let his hair down with his colleagues.'

'A rather unfortunate start to the evening, Ma'am,' Rafferty commented sympathetically.

'Yes.' She sighed. 'Of course, in the way of such things, it got worse. The lights on my car had been accidentally left on and the battery was flat. Anthony rather blamed me, but both he and my son, when he's home, tend to use my car as a spare. Anyway, after some completely pointless recriminations, we borrowed a spare battery from the cook. By the time we finally got going, it was rather late.'

'It might have been a better idea to borrow the cook's car in the first place,' Llewellyn commented dryly.

'I did suggest it, of course—it's an automatic like mine, but it's a little old and shabby, and my husband feels he has a position to maintain. He didn't want to arrive in such an...unsuitable vehicle.' She went on. 'But as it happened, it wouldn't have mattered. By the time we got to *The George*, the car park was full, and the attendant wouldn't let us in. We had to drive round and round the streets till we could find a parking place. Anthony wasn't very pleased. He gave the door-man rather a hard time, though, of course, it wasn't his fault, poor man.'

Rafferty could imagine how Anthony Melville-Briggs would take such an affront to his dignity. No wonder he had been so sure the door-man would remember them. The good doctor in a rage would certainly be a pretty spectacular sight.

He swallowed the appreciative chuckle and glanced over at Llewellyn. The Welshman's dark head was bent over his notebook as though its contents engrossed him, and, for a moment, Rafferty wondered if it was possible that his uptight sergeant shared his amusement.

Then he dismissed the possibility. Llewellyn suffered from a sense of humour failure on an epic scale and had already made it clear where his sympathies lay.

Although the day outside had turned bleak, and the old house groaned from the buffeting of the wind blowing straight off the North Sea, the winter parlour was warm. The paneled walls reflected the glowing red and gold flames from the heaped logs burning steadily in the hearth. They had Rafferty mesmerised. He felt lethargy begin to steal over him and he gave himself a mental shake. Curious to discover more than his quick perusal of the guide-book had revealed, he asked, 'Has Elmhurst Hall always belonged to your family, Ma'am?'

'No, only since the late Fifteenth Century,' replied Lady Evelyn. 'My great, great, great, etc, grandfather, a landless knight, backed Henry Tudor at the Battle of Bosworth, and as you probably know, the Tudor won the day.'

'And your family were rewarded with the Hall?'

'In a roundabout way. Henry Tudor was reluctant to give rewards out of his own pocket, being a mean man by nature, but Edward Melville was given something even better – a rich heiress in marriage – Lady Cecily Aimering. It was through her that we acquired the Hall, amongst other things. At that time, of course—' she broke off, and he looked enquiringly at her.

'I'm sorry.' She gave an apologetic smile. 'I didn't mean to give you a history lesson.'

Rafferty glanced slyly at Llewellyn to see if this sensitivity had penetrated. Llewellyn met his eyes with the inscrutable expression of a Merlin as Lady Evelyn continued. 'My husband tells me I bore people to death talking about the house.'

'You're not boring me,' Rafferty assured her. He managed to get a little dig in for Llewellyn's benefit. 'Give me someone who knows their stuff and can tell it without talking down to people and I'm happy. Besides, I'm a bit of a history buff myself.

'Houses are a hobby of mine,' he explained, 'and history tends to go with the territory.'

But there was work to be done, he reminded himself. He signalled to Llewellyn as he got to his feet. 'We'd best be off. Thank you for your hospitality, Ma'am. If you could possibly pop into the station some time and sign the statement?'

'Of course. Tomorrow morning? About ten?'

He nodded. 'That'll be fine.' Rather sheepishly, he pulled the little library book about the Hall from his pocket as they headed for the door. 'I understand you occasionally open your home to the public, Ma'am? I wouldn't mind seeing it myself when this case is over.'

'Why don't you give me a ring when you're able to make it and we'll arrange a time?'

Rafferty was happy to agree and finally they left. But he couldn't help wondering if Lady Evelyn would still be willing to show him round her home if the case ended with her husband being arrested for murder. He rather doubted it.

In spite of his air of confidence, Melville-Briggs's alibi wasn't nearly as sound as he'd led them to believe. If his own wife couldn't vouch for him for the whole evening, was it likely that anyone else could?

Chapter Seven

Llewellyn looked up from his study of the Hospital Yearbook as Rafferty entered their temporary office the next morning and flung himself into a chair. 'Still no sign of the murder weapon?'

Llewellyn shook his head. 'They should finish searching the hospital and its grounds today. Has Dr. Dally been able to give you any idea what the weapon might be?'

'Hasn't a clue.' Rafferty pulled a face. 'Won't admit it, of course. I don't suppose any blood-soaked clothes have shown up, either?'

Llewellyn shook his head again. 'And we're still waiting for any match on the fingerprints. Staffing problems. Fraser said he'll ring back if they come up with anything.'

Rafferty nodded. 'Perhaps I should ask my old Ma to light a few candles for us? We'll need all the help we can get to solve this crime if we can't even discover who the victim was. You'd think someone would have missed her by now.'

Llewellyn tapped lean fingers on the book lying open on the desk in front of him. 'The Holbrook Clinic, that Dr. Melville-Briggs mentioned, sir, it's only about three miles away.'

Rafferty grunted. 'I know. I asked Gilbert. But never mind that for now. Whittaker isn't going anywhere. If he intended to, he'd have gone by now, and he hasn't. I checked.' He got up restlessly. 'Get on to the station, please Dafyd. I want more men up here. I don't care how many officers you have to drag off leave. I want those clothes and the weapon found.'

After Llewellyn had organised the extra manpower, his probing dark eyes studied Rafferty. 'Do you really think there's anything in this professional jealousy theory of Dr. Melville-Briggs's, Sir?'

Llewellyn's voice sounded doubtful and, sensing an unspoken criticism, Rafferty frowned. Aware that he was being over-sensitive, but unable to stop himself, he took a high moral tone. 'An experienced policeman keeps an open mind, Sergeant,' he replied loftily. 'There certainly seems to be a lot of bad feeling between the two men. According to Gilbert, they nearly came to blows a month ago, apart from their disagreement on the night of the dinner. Seems Whittaker accused Melville-Briggs of spreading malicious rumours about him. Gilbert swears Whittaker hadn't obtained a key to the side-gate from him, but he did drop a heavy hint that Miss Gwendoline Parry, the Administrator here, is rather sweet on Whittaker and she has a key. She's on leave till Tuesday. She'll keep. We've plenty to occupy us till her return.'

The phone rang just then. Rafferty snatched it up, hoping there might be some good news at last. A delighted grin split his face as he scribbled a few quick notes on the scrap pad in front of him. 'Yes, yes, I've got that. Thanks. Thanks very much.' He replaced the receiver slowly, as though savouring the moment, and gave Llewellyn an elliptical glance.

'Good news, Taff.' The use of the nickname was quite deliberate. As he had guessed, the Welshman didn't take kindly to it—well; *he* didn't take kindly to being thought of as an ignorant Mick. Maybe Llewellyn would take the hint and stop acting so damn superior. Rafferty tilted his chair back at a dangerous angle, and challenged, 'I bet you a pound to a pinch of shit that this'll bring a smile to that mournful Welsh mug of yours.'

Llewellyn merely murmured, 'Oh?' before issuing a cautious warning, 'I wouldn't tip your seat back like that, Sir. These old hospital chairs aren't up to such rough treatment.'

Rafferty waved the caution aside. 'That was Fraser on the phone. He's matched the prints, so Ma won't have to light those candles after all. The victim's identity will point us to the man who killed her. It's bound to.'

Llewellyn's expression didn't alter, but his laconic reply succeeded in wiping the smile off Rafferty's face. 'I wouldn't be so sure. Identifying a victim does not a murder solve.'

Rafferty scowled and brought all four legs of his chair back to earth with a crash. The crack of splintered wood proved Llewellyn's forebodings correct. Rafferty landed in an

DEAD BEFORE MORNING

undignified heap on the floor as what was left of the chair collapsed under him.

A faint smile took fleeting possession of Llewellyn's features, and he murmured softly, "'Pride goeth before destruction, and an haughty spirit before a f—'"

'Oh shut up!' Rafferty retorted childishly. Bloody sanctimonious know-all, he silently cursed his sergeant. He got up gingerly. The legs of the chair had parted company with the seat—permanently by the look of it. He pushed the evidence of his vandalism into the adjoining lumber-room and shut the door on it. Not that Dr. Melville-Briggs was likely to show his face down here, but you never knew. It would be just like him to send in a bill for the damage. Rafferty thrust his hands into his pockets, and demanded belligerently, 'Don't you ever look on the bright side?'

Llewellyn gave a tiny shrug. 'I don't believe in courting disappointment.' He paused. 'There is one thing I don't understand though.'

'Only one? You surprise me. And what might that be?'

'Why you assume the murderer was male.'

Rafferty hadn't assumed any such thing, the use of the male pronoun had just seemed the most obvious in the circumstances, but now he felt stung to defend his choice. 'Elementary, my dear Llewellyn,' he replied loftily, determined to regain the advantage which he had so abysmally lost. 'The victim, Linda Wilks, was on file for prostitution.'

Just then, he heard a faint shuffling noise outside the door. He put his finger to his lips, crept to the door and quickly hauled it open. Gilbert was standing there with a tea-tray. Startled, he nearly dropped the lot.

'What do you want to go and do that for?' he complained. 'Gave me the fright of me life.'

Rafferty's eyes narrowed. 'Have you been listening?' He wouldn't put it past him. Perhaps that was why Dr. Melville-Briggs hadn't sacked him yet. Men like Gilbert had their uses.

Gilbert got on his high horse. 'I've got better things to do with me time. Mrs. Galvin thought you'd want tea and asked me if I'd be good enough to oblige.' He sniffed. 'But I shan't bother again.'

Rafferty took the tea-tray. 'Thank you, Gilbert.' He stood pointedly in the doorway, waiting for the porter to go. 'Was there anything else?' he asked.

Grumbling to himself, Gilbert took the hint.

'We ought to get a key to that outside door, sir,' Llewellyn suggested quietly once the porter had gone. 'We don't want him or anyone else eavesdropping on our discussions of the investigation.'

'I'm aware of that, Sergeant,' Rafferty replied tartly. 'Unlike you, I'm also aware that Gilbert's likely to have duplicates to all the keys in the place. It's a bolt we need.' There was one on the inside door, he noticed. He'd better bring a drill and screwdriver in with him tomorrow and move the bolt to the outside door if they didn't want the entire staff to be privy to their discoveries.

He slammed the door and set the tray down on the table. 'You can be mother. Three sugars in mine. Now,' hooking his foot beneath the front rung of another chair, he dragged it towards him and sat down. 'Where was I?' he asked.

'You were explaining why you think the murderer is a man, sir,' replied Llewellyn expressionlessly as he handed him his tea.

'So I was.' Rafferty stirred his tea vigorously, laced his fingers behind his head and assumed his most nonchalant pose. But he wished he hadn't started this conversation as Llewellyn could be relied upon to pinpoint any flaws in his hastily-constructed theory. 'How likely is it that a London prossie would come all the way out to deepest Elmhurst to see a woman?'

Llewellyn replied coolly, 'More likely, I would have thought, than coming all the way out here for just one client.'

'Unless he could pay well enough to make it worth her while,' Rafferty countered swiftly. Which ability, in his book, put Melville-Briggs back as odds-on favourite.

He was savouring this thought along with the hot, sweet tea, when Llewellyn, true to form, spoiled the flavour of both. 'High-class then, was she, sir?'

'Not exactly, no,' Rafferty replied. He regretted his desire to put his sergeant in the wrong. He might have known that Llewellyn would immediately put his finger on the weak spot in his argument. It was probably his university education. Resentfully, Rafferty was forced to concede that his theory might have a few holes in it. Because Linda Wilks had been far from high class if the Met were to be believed.

Although he accepted that it was a bit early to jump to conclusions, Llewellyn's criticisms made him reluctant to wave goodbye to his conjectures entirely. Particularly if there was a chance of involving his favourite medical man in a juicy murder trial. The starring role in such a case would take the satin finish from Melville-Briggs's smoothly-emulsioned mug with all the efficiency of a blow-torch. It would even be worth suffering Llewellyn's scepticism to see that.

Aware that his own personal feelings ought not to come into it yet determined not to let his sergeant get the better of him entirely, Rafferty added, 'Let's just say she was an obliging sort of girl – went in for the kind of parlour games that stimulate jaded sexual appetites – whips, chains, that sort of thing. Saucy outfits too, apparently. When Streatham nick picked her up last time, she claimed she was an actress.'

He snorted. 'A likely story. The only acting she did was when she played Madam Whiplash for a paying customer. Fancy a guess as to who the customer might be?'

Llewellyn didn't take him up on his offer.

'Who do we know who's got a nice cosy flat, right on site? Whose sexual appetites – according to friend Gilbert – have had a surfeit of sweeties? Who's high-powered enough to enjoy the titillation of a little role reversal? The great, the greedy, the goose-egg gatherer himself, that saviour of womankind, Dr. Anthony Melville-Briggs, that's who. No wonder he tried to dump our suspicions elsewhere. It's well known that the rich are a weird lot where sex is concerned. Their goings-on swamp the pages of the Sunday tabloids every week. You must remember Madam Cyn from Streatham, the Luncheon Vouchers bordello queen, even though it was some years ago.'

Llewellyn looked down his long nose at the suggestion. 'I make a point of avoiding such sordid sensationalism.'

You would, thought Rafferty, as he murmured, 'That's rather a pity. I've always thought a policeman should keep up with the scandal sheets. All in the line of duty, of course,' he added. 'Call it a 'getting to know' our future customers exercise, if you like. Anyway, Madam Cyn's main business came from the intellectual type's fancy for "correction".' Rafferty eyed Llewellyn mischievously as he got the dig in. 'Same sort of line as Linda Wilks.' He grinned. 'Perhaps the good doctor likes to be tied up by a bit of rough trade occasionally and smacked on his plump, pink behind?'

'Aren't you being a trifle melodramatic, Sir?' Llewellyn questioned deflatingly. 'We've only just discovered the victim's identity. It might be advisable to find out first if there was any connection between them before jumping to hasty conclusions based on suppositions and hearsay. Besides, we've still got the rest of the skeleton staff to interview yet. We can't begin to settle on a suspect until we've got an overall picture.'

Rafferty sighed. Trust Llewellyn to want to go by the book. Rafferty had always found it made a case much more interesting if he ignored the book. There was nothing wrong with a bit of good, dirty speculation, he told himself. As far as he was concerned, he'd be delighted if old smarmy-pants proved to be a mass of nasty perversions, and a murderer to boot, friend of the Chief Constable or not. If he was their man, Rafferty wouldn't allow such a consideration to prevent him making the arrest. Besides, the CC would be pretty quick to distance himself from the doctor if he was the culprit, so Rafferty's job should be safe enough.

He couldn't resist teasing Llewellyn a little more. 'Perhaps she decided to up her rates and he wasn't keen. I like it,' he added decisively as the grin stretched even further.

Of course, Llewellyn wiped the grin off his face with his usual efficiency. 'I doubt the Chief Constable would—not without some proof, and so far, there isn't any.'

'Not yet,' Rafferty conceded. 'But as you so rightly pointed out, we haven't finished interviewing yet. Lady Evelyn didn't give her husband the fool-proof alibi he probably hoped for. Perhaps the others at that medical dinner won't either.'

Like the voice of conscience, Llewellyn immediately piped up. 'Sam Dally was there. And he didn't remark on any obvious absences on the part of Dr. Melville-Briggs. He was the Chair, don't forget. He'd be sure to be missed.'

Rafferty scowled. He'd forgotten that Sam Dally had mentioned his prime suspect headed the committee responsible for organising the annual dinner, and probably responsible for making sure that everyone, especially himself, had the whale of a time. No wonder Melville-Briggs had been so unlovable yesterday morning. He'd probably been nursing a hangover as formidable as Rafferty's own. He could almost like the man for that, almost, but not quite. 'It's not far to drive from *The George,'* he pointed out. 'He could still have nipped out during the evening, driven back here, killed the girl and nipped back. I imagine there was a large crowd. Nothing could be easier than to disappear for half an hour or so, especially once the dinner was over and he started to mingle.'

But apparently, Llewellyn had pumped Sam Dally a little more, and now he wasted no more time in giving Rafferty the rest of the good news. Apparently, the role of chairman called for a lot of speechifying and prize-giving; Dr. Melville-Briggs had been centre-stage during the greater part of the evening, no doubt holding forth on his favourite topic—himself, thought Rafferty begrudgingly. And as Llewellyn had said, even Sam hadn't been able to recall any great gaps in his presence.

With regret, Rafferty put his suspicions of Melville-Briggs temporarily aside. He couldn't even console himself with his madman theory. It seemed the pyjama-clad denouncer of women had several strange habits, one of which consisted of covering his hands with blood, any blood, he wasn't particular. Yesterday morning, before the nurse could stop him, he had dashed out of the day room and entered the kitchen where he had smeared his hands with blood from a large joint of beef which was just about to go in the oven.

'Did you check with Charge Nurse Allward about the possibility of the rest of the patients being able to get out of the bedroom block?'

Llewellyn nodded. 'Nothing there. He told me that either himself or the little Filipino girl, Staff Nurse Estoce, sat at the end of the block, right by the locked door all night. No matter how devious they might be, none of the patients could get out without being seen. The patients can't open the windows. I haven't yet spoken to the Staff Nurse, but I imagine she'll confirm what Allward said.'

Disappointed, Rafferty nodded and bent back to his lists. There was no way they were going to avoid checking out everyone's movements. 'Right,' he said. 'Let's get on. We'll have Friday night's duty doctor in, please, Llewellyn. Dr. Simon Smythe. Round him up, there's a good man.'

Left alone, Rafferty leaned back in his chair and gazed at the small square of blue sky visible through the window. Someone had opened the side gate and let the girl in, presumably, someone who was expecting her, and despite Llewellyn putting the dampers on his theory, he still thought it most likely to have been a man that the girl had come to see.

All right, he admitted, Sam had said that a woman could have killed the girl, but it didn't seem a woman's crime somehow. It would, he was now convinced, turn out to be a relatively simple case. Maybe some member of the night-duty staff had organised Linda's visit as a bit of light relief during the long shift. If so, it had gone badly wrong, and frightened by what he'd done, he'd panicked and smashed her face, perhaps hoping to divert suspicion to one of the more violent patients. Though, he mused, if so, surely, he'd have had the wit to arrange an escape?

Just then Llewellyn opened the door and ushered Simon Smythe into the room.

A long and bony man, Dr. Smythe looked to be in his late twenties. His old-fashioned horn-rimmed glasses seemed too heavy and overwhelmed his face. Already, he'd lost most of his blond hair; what remained was stretched lankly across as much of his scalp as it could cover.

Rafferty summoned a smile. 'Thank you for coming so promptly, Doctor. Won't you sit down?' Smythe did so, and Rafferty sat companionably beside him on the desk, while Llewellyn and his notebook took the other chair. 'Now, then, Doctor, as you probably know, we're interviewing all the staff and patients about the murder.' Smythe nodded. 'I understand you were duty doctor on Friday night?'

'Yes, yes, that's right.' Smythe's watery eyes looked quickly at Rafferty and away again. 'I—I generally am at holiday times like this.' A tinge of resentment crept into his voice. 'Dr. Melville-Briggs likes to get away, but even when he's in the flat here, he becomes very annoyed if I disturb him.'

Understandably, if he was "entertaining", thought Rafferty. 'I see. So, you were the only doctor on the premises?'

Smythe nodded quickly, as though he would prefer to deny it. His hands began to tremble slightly; he tucked them in the pockets of his white coat out of sight and cleared his throat. It sounded very loud in the small and otherwise silent room. Its echo seemed to agitate him.

'It must be a great responsibility.' It was clear he'd touched a raw nerve, as Smythe immediately launched into a string of complaints.

'It is. A great responsibility, Inspector.'

Rafferty nodded sympathetically as Smythe began to pour out his grievances

'Of course, in an emergency I can always contact Dr. Melville-Briggs, but,' his mouth turned down like a sulky child's, 'he doesn't always agree what constitutes an emergency. He can become quite abusive if one disturbs him unnecessarily.'

'Bosses aren't always very understanding, Sir,' he commiserated. A picture of Superintendent Bradley in full hectoring mode came into his mind, and he added quietly, 'It's much the same everywhere—the way of the world.'

Smythe gave a slow nod, as if Rafferty had revealed a great truth and for a few moments they both pondered the extent of his profundity.

Judging the moment propitious to press on, Rafferty asked quietly, 'Can you remember anything unusual about that night, Sir? Anything at all?'

Smythe hesitated, and then shook his head. 'No. It was a quiet night. That's why—' He broke off and looked guiltily at Rafferty.

'You were saying, Sir?'

'Nothing. Really.' Smythe clamped his lips tightly together as though scared he might say more than he intended. 'It, it's just that I still can't quite believe it. That poor girl must have been murdered while I was watching the late film.'

Strange, thought Rafferty, the approximate time of death hadn't been revealed. However for the moment he didn't pursue the point. He gazed thoughtfully at Smythe, and replied, 'She died quickly. It's not as though you could have done anything to help her.'

Smythe brightened at this. 'You're right, of course. I couldn't have helped her, even if...' His voice fumbled into silence once more.

'Just a few more questions. When you're on call, I imagine you're expected to stay on the premises?'

Smythe gave another slow nod. His gaze slid away again.

Curious that he should behave as guiltily as a shop-girl caught with her hand in the till, but confident that he would winkle his secret out of him sooner rather than later, Rafferty contented himself with continuing the interview rather than pursuing the point. 'And when you're on call, where would you usually be?'

'I'd be either in my office or the staff lounge. They're both in this building on the first floor,' he added helpfully, as Rafferty consulted the plan of the hospital which was open on the desk. 'I carry my bleep, so I can always be contacted straight away, no matter where I am. It reaches several miles.'

'I see. And how long would you be on call?'

'From nine at night to seven in the morning. I was in my office when Gilbert found the body and came to get me.'

'So, you'd be available the entire night and either in your office or the lounge—is that correct?'

Smythe blinked owlishly, and then nodded.

Rafferty wondered if he had filled in part of the long night with bashing in Linda Wilks's head. He seemed the type who would need to turn to a prostitute for sexual gratification. Of course, he reflected, Smythe's odd behaviour mightn't have anything to do with the murder. A lot of nervy types worked themselves into a state when the police interviewed them.

After a few more questions, he terminated the interview. Smythe's eagerness to be gone was apparent, as was his dismay when Rafferty let him get as far as the door before he called him back, Columbo-style. 'Just as a matter of interest, Doctor. Does the name Linda Wilks mean anything to you?' If he had hoped to startle Smythe by the revelation that they knew the dead girl's name, it was a wasted effort. Perhaps Gilbert had already spread the word?

Smythe's red-rimmed eyes looked blankly back at him through the thick lenses. He shook his bony head vigorously, as though relieved he had been asked a question that held no fears for him. 'Should it?'

Rafferty smiled at him. 'Probably not.' If he had known the victim, he mightn't have known her by that name. Vice girls commonly used several aliases to keep one step ahead of the law. This time, Smythe made it safely through the door.

Chapter Eight

'He could have done it,' said Llewellyn. 'He was here alone. He said himself it was a quiet night. He could have slipped out, or even brought the victim into his office, with nobody being any the wiser. Even if he didn't do it, he might have seen who did.'

Llewellyn leaned over the plan of the hospital and pointed with a long, elegant finger. 'I've been checking the layout of the house, and from both his office and the staff lounge you can see over the side-gate. Of course, even with the outside lights, it would be dark, but he could still have seen something or someone.'

'We'll have another word with him, but not just yet,' Rafferty decided. 'If he knows something, it shouldn't be too difficult to get it out of him. We'll have Staff Nurse Estoce in next, and then Charge Nurse Allward. They were both on duty on Friday night. You'll probably find them waiting in the staff lounge if you give it a ring.'

With her flawless skin and graceful movements, Staff Nurse Estoce was quite exquisite, thought Rafferty, but as with so many Oriental girls, she was shy and self-effacing.

Still, she managed to answer their questions clearly enough; at least, until they asked about her duty colleague on the night of the murder, then her eyes became clouded, and Rafferty had to remind himself to concentrate on her answers rather than her face. It didn't take many more questions before she revealed something interesting.

'You say that Charge Nurse Allward was late back from his early break, Staff. Did he give a reason for that?'

She nodded. 'One of the patients had a bad dream. Charge Nurse Allward settled him and stayed with him till he slept.'

'He didn't ask for your help?' She shook her head. 'So you didn't see the patient at all during this time?'

'No. I checked on him later, of course.'

'And you say Mr Allward returned at 11.45 p.m.?'

'Yes. I noted the time particularly before I went for my own break as I do not like to be late back.'

'Didn't you hear the patient cry out yourself?' Again, she shook her head. 'Why was that?'

She gave a tiny shrug. 'I imagine it was only a little cry and Mr Allward comforted him before he became too upset. I was checking on another patient and spent a little time with him.'

'You didn't notice anything unusual that night? You didn't hear a scream for instance?'

'No. But, in a hospital such as this screams are not so unusual.'

'Have you any idea what the victim might have been doing in the grounds?'

Interestingly, a delicate rose colour tinted her olive skin and her reply was defensive. 'N—no. I couldn't say.'

Couldn't—or wouldn't? 'You don't seem very certain, Staff,' Rafferty remarked gently. 'The victim's name was Linda Wilks. She was about your age. Perhaps you'd like to think about that and get back to me?'

She nodded once, and her eyes looked anxiously at the door, before returning to his face.

Why was it that everyone was so anxious to get away from him today? First Simon Smythe and now Staff Nurse Estoce. If this kept up he'd have to seriously consider changing his deodorant, which would be a pity, as he still had twenty bottles of the stuff that his Ma had got wholesale. At least, she'd said they were wholesale, he remembered uneasily.

Staff Nurse Estoce was still staring at him with her great dark eyes, making him feel like a thug, and he let her go. It was obvious something was worrying her. What on earth could she be hiding? Was she protecting someone?

'Find out if she's got a boyfriend amongst the staff,' he instructed Llewellyn. 'Let's have Allward in now.'

There was nothing meek or self-effacing about Charge Nurse Allward, Rafferty noted. He couldn't have presented a greater contrast to Simon Smythe or the little Staff Nurse.

Allward was in his early thirties, and only about five or six years older than the other man, but they might have been light years apart. He was tall and elegant from his glossy, expensively-styled, brown hair to his burnished black shoes. He seemed completely at his ease. He sat on the hard hospital chair with a faintly sardonic air, as though he found it amusing to be interviewed by the police.

'The sergeant said you wished to see me, Inspector?'

'That's right, Sir. Just a few questions.' After going through the previous spiel that he'd used with Smythe, he asked Allward for his movements on the night of the murder.

'As you probably know, I was on duty in the male bedroom block, with Staff Nurse Estoce from 8.45 p.m. till 7.00 a.m.'

Rafferty nodded. 'I understand you were late returning from your 11.15 p.m. break? Fifteen minutes late. Why was that?'

Allward's sardonic expression became more thoughtful at this. He sat up a little straighter, as though realising he should treat the interview more seriously. Perhaps he hadn't expected his loyal little Staff Nurse to mention his lateness.

'I was delayed by one of the patients,' Allward smoothly explained.

'Which one?'

'Old Mr Tompkinson. His room's at the end of the corridor, near the little cubby-hole where we make the hot drinks.'

'I see. What was the matter with him?'

'Just a bad dream.'

'You didn't need to give him any medication?' He knew that would have to be entered up on the patient's records.

'No. I just got him a drink and settled him down again.' He smiled easily. 'He's a nice old boy. Pathetically grateful for anything you do for him. He and I came here on the same day, so I've always regarded him as one of my special charges.'

'You didn't see anything unusual that night?'

With a grin playing around his mouth, he said. 'Depends what you mean by unusual. This is a psychiatric hospital, Inspector,' Allward gently teased.

Rafferty didn't smile. He simply looked at Allward, and said sharply, 'You don't seem to be taking this seriously, Mr Allward. A young woman was brutally murdered just yards away from this room. Does her death amuse you?'

'No, of course not. I'm as shocked as the rest of the staff.'

'You have a funny way of showing it.'

Allward just shrugged and went back to admiring his shiny shoes.

Rafferty bit back a sigh. 'Okay. Let me put it another way. Did you see anything out of the ordinary?'

Allward shook his head. 'No. But then I didn't look out of the windows, if I had I might have seen something, I suppose. I'm afraid I can't help you, Inspector.'

He even managed to look and sound as though he was genuinely sorry not to be of more assistance, which made Rafferty feel an unreasonable irritation. But Allward was far too smooth for his taste, and he too human to keep his feelings completely hidden. Rafferty wondered how it was that Llewellyn's professional composure never seemed to be ruffled by personal antagonisms. The thought added to his irritation.

'The victim's name was Linda Wilks. Did you know her?'

For a moment, he thought he saw a brief flicker of – something – in Allward's eyes, but it had vanished before he could decide whether it had been recognition, fear or surprise at their speed of identification that had caused it.

'I'm afraid I can't help you, Inspector. But, of course, if she was a visitor to one of the female patients, I'd be unlikely to meet her. Perhaps one of the porters would know her?' he suggested helpfully. 'They get to see all the visitors.'

'Surely, Gilbert's told you they didn't know her? That they had no idea what she was doing here. Neither has anyone else—or so they say. She's a regular mystery woman. Very strange. She wasn't a member of staff or a patient. She wasn't a visitor—at least not an official visitor, which, given what we've found out about her, leaves me to conclude she had a less than above board reason for coming here. She was a prostitute, Mr Allward,' Rafferty told him bluntly. 'Who do you think might have booked her services that night?'

Allward met his eyes squarely. 'I can't imagine.'

'Try,' suggested Rafferty. 'There were six members of staff on duty that night. One of them yourself, three of the others were women, which would seem to rule them out, and the others were Dr. Smythe and Fred Brown, the night porter. A limited field for your imagination to work in, I think.'

'Are you inviting me to smear a colleague, Inspector? Hardly ethical. Besides, any of the other members of staff could have returned easily enough. The hospital would be a convenient place to take such a woman, I would have thought, away from prying families, especially as most of the patients are away at the moment and there are plenty of empty bedrooms.'

'They've already been exonerated, Sir,' Rafferty told him with satisfaction. But it was clear that Allward wasn't about to confess.

After Allward had gone, Rafferty pulled his coat off the back of the chair and shrugged into it. 'We'll do the rest of the interviews later. Guess who's got the happy task of breaking the news to the dead girl's parents?' He headed for the door but stopped when he heard the swiftly indrawn breath behind him.

'Can't the Met can do that?' Llewellyn asked sharply. 'Surely we're not expected to go all the way to London to break the news. I hate—' He broke off and closed his mouth tightly, as though aware that he'd already said too much.

Surprised at this unexpected outburst, Rafferty eyed Llewellyn with a certain degree of sympathy. Breaking news of sudden death was one of the more unpleasant aspects of police work. Nobody liked it. But he was startled to see the usually controlled Welshman show his distaste so openly.

Llewellyn's pale face flushed, and he made an awkward attempt at an explanation 'It's just that, as a child, I had often to accompany my father when he broke the news of sudden death. He was a minister,' he went on in a strange stiff voice. 'He told me it was part of my training for when I went into the ministry myself.' The flush had faded now, leaving his pale face starkly etched with lines of pain. His lips twitched in a ghostly semblance of a smile. 'I've hated having to break such bad news ever since.'

Embarrassed, Rafferty remarked gruffly, 'Bit of a problem that in our line. How have you managed?'

'It wasn't too bad in the little country town where I was stationed before. Most of the sudden deaths were of farmers driving home intoxicated at the end of market-day and the uniformed branch dealt with them.' He squared his shoulders. 'I suppose I've become a bit rusty, especially since my father died.'

'Look,' said Rafferty diffidently. 'If you'd rather, just this once, I can take a WPC along.' He shuffled his feet awkwardly and avoided Llewellyn's eye. 'Ease you into it gradually, like, especially as this job's likely to be particularly gutty.'

'Thank you for the offer, sir, but no.' Llewellyn's stern self-control was back in place—just. 'Avoidance is no answer. I'd rather get it over with.'

Rafferty nodded, 'As you like.' He returned to Llewellyn's previous remark, glad to get away from such an uncomfortable topic. 'I didn't know you had a religious vocation, Taff.'

'I haven't.'

'Ah.' But it sounded as if Llewellyn had a pushy father in his youth, who took it for granted that his son would follow in his footsteps. It must have been quite a tussle for him to join the police service. Well, if Llewellyn wanted to confide in him, he would do so. Not that he showed any sign that he was about to fall on Rafferty's manly bosom.

Thankful for that, and relieved to have discovered a more human side to his sergeant, Rafferty felt the stirring of a little fellow-feeling, and as they went out to the car, he explained, 'The victim rented one of those anonymous and tacky bed-sits in Streatham for her trade. But her family live near here, according to the Met. Only about half a mile from the hospital. Perhaps the victim was visiting her parents and decided to earn a little extra while she was here?'

Llewellyn had brought the car round to the front earlier, and now it stood gleaming in the brilliant April sunshine. The

Welshman seemed to Rafferty to take little pleasure in much else, but cars appeared to be the joy of his life; this one was certainly cleaned to within an inch of it. He probably offered such ritual cleanliness up as a sacrifice to his dour Welsh god, thought Rafferty, and his earlier sympathy dissolved a little. 'I'll drive. Got the car keys?'

Reluctantly, Llewellyn handed them over. Rafferty knew he didn't like anyone driving "his" car—particularly him, whom Llewellyn considered both fast and reckless.

His expression resigned, Llewellyn got in. He visibly winced as Rafferty revved up.

Rafferty reached to take his cigarettes from his pocket. Then he remembered he'd given them up. Instead, he pulled out a bag of boiled sweets, unwrapped one and popped it in his mouth.

Glancing at Llewellyn, Rafferty noticed that the Welshman's eyes were still shadowed, even though he kept his gaze stiffly 'eyes-front'. He declined the proffered bag of sweets with a taut shake of his head. Anxious about the coming interview, Rafferty surmised, sucking hard on his lemon sherbet. That made two of them.

***

The privet hedge surrounding the Wilks's small front garden was fussily neat and clipped as efficiently as a sergeant-major's moustache, but to Rafferty it had more of the appearance of a green, plastic wall, than a living thing. As he advanced up the path, he took in the sparkling white nets draped across the louvre windows of the terraced house, each of their full folds a neat one inch from its neighbour, and he sighed. The short back and sides on the hedge had hinted at it, but the curtains confirmed that he and Llewellyn were likely to be regarded by the murdered girl's parents as little better than murderers themselves: murderers of reputation, respectability, and pride.

Rafferty glanced anxiously at Llewellyn as he raised the door-knocker and realised from the Welshman's stiff face he had come to the same conclusion. But before he could stiffen the other man's spine, the door opened a bare three inches and a woman's face appeared. Rafferty felt a momentary shame at the relief that flooded him when he saw her eyes were red-rimmed with weeping; they must already know, he concluded, mystified as to how, but grateful that someone else had broken the bad news to them.

'Who are you? What do you want?'

'Police, Mrs. Wilks,' Rafferty explained in a low voice, holding up his identity card for her to see. He cleared his throat of a sudden frog. 'It's about your daughter, Linda.'

Her head shot up. 'Linda? What's happened? Has she been arrest—' her voice broke off abruptly. She bit her lip, and, with evident reluctance, she opened the door wider. 'You'd best come in.'

Rafferty and Llewellyn exchanged puzzled glances as they followed her past the well-buffed horse-brasses and flower-patterned carpet of the hall. Rafferty concluded they must have had other bad news; something totally unconnected with their murder investigation.

Although it was still bright outside, the curtains were pulled across the windows, and the living room was shrouded in gloom. But the curtains were unlined and allowed sufficient filtered light through for Rafferty to confirm his earlier conclusions about the Wilks's respectability from a swift survey of the room. Everything was spotless and fussily neat. No books or newspapers created the usual friendly muddle that filled most people's homes. Each item had its place and remained in it. There were still more flowers here; on the fitted carpet, full-blown pink roses on the faded chintz-covered suite, delicate, tightly-enclosed buds on the wallpaper.

Rafferty felt Llewellyn give a start, when behind them, and so far unnoticed in the gloom, a man's figure rose to his feet. Linda's father, Rafferty guessed and introduced himself and Llewellyn. Like his wife, Mr Wilks didn't seem surprised to see them. What was going on here?

Sidney Wilks was not an impressive man. Short and wiry, under sparse pepper-and-salt hair, his face was brick-red, and a curious selection of expressions passed, one after the other over his features – shame, resentment, anger – and a quickly hidden fear, which Rafferty found even more baffling.

Invited to sit down, they eased themselves gingerly on to the edge of the chintz settee, Rafferty now almost as anxious as his sergeant for the job to be over and done with.

'Well?' Sidney Wilks barked at them suddenly. 'Why don't you get it over with? What's stopping you? Though I don't know why it takes two of you.'

Beside him, Rafferty felt Llewellyn jump, and he quickly found his voice in case his sergeant's stern self-control gave way and he said something they'd both regret. 'I'm sorry, Sir. It's just that I thought you knew, Mr Wilks,' he began. 'You seemed—'

'Knew? Of course we knew,' Daphne Wilks broke in before Rafferty could continue. 'Why else would we be so upset?' She glared at him, then, slowly, her gaze swung to Llewellyn, and her face changed as though she saw something in the Welshman's stiff, white demeanour that suddenly made everything clear to her. All at once her face became ashen; she sat abruptly on the armchair behind her and gazed accusingly at Rafferty.

'You're the one in charge of the murder. It was in the local paper.' Her voice was now no louder than a whisper. 'Oh, my God, no! It's her isn't it? The girl found murdered at that hospital—it's our Linda. That's why you're here. And I thought—' She gave a faint, hysterical laugh. 'Stupid of me. Why else would you come to see us? She is—was of age after all. What concern is it of the parents if a girl decides to pros—?'

'Mother!' Sidney Wilks's sharp voice cut across her words. 'They're not interested in that. That's our business.' He scowled a warning at her before he turned to Rafferty with an apologetic smile. 'I'm sorry. She's not herself. It's her age, you know?'

Rafferty stared at him, conscious that he'd made a terrible blunder. Did Sidney Wilks really imagine they were unaware of their daughter's extra-curricular activities? The way he had shut his wife up, suggested that was exactly what he did think.

Mr Wilks gave his hand-knitted cardigan a tug downwards as if to say, 'Glad I've got that out of the way', before he met Rafferty's eyes once more. 'Was she right? About Linda being the murdered girl?'

Rafferty nodded, and mumbled, 'We know what your daughter did, Mr Wilks, there's no point in trying to hide it. I'm sorry.' But Wilks gave every appearance of not hearing him, and he lapsed into silence.

'Perhaps these gentlemen would like some tea?' Wilks suggested to his wife, in the voice of a man determined to observe the civilities. His daughter might have been murdered, its tone implied, but that was no reason to forget one's manners. Mrs. Wilks cast a reproachful glance at her husband before going out and shutting the door behind her.

Rafferty found himself watching Wilks with a kind of horrid fascination. Unlike his wife, he didn't seem shocked by his revelation of their daughter's murder. Of course, shock came in many forms, but Sidney Wilks was a shade too accepting, too unemotional, and Rafferty wondered if he'd already known that his daughter was dead. How could he? Unless...?

But he was jumping to conclusions again, he chided himself. It might just be that he was one of those men who considered it unmanly to show strong feelings. He was of the generation to feel that way. And it seemed likely that Linda would have been the sort of girl to think nothing of disappearing for a few days without a word to her parents.

Even so, his manner made Rafferty feel increasingly uncomfortable. He opened his mouth to speak when Wilks's lack of emotion was dispelled in an outburst that was as sudden as it was furious.

'Wanted to be an actress!' His voice scorned such an ambition. Now he seemed to need to talk, to explain feelings he had been keeping pent-up. 'I told her not to be so stupid, as if such jobs were for people like us. Security, I said, that's what you need, my girl. Told her if she persisted no good would come of it, and I was right, wasn't I? No good has come of it.'

He sounded satisfied that his prediction had been proved correct. Perhaps he realised how this must appear, for his voice became quieter, more intense. 'I fixed her up with a good job at the local offices of one of the power companies when she left school,' he told them, as though he still didn't understand why his daughter should reject what had been good enough for him for forty years. 'Typing. They were even willing to train her on the 'phones in their Customer Service Department. But no—that wasn't good enough for Madam Linda. She had ambitions, she told us. Ambitions!'

Mrs. Wilks came back with the tea. Rafferty wasn't surprised that the bone china tea service had been brought out. More roses decorated the matching teapot and crockery. He was beginning to find the flowery theme of the room oppressive; he longed to loosen his tie and fling the blinds back.

Mrs. Wilks poured the tea and passed it round. The hot beverage seemed to restore her, for now she began to explain 'We had a row, the night—the night before she was found in that hospital. When I heard about it, I wondered if it could be our Linda. She hadn't come home, but then that wasn't unusual.'

'Used this place like a hotel,' Sidney Wilks interrupted. 'Thought her mother was a launderette and restaurant combined. I told her—'

'Please Sidney.' Obviously distressed, his wife cut off his flow, before she quietly continued. 'Besides, I didn't want to think about it. I persuaded myself it couldn't be her. I didn't want to face—' Her voice trailed away.

Rafferty felt sure that Daphne Wilks would always shy away from unpleasant reality. In this instance, he couldn't really blame her. The death of a child, whatever their age, was more than most parents could come to terms with. 'She died very quickly, Mrs. Wilks,' he told her, in a futile attempt at comfort. 'She couldn't have known anything about it. The – rest – happened after death.'

Mrs. Wilks nodded mechanically, as though she hadn't really taken in what he had told her, and she went on as if he'd never spoken. 'After the row, Linda ran out, and Sidney went after her.'

'I couldn't catch her,' Sidney Wilks quickly broke in again. 'She'd disappeared by the time I got to the end of the road.'

'I don't know why you didn't come straight back,' complained his wife. 'When you knew how upset I was.'

'I was upset too,' he defended himself aggressively. 'I wanted to be alone for a while, to think what was best to do. She told us she was moving out permanently,' he explained for Rafferty's benefit. 'She wasn't here much at the best of times. Staying with friends, she used to tell us she was. Anyway, she said she'd fixed up to move into a flat in London with some girlfriends. God knows who they were, she never mentioned any names. Had it all planned and not a word to us.'

'Was that what caused the row?' Llewellyn asked quietly, apparently having got himself back under control.

'No,' replied Mrs. Wilks. 'It was the—other business. You see I found her diary—'

'Mother!' Sidney Wilks's voice sharpened again. 'They don't need to know about that.' He turned back to the policemen, as though his word settled the matter, but Daphne Wilks had decided to face facts and she overruled her husband.

'It's no use, Sidney,' she told him. 'We can't hide it. Linda must have had a criminal record, don't you see? How do you think they were able to identify her? According to the papers...' She took a shuddering breath. 'Anyway, it might help them find out who did this dreadful thing. I owe her that much. We both do.'

She ignored her husband's ugly red flush, turned back to the policemen, and said, 'I found her diary, you see. Usually she locked it away, but that evening she must have forgotten. 'I was so stupid,' Daphne Wilks went on. 'At first, I thought she'd written a series of little plays. They were all set out like that, you see. But they were all on the same theme. That was what made me suspicious. She always took a particular case with her when she went up to London. Her "auditioning" gear, she told me it was. I forced it open. She kept it hidden at the back of her wardrobe. No wonder. Inside there were the most—'

She stopped for a moment to wipe her reddened nose with a damp handkerchief, and then went shakily on. 'All I could think was "why?" What could have made her do this to us?'

Mrs Wilks gave a half-shamed glance at her husband, before she went on. 'Sidney had been in the garage, working on the car, and when I heard her come home, I fetched him, so we could confront her together. I was in such a state; I didn't even make sure he washed his hands first. He left a dirty smear on the wallpaper.' Her mouth formed into lines of reproach, as if she believed that, by concentrating on mundane resentments, she could push the horror to the back of her mind. 'I haven't been able to get it out—'

'Can I see this diary?' Rafferty interrupted before the pair started on mutual recriminations.

'We burnt it,' said Sidney Wilks quickly. But not quite quickly enough, as his wife reached beneath the seat cushion of her armchair and brought out a large and expensive looking calf-skin-bound book and handed it over.

'You promised you'd burn it!' her husband accused.

'I know.' Her head drooped. 'I couldn't.' Slowly, she raised her head and looked at Rafferty. 'We've just got the gas fire, you see,' she explained with an air of apology. 'I'd have had to burn it out in the garden, and I kept thinking what the neighbours would say if any of the pages were to blow away.'

Rafferty guessed that what the neighbours would say had largely governed their lives. Sadly, he reflected that the neighbours would now have enough scandal to keep their tongues wagging for many a long day.

Mrs. Wilks was right, he saw, as he flicked through the diary. Linda had set it out like a play or a film script, or as near to them as either of them would recognise. The diary contained Linda Wilks's dreams; the film-script-like layout had helped to clothe the sordid reality of what she was doing in the soft-focus lighting of a film seduction scene. Had she managed to convince herself as well that she was merely acting out a role? Had she persuaded herself that should the acting become too brutally real the director would shout "Cut"?

He turned back to the first few pages. Slowly, he began to read.

ACT 1 SCENE 1

The scene opens in a book-lined study. We see an elderly man dressed in a school uniform sitting in front of a desk.

CUT TO: A young woman wearing a cape and mortar-board enters. In one hand she is carrying a cane which she hits into the other palm. She walks slowly forward till she is standing in front of the elderly schoolboy.

GIRL: You've been a naughty boy, haven't you, Simpson?

MAN: (Cringes). Yes Miss.

GIRL: Do you know what happens to naughty boys?

She swishes the cane.

MAN: Oh, yes Miss. I know.

The man's face goes pink. Now he seems suddenly excited.

GIRL: Lower your trousers then, Simpson and bend over the desk.

The man does as she says.

GIRL: It's six of the best for you.

Her cape swings open. Underneath she is naked. She gazes at the quivering buttocks of the man and raises her arm—

Rafferty snapped the diary shut and glanced quickly up as though he had been caught doing something dirty. From his brief flick through, the entire diary seemed filled with similar scenes. That one had been quite tame. But others... 'I'll have to take this,' he told them apologetically.

Sidney Wilks hissed at his wife. 'You should have destroyed it, as I said. Now the whole world will know exactly what sort of little trollop your daughter was.'

Rafferty wasn't altogether surprised at the speed with which Wilks distanced his own relationship with the girl. The theory was that tragedy brought people together. It didn't—more often it tore them apart in a manner as savage as the original crime. He'd seen it many times and it never failed to depress him. Grimly, he looked at Wilks as he began to taunt his wife.

'At least when they catch the man who killer her, and that's read out in court, the papers won't need to make up anything worse,' he told her, voice spiteful. 'This'll give the neighbours something to talk about all right.'

Mrs Wilks gasped. Her hand clutched at her bosom and the look she gave Rafferty was beseeching. 'Is he right? Will everyone hear all the details of what Linda—what she did? I thought you'd be able to keep it quiet.'

Rafferty looked from one to the other and swallowed hard. How could he tell her the truth? It would be kinder to let it dawn gradually on her. 'It depends,' he temporised. 'The way she earned her living may not have had anything to do with her murder, of course, in which case—'

'You don't really believe that though, do you, Inspector?' Sidney Wilks derided. 'It'll come out, especially as she was going to meet another of her men that night.'

Rafferty felt Llewellyn tense beside him before he made his second contribution to the interview. 'How do you know that, Sir?' he asked.

'She had a phone call, didn't she? About half ten that night, a few minutes after she came home. Taunted me with it when I demanded to know who it was. "One of my men friends," she said. "A medical man".' He glanced at his wife's huddled figure. 'Of course, you know we'll never be able to hold our heads up again,' he spat at her. 'We'll have to move.' This was said with such spiteful satisfaction that Rafferty felt his whole body cringe.

Mrs. Wilks's face seemed to crumple as she realised her husband was right. Fresh tears filled her eyes. She looked around her oppressively tidy living room with a tragic expression, shaking her head all the while, as though that loss, to her, was more unbearable than her daughter's death.

'Could we perhaps have a photograph of your daughter, Mr Wilks?' Rafferty put in abruptly. He needed to get out of this stifling atmosphere and breathe some fresh air. 'It might help us to catch her killer.'

'Have one?' The voice was tart. 'You can have them all. What do we want with them now?'

One by one, he pulled every photograph of Linda from the fireplace wall and dropped them with a clatter on the low table in front of the settee on which the two men sat. His wife made no protest, but just sat rocking herself backwards and forwards staring sightlessly at nothing, as though she had retreated to a secret refuge where sordid reality couldn't touch her.

'Ahem, Mr Wilks?' Rafferty began tentatively. 'Can you give us any reason why your daughter should dye her hair dark?'

Sidney Wilks blinked rapidly as he gazed down at the photographs; family snaps taken in happier times of Linda as a baby propped up with cushions, as a toddler, as a gap-toothed and wriggling tomboy sitting on her father's lap, school photos as a teenager where she looked with sultrily half-closed eyes into the camera—perhaps even then convinced she would be a great actress.

'It was for those acting roles she kept going for,' he told them in a flat voice. 'She thought she'd stand more chance if her hair was the same colour as the character she was trying for.' He reached out a shaking hand, picked up one of the most recent photographs and rubbed his thumb over the glass. 'That was my little girl,' he told them bleakly. 'My pretty, innocent little girl.'

He took out a large white handkerchief, and after blowing his nose, put it carefully back in his pocket. For a moment, he looked bewildered, as though he hadn't quite grasped what a cataclysm had wrecked his orderly little world. Then, without any warning, his face contorted, and he smashed the glass of the frame against the corner of the mantelpiece, yanked out the photo, and threw it at Rafferty.

'Take it. Take them all. We don't want them back. Wearing those short skirts of hers, flaunting herself, the bitch asked for it. She deserved all she got. Deserved all she got,' he repeated, as though trying to convince himself of it.

Silently, they stood up, and Rafferty picked up the photograph. Mrs. Wilks was still in a world of her own and took no further interest in the proceedings. 'I'd like to look at Linda's bedroom, Mr Wilks, if that's all right?'

Sidney Wilks just nodded. He'd washed his hands of his daughter, his expression said. They could do what they liked.

'Perhaps, while I'm doing that, you could let my sergeant here have a description of what Linda was wearing that night?' he suggested.

Llewellyn shot him a reproachful look and sat down again. Slowly, he pulled his notebook back out and began to write as Sidney Wilks' voice, drained now of emotion, described what his daughter had been wearing.

Rafferty went upstairs. It was evident which room had been Linda's. A riot of clothes in a tawdry kaleidoscope of colours littered the room as if in defiance of the order in the rest of the house. He saw a worn teddy on a shelf, tattered film scripts of old television series, make-up scattered across the top of the dressing table. His search was brief, but thorough.

He found the case that Mrs. Wilks had referred to, but it was empty, all the usual erotic items of a prostitute's art removed. Sidney Wilks had obviously been here before him. He must be cursing himself that he hadn't been quite thorough enough.

Rafferty returned to the living room to collect the stiffly-perched Llewellyn. And after drawing Sidney Wilks back from whichever hell he had retreated to, they said their goodbyes and speedily left.

Chapter Nine

Llewellyn expelled a long held-in sigh as the door closed behind them. His eyes curtained by the fall of thick black lashes, he gave himself a little shake, and the controlled expression was back in place, the deep emotions that had flickered across his features safely stowed away once more. 'An unhappy man,' was his taut comment. 'He loved her very much, in his own way, you could see that.'

Rafferty was about to disagree, then he realised his sergeant was right. Love came in all shapes and sizes; he, of all people should know that. His expression bleak, he began to flick through the diary once more as they made for the car.

Back to normal, Llewellyn found a mournful quote to enrich the experience still further. '"*Love is a sickness full of woes*",' he began. But Rafferty's involuntary groan caused him to break off mid-flow. 'Samuel Daniel, 1562—1619,' he muttered under his breath.

'Miserable git he sounds. Bet his family held one hell of a coffin-dancing Wake when he died.'

'Curious that Wilks didn't come straight back when he didn't find his daughter,' Llewellyn remarked after a brief silence. 'It would be more usual for parents to share the shock of such a discovery together.'

'You saw them. There was precious little attempt at comforting one another.

'They live only half a mile from the hospital,' Rafferty went on thoughtfully. 'Discovering that his daughter's on the game would be enough to make any man mad with rage.'

At least he assumed so. Not having ever experienced the dubious joys of fatherhood, he had only his imagination on which to draw. It was certainly a strong motive for murder. 'He could have followed her—he'd been tinkering with the car when his wife found the diary and called him into the house. Perhaps, when Linda ran out, without thinking, he carried the spanner he had been using to work on the car and went after her.'

'He couldn't have done it, of course.' Back in his stride with a vengeance, Llewellyn threw cold water over the idea with the ease of long practise. 'Linda was found inside the hospital grounds, not outside. Where would he get a key to that gate?'

'Perhaps he didn't need one.' Rafferty's head rose from his perusal of the diary, pleased he'd succeeded in coming up with a theory that Llewellyn wouldn't find so easy to fault. 'Maybe the person she was meeting let her in and left the door unlocked by mistake?'

He tapped the slim book with a forefinger. 'Or perhaps, if she had a regular customer at the hospital, he might have given her a key. Her father said she was going to see a medical man that night, and there's no reason why she shouldn't occasionally earn some money locally during a visit to her parents.'

Llewellyn nodded thoughtfully. 'And her father pushed through after her once she'd unlocked the gate? You could have something there, sir. Wilks seems the type to have a complete brainstorm. All that determined respectability is unnatural.' He gave Rafferty an inscrutable glance. 'As Freud said—'

'Never mind what Freud said,' Rafferty broke in before Llewellyn had a chance to start on all that psychological mumbo-jumbo. 'We'd do better finding out what her prospective flat-mates have to say. Now that we've got her name and photograph I'll get on to the media. I shouldn't think we'll have long to wait before her girlfriends contact us.' He sent up a silent prayer for forgiveness after his comforting lies to Mrs. Wilks. 'I agree the father's a possible suspect, but at this stage, we can't afford to concentrate our investigations too much on one person.'

Llewellyn askance at this, as well he might, given Rafferty's enthusiastic concentration on Melville-Briggs.

'Her girlfriends might know if Linda had a regular customer at the Elmhurst Sanatorium, particularly if they were on the game themselves.'

He opened the driver's side door of the car and was about to get in, when he saw Llewellyn's unhappy expression and relented. 'All right, you drive,' he said. He pressed the button to unlock the car, handed the fob over, walked round to the passenger side and got in.

Llewellyn fumbled with the ignition fob and Rafferty chivvied him. 'Hurry up man. Let's get back to the station. We've got a lot to do.'

He brandished the photograph of Linda. 'I want you to get copies made of this and give them to the house-to-house team. They'll have to start over again now. And I'll want posters of her put up at bus and train stations. I want everyone within a twenty-mile radius to know her face. Get the photo off to the Met. She presumably found most of her johns there, and it's possible there's someone in town who knew her in both identities.' Certainly better than her parents seemed to, he added silently to himself.

Llewellyn was still applying his logical mind to Rafferty's previous idea. 'If her father did do it, why would he strip her?'

Rafferty glanced back at the house as Llewellyn started up the car. Someone had been watching them. As he turned his head, he just caught a quick movement as the nets were twitched back into place.

'He said she dressed like a tart. Perhaps he thought, naked, she looked more respectable, more innocent than she ever could in her working gear. If it was him, I wonder what he did with her clothes. He wouldn't have been able to burn them easily with no open fires in the house. Perhaps he buried them or threw them in the sea? It's only about a fifteen-minute walk from their house. I want you to notify the search teams to be on the lookout for anything washed up by the tide.'

Llewellyn slipped in a little philosophical comment as he slid the gear stick into first. 'He'll blame his wife for the girl going to the bad, of course. That type always does.'

'Well, he's got to blame someone. I bet your friend, Freud, would agree it's human nature. Especially if he did do for the girl. And who else is there to blame?'

Perhaps, he mused, if Linda's mother had been a different sort of woman, her father would have been a different sort of man, and Linda would still be alive. But of course, he reminded himself, you could say that about anyone.

***

Rafferty was gratified to find he was in the right for once. They'd passed Linda's photograph to the media in time to catch the Monday papers, and Linda's girlfriends had seen the item and the request for information. He and Llewellyn were soon en route to south London to see them.

'Let me do the talking,' he warned Llewellyn. If, like Linda, they were part-time hookers, he didn't want Llewellyn going all moral on him and putting the girls' backs up before they shared what they knew.

Despite making good time, it was nearly noon when they reached Streatham, and then Rafferty spent twenty minutes circling round before he could park.

Finally, ignoring Llewellyn's stern exhortations about policemen not being above the law, he left the car on a double yellow line. He gave Llewellyn a smug smile as he dug in his back pocket and slapped a 'Police' sticker on the windscreen, a la 'Del Boy' Trotter with his 'Doctor on call' homemade effort.

"'Be prepared", is my watchword, Daff.' The Welshman wasn't the only one who could come out with quotations, even if his own weren't of his sergeant's preferred highbrow sort. "'Dib, dib, dib, dob, dob, dob.'"

Llewellyn's aquiline nostrils quivered a fraction at this, but he said nothing, beyond the accurate observation, 'You were never a Boy Scout.'

'True. I didn't fancy sewing on all the badges I'd have won. Bet you were, though.'

Llewellyn didn't deny it.

Rafferty cursed when he saw the flat. It formed part of a large house, with a tarmac front garden that provided ample space for parking and would have saved them the half-mile trudge back to the car. He should have guessed. Many of the large, formerly family homes around this area had been converted into flats.

Rafferty straightened his dazzling orange and magenta tie, ignoring the sombre-suited Llewellyn's wince of pain, and studied the array of cards and bells by the front door. He pulled a face when he realised they wanted the top floor. 'I hope they've got a lift,' he muttered as he rang the bell.

The grill spluttered into life, he shouted his business and the door was released. Rafferty cursed again as he saw the 'lift out of order' sign.

By the time he reached the top floor, his breathing was phone-pervert heavy, and he had to hang on to the banisters for a minute, with nothing but a helpless grin to ward off the wary looks of the two young women at the door. While he clung there, Rafferty had time to reflect that he had probably stopped smoking none too soon. His lip curled as he noted Llewellyn's breath was perfectly measured. The Welshman's body was as disciplined as everything else in his life, and he worked out twice a week in the police gym; something which earned a few ribald comments from the canteen cowboy beer guts at the station.

The girls looked nervously, first at each other, and then at him. 'Inspector Rafferty?'

Still gasping, he could only nod. Did they really think any self-respecting rapist likely to knacker himself by climbing all those stairs?

As the girls still regarded him with suspicion, he pulled his identity card from his wallet; wordlessly, he thrust it at them.

Reassured, they now became concerned at his speechless condition, and one of the girls asked, 'Are you all right?'

'Really, I'm fine,' he gasped, when he was finally able to get a word out.

'The stairs are tough on older people,' she sympathised artlessly, while behind him, he heard a muffled snort from Llewellyn, who was still – just – the right side of thirty.

Her comment did nothing to boost Rafferty's ego. Dammit all, he was only thirty-seven, not seventy-seven. He supposed along with giving up smoking, he ought to start taking more exercise, watch his diet, cut down on alcohol; in short, make himself as big a misery as Llewellyn.

Apparently, the three girls all made a somewhat precarious living on the fringes of show business, and although Linda had not only been a friend of sorts, but had also been about to move in, they could tell them little about her. It seemed that none of them enquired too closely into the affairs of the others.

'Please try to remember,' he pressed. 'It's very important. Did Linda say anything, anything at all, about any regular men she might see at Elmhurst, or where they might meet?'

They looked at one another and shook their heads. The blonde girl, Patsy, said, 'We knew she must have some men friends down there, of course, because sometimes, when she came up to town, she had quite a bit of money with her, money she wouldn't have been able to earn otherwise. But who they might have been, I've no idea. Perhaps Tina would know more, she's known Linda a lot longer than either of us two.'

Rafferty looked about him hopefully.

'She's not here. She had a very early flight to the States last Saturday morning. Tina's a dancer,' Patsy explained, 'and her agent managed to get her a tour booking as a replacement at the last minute.'

'Would you have a number where I could contact her?'

'She forgot her mobile in the rush to make the flight. You could try her agent.' Patsy picked up the phone book and read out his name and number as Rafferty jotted the information down.

'You don't happen to know the names of any of her men friends here in London?'

Patsy shook her head. 'She rarely mentioned anyone. Men were just – men – to Linda, unless she met someone who could help her career.'

'It was that important to her?'

Patsy smiled at him. 'Oh, yes. In fact, you might say she spent her whole life playing a part.' She handed him a photograph from the sideboard. 'That's Linda, in the middle.'

The Wilks's family photographs hadn't really captured the dead girl. This photo gave far more of an idea of the real Linda. As Patsy had said, she was pretty enough, in a pale, unhealthy sort of way. Her hair hung over her face in the expected provocative manner, and though her mouth held a matching pout for the camera, there was a hint of desperation in her eyes.

'When was this photo taken?' asked Llewellyn, obviously determined to get in on the act, despite Rafferty's warning.

'Last year. She had a small part in a film, and we went to see her on set. She was so excited about breaking into films, was sure her big chance would come from it. But it was never released. They ran out of money.'

'Did Linda ever mention the Elmhurst Sanatorium?' Rafferty queried. He didn't have much hope anything would come of it, but he had to ask. They shook their heads. 'What about Dr. Anthony Melville-Briggs or Dr. Simon Smythe?' No, they'd never heard of them either. He ran a few more names past them, but they, too, were unknown to them.

Still, that proved nothing, Rafferty reassured himself. Linda had not been forthcoming about her men friends. He held up the photograph. 'Is it all right if I take this?'

Patsy nodded.

'I'll let you have it back as soon as possible.' He fished in his pocket for his card and handed it over. 'If you think of anything, please phone me.'

Patsy showed him out. 'Poor Linda. All she wanted was the big break. She never talked about anything else.' She shook her head. 'It's funny, but the last part she played was that of an angel. Another flop.' Her eyes flickered upwards. 'Strange to think that if she's managed to get up there she'll be auditioning for the same part right now. You will get the man who did this to her, won't you, Inspector?'

Rafferty did his best to reassure her on that point. He wished he felt half as confident as he sounded.

He was thoughtful as he and Llewellyn walked back to the car. They had learned little and the thought depressed him, but he cheered up a bit when he discovered they hadn't been given a parking ticket. He even let Llewellyn drive, and as they left the quiet residential street behind, he sat staring restlessly out of the side window. The traffic lights changed to green and they rounded the corner. His ears pricked up as he heard the familiar sound of a concrete mixer. Hadn't his Uncle Pat said he was working on a building site around this way?

Rafferty looked at his watch and grinned. Five to one. Couldn't have timed it better if he'd tried. 'Pull up here,' he instructed.

'But it's a double yellow line, Sir,' Llewellyn protested for the second time. 'I really can't just—'

Rafferty sighed, unwilling to go through that all over again. 'I'm only asking you to pull up for a minute, not take up squatter's rights.'

Llewellyn muttered under his breath but did as he was told.

In spite of feeling he was beginning to know and understand his sergeant better, Rafferty still found his unrelenting company something of a strain, and he needed a break, however short. The craving for a bit of light relief made him feel guilty, and the sharp edge had gone from his voice as he added, 'Get some lunch and come back for me in an hour. You'll find there's a decent pub near the common. They serve hot food and they've got a car park, with no double yellows in sight.'

He got out of the car and slammed the door with the enthusiastic vigour of a convict out on parole. He crossed the pavement and skirted the barriers guarding the building site.

A pleased smile settled on his face as he took in the beginnings of a block of superior apartments rising from the dust and rubble of some previous building. He stood and watched for a little while, taking pleasure in the almost symphonic movements of the foreman and his men as they laid their bricks. Then, as though obeying the commands of some invisible conductor, they all laid down their trowels at virtually the same moment, and with a purposeful air, they followed one another down the ladder secured to the scaffolding. Lunchtime.

Rafferty strolled over. Already he could feel his spirits lifting. Building sites always had that effect on him. He had done some of his best thinking whilst surrounded by the roar of machinery and the good-natured cussing of a building crew.

'Hello, Uncle Pat.' It was a courtesy title as Pat was really a first cousin; his oldest and favourite cousin, in spite of the fact that he was always ready to take a rise out of him. At least he didn't hold his job against him.

The black-haired giant glanced round and his broken-toothed mouth curved into a grin. 'Joseph Aloysius! It's yourself, is it?' His eyes twinkled as he clapped him on the back with a heavy hand. 'What's this I hear about you and our Maureen? Your Ma's told me you're sweet on her.'

Rafferty sighed. Maureen was Pat's eldest daughter, and his second cousin. She was very bright and usually managed to reduce Rafferty to tongue-tied inanities in ten seconds flat, an obstacle to love that his Ma seemed happy to ignore in her desperation to see him married again.

The trouble was that his Ma couldn't see beyond the fact that, in a country of increasing non-believers, Maureen was a "good Catholic girl", and likely to encourage the religiously lax Rafferty back to the paths of righteousness.

As if that wasn't recommendation enough for his mother, she came from a good breeding family—his own. Hadn't his Ma drawn his attention to Maureen's child-bearing hips more than once? Unfortunately, for his Ma, they seemed to clinch that the match was made in heaven.

'When's the wedding?' Pat enquired, still grinning. 'Sure an' it'll be useful having a policeman as a son-in-law.'

Rafferty managed a sickly grin.

'Don't look so worried, lad. It's only pullin' your leg, I am. My girl knows her worth, her ma's made certain of it. Surely, you know she goes for the intellectual type?'

Rafferty hadn't, but, as he did his best to stay out of her way, that wasn't surprising. Still, he made a mental note, just in case this fact should come in useful one day.

'She's on the hunt for a professor, at least,' Pat went on. 'I'll give you ten to one she wouldn't think of throwing herself away on a skinny carrot-top copper, whatever your ma hopes. It's my bet you'll stay on the shelf a while yet, Joseph.'

Amazingly, Pat had married an educated woman with ambitions, and, after twenty-five years together, they were still happy. It must be the attraction of opposites, mused Rafferty, uneasily reminded of Maureen.

Pat put his great arm round his shoulders and gave him the same disarming grin that had persuaded the middle-class highbrow, Claire Tyler-Jenkins, up the aisle and into his arms.

'Chin up, son. A little disappointment in love is good for a man. Sure and you'll get over it.'

Since being bowled over by his uncle's determined romancing, Rafferty's 'Auntie' Claire had transferred her ambitions to her children. Rafferty was grateful to have confirmed his conviction that none of those ambitions included marrying one of her daughters to him.

But he still suffered a twinge of unease. Because his Ma was also a woman of ambition. And Kitty Rafferty had a way of eroding a person's resistance that was positively tidal.

'Enough of this mournfulness.' Pat punched him playfully on the shoulder with sufficient force to break a bone. 'Come away in the hut and have a bite to eat with the lads.'

As he sat in the hut, wedged between his Uncle Pat and his son, Sean, Rafferty for the moment forgot his troubles. The atmosphere in the hut was cheerful, the tin mug in his hand, held tea, strong, sweet, and piping hot, and his Ma, Llewellyn, The Elmhurst Sanatorium and Dr. Melville-Briggs seemed a million miles away. For the moment, he was content.

Chapter Ten

Although the A11 was fairly quiet, it was late afternoon by the time they got back to Melville-Briggs's sanatorium and their dreary little office.

'Get hold of Dally,' Rafferty instructed the Welshman. 'Remind him that I'm still waiting for the results of the post-mortem. Anyone would think he had a conveyor-belt of corpses awaiting his attention.'

Of course, there was no answer from Sam Dally's end. And as he listened to Llewellyn leave a message Rafferty checked down his lists. 'We'd better get on. We've only one or two more members of staff to go, and three more patients. Right, let's have—' He paused, unable to read his own handwriting. 'Nurse White.'

'Nurse Wright, is, I think you'll find, the young lady's name, sir,' Llewellyn supplied confidently, secure in the ivory tower of his own perfect script.

'Whatever,' Rafferty mumbled. 'Let's have her in.'

Nearly three quarters of an hour later, Rafferty knew he was in no danger of ever forgetting the wretched woman's name. He felt like cursing it and her from Llewellyn's ivory tower.

Nurse Wright mightn't have been sufficiently academic to have studied for the higher, RMN qualification, Rafferty reflected, but she was smart enough to know on which side her bread was buttered. It had taken him all that time to drag her story out of her and, even then, it came reluctantly. Disgruntled, he wondered if she was hoping for promotion to Melville-Briggs's bed.

Nurse Wright told them a young woman had handed her a note for Melville-Briggs just as she had arrived at the side gate for duty on the night of the murder. Of course, she hadn't thought to give it to them when Linda Wilks's body had been found the next morning. She'd actually thrown it away. Or so she said.

She also said this young woman had told her she would wait till 11.30 p.m. for Melville-Briggs to contact her on her mobile. But as Nurse Wright claimed it was only when she got no answer to her knock on the door of Melville-Briggs's hospital flat that night that she realised it was the night of the Doctors' Do, so had thrown the note away.

***

Of course, the note had vanished. Rafferty wondered if she'd handed it to Melville-Briggs at the first opportunity and hadn't thrown it in the waste-basket at all. He cursed as he thought of the hours be wasted raking through dustbins. He'd had to take men off the other search teams to look for it. Remembering

Nurse Wright's tight white uniform and the fashionably tousled blonde curls under the saucily-positioned cap, he hoped Melville-Briggs would be grateful for her attempted discretion. They deserved each other.

They'd almost certainly lost the element of surprise in questioning Melville-Briggs about the matter. He'd be expecting them to demand an explanation. Well, Rafferty determined, he wasn't going to—at least not yet. Apart from his Boy Scout motto, Rafferty had another one: never do what people expect you to do. It left them unbalanced which was just what he wanted. He'd see Gentleman Jim when he gauged vertigo was ready to tip the doctor over into some useful disclosures, and not before.

***

Tuesday morning was fresh and bright. The tantalising intimation of spring made Rafferty reluctant to head straight for their grim temporary office. Instead, he lingered in the hospital grounds for a few precious moments of peace. But at a sound behind him, he realised that brief respite was to be denied him.

'Psst.'

Rafferty stopped and turned, but there was no-one in sight. He shook his head and told himself he'd be seeing pink elephants next.

'Psst.'

There it was again.

It seemed to be coming from the trees bordering the perimeter wall, and he tried to peer through this newly-leafed bower. 'Who's there?' he called.

'Shh. Be quiet, can't you?' he was asked in a furious whisper. The voice sounded whinily familiar. 'Come over here, for God's sake, before somebody sees you.'

Rafferty put his hands in his pockets, and after a casual glance around to see if he was being observed, sauntered as nonchalantly as curiosity permitted, towards the trees and the urgent, whispered summons.

He wasn't altogether surprised to find that it was Gilbert, the gate porter who had found the body, who was indulging in such James Bondian tactics. 'Not got the sack, yet, then?' he enquired dryly, which conversational gambit only earned him a scowl. 'What do you want, Gilbert?'

'Got something that might interest you, 'spector,' said Gilbert, with a quick, furtive glance over his shoulder. 'I meant to tell you before, like, only it slipped me mind.'

What dreadful secret could be pummelling Gilbert's flexible conscience? Rafferty had told the little man to consider him as a priest; perhaps he was now to be treated to a confession? He hoped Gilbert didn't realise that full confessional secrecy was not something that he personally had any truck with. 'I'm listening, Gilbert,' he responded, assuming as pious a stance as he could muster. 'Go on.'

'I wanted to tell you about who I saw in the local pub the night the girl was killed. As I say, I meant to tell you before—'

'And who might that be?' Rafferty interrupted.

'Simple Simon.'

'Dr. Simon Smythe do you mean?'

'That's right. Simple Simon. Only he didn't meet a pie-man.' Gilbert sniggered at his own wit.

Rafferty smiled obligingly and waited for him to elaborate.

'He met a girl. And 'im meant to be on duty, too.' He sniffed, adopting the self-righteous tones of a man who knew his duty and did it, come what may.

'You're sure it was the night of the murder?'

'Course I'm sure. He was in the small, private bar; knocking back whisky like it was going out of fashion. He didn't see me as the angle was awkward, but I saw 'im all right. I only caught a glimpse of the girl, though.'

'This girl—are you saying it was our murder victim, Linda Wilks?'

'I'm not saying nothin'. I'm just tellin' you what I saw, ain't I?'

'But Linda Wilks was a local girl and Elmhurst's a small place. Are you saying you didn't know her?'

'I wish you'd stop tryin' to put words into me mouth,' Gilbert complained. 'I didn't say I didn't know Linda. I did.' Hastily, in case, Rafferty should think he had murdered her, he added, 'Just to nod to like, when she was 'ere, which wasn't often.

'Anyway, all I'm sayin' is that the girl I saw could 'ave been Linda. But as I only caught a glimpse of the back of 'er 'ead, before the landlord came and served me and blocked me view, I can't swear to it. I can't be sure who she was. But Linda must 'ave been in Elmhurst that night, mustn't she?' he remarked slyly. 'She managed to get 'erself murdered, after all. Bit of a coincidence that, to my way of thinkin'. Mind, I'm not sayin' that Simple Simon done it. That's fer 'im to know and for you to find out, ain't it?'

Rafferty sighed. Who'd have suspected that Gilbert had such delicate scruples? For some reason, he wanted to drop Simon Smythe in it, but his strange code wouldn't let him make a proper job of it, wouldn't let him say anything definitely helpful to the police.

'Mind,' Gilbert went on, confidingly. 'If it was Linda Wilks, we all know what 'e was doin' wiv 'er, don't we? Simple Simon rarely 'ad a girlfriend. Not a proper one, like.' He sniggered. 'You might call Linda Wilks more an improper one, mightn't yer?'

Ignoring the salacious look in Gilbert's eye, Rafferty asked, 'Did they come in together?'

Gilbert shrugged. 'Don't know. I only noticed them at the last knockin's. Landlord called time five minutes later.'

'Can you describe this girl?'

Gilbert screwed up his face, as though to emphasise the difficulty of casting his mind back in time the vast distance of four days. 'Let me see. She had long, dark hair,' he at last revealed. 'Admittedly, Linda Wilks was blonde the last time I saw 'er, but I generally never saw 'er with the same colour 'air twice in a row, so that don't mean nothin'. Bit on the skinny side. Meself, I prefer a woman with a bit more meat on her bones.'

'Never mind about that. Get on with it.'

Gilbert tutted. 'I'm tellin' you ain't I? She was about nineteen, twenty, I'd say. Quite tall, about 5' 7".'

Gilbert seemed to be having few problems with his memory now, Rafferty noted. He suspected that the real reason he was the recipient of Gilbert's news was that the porter had tried to get Simon Smythe to cough up in return for keeping quiet and had been refused.

Smythe's hitherto unsuspected bravery surprised him. Unless it was that the poor sap just hadn't had the wherewithal to buy the porter's silence.

Gilbert continued in an even more confiding tone. 'I'm not normally a man to snitch, like, but if 'e done it, then it's my duty to 'elp the police ain't it? 'Ere,' he looked sideways at Rafferty. 'Isn't there usually some sort of reward offered for 'elping the police? Not that I'm doing it for the money,' he added hastily, as he saw Rafferty's frown. 'But if it's my entitlement, I might as well 'ave it.'

Rafferty's lips tightened. Gilbert struck him as the sort of man who would milk a system for every penny of his entitlements, whether he deserved them or not.

Not without a certain amount of satisfaction, he said, 'I'm sorry, Gilbert, but you must have been watching too many cops and robbers programmes on the telly. You're thinking of insurance companies. They're the ones with money to burn on financial rewards for informants, not the poor copper.'

Gilbert looked as if he regretted his confidences now the chance of any profit was gone. Rafferty decided it was time to get tough with him. 'I must say, I'm surprised it's taken you so long to "remember" what you saw. What's the matter, Gilbert? Did Smythe tell you to go to hell?'

Gilbert stiffened, the image of injured innocence. Unfortunately for him, it was at odds with the shifty look in his eyes. 'I don't know what you're talkin' about,' he retorted belligerently. 'I'm only tryin' to do me duty. But if all you're goin' to do is make nasty 'sinuations, I won't bother.' He clamped his mouth tight shut and made to go. But Rafferty grabbed his arm and held it tightly.

'Not so fast, Mr Gilbert. If there's any more I want to hear it.' He smiled grimly into the man's sharp, weasel features. 'After all, you want to do your duty, don't you?'

Evidently Gilbert thought better of playing hard to get. Sticking out his bottom lip, he remarked plaintively, 'I was just about to tell you, wasn't I? You don't give a man a chance.'

'So, I'm giving you the chance now. Take it.'

'All right, all right, keep yer 'air on,' Gilbert complained. 'Though I don't know what else you expect me to say. You coppers are always putting words into a man's mouth. I don't want you to think—'

'Never mind what I think. Did they leave together?'

'No,' Gilbert reluctantly admitted. 'They seemed to have a bit of a row, and she just upped and left. He hung about for a minute, then he followed her out. He could 'ave caught up with 'er easily enough, what wiv those great long, gangling legs of 'is.' He eyed Rafferty speculatively. 'Gonna arrest him are yer?'

Rafferty tapped the side of his nose with his finger. 'That's for me to know and you to discover, Gilbert.'

The porter scowled, and Rafferty eyed him thoughtfully. It seemed that Gilbert had noticed rather more than a second's glimpse would reveal. It didn't surprise him. Smythe was supposed to be on duty at the hospital, and Rafferty could imagine the porter's shifty eyes out on stalks when he saw Smythe in the pub. Gilbert's grubby little mind must have worked overtime, calculating the nice little profit he'd receive for keeping his mouth shut. It was surely only a base spite that had made him tell Rafferty what he'd seen when any blackmailing demand he'd attempted had been refused.

He eyed the man with distaste. 'Would you recognise her again?'

'Doubt it. I told yer, I only saw—'

'The back of her head. I know. I just wondered if any more of your memory had inexplicably returned.'

'I'd tell yer if it did, 'spector,' Gilbert protested, with a show of hurt pride. 'You needn't sound as if I forgot deliberately. I reckon it must 'ave been the shock that made me forget. Yes,' he added firmly, glad to have found a believable excuse for his memory lapse. 'That'll be it. Shock can do funny things to a man's memory, you know. You learn things like that workin' in an 'ospital.'

'Really? Well, we must just be glad that the shock's started to wear off, then, mustn't we?'

Gilbert scowled again, and his face fell into disconsolate folds. Rafferty ignored him and concentrated on the implications of what the porter had just told him.

If Linda Wilks had been with Smythe just before she was murdered, it looked as if Melville-Briggs would be off the hook, which was rather a pity. He'd been looking forward to tackling him about the disappearing note. He still might do it, though, he promised himself, as a small reward for putting up with the doctor's increasing harassment. He seemed to expect Rafferty to debrief him on their results at the end of every day and he was getting fed up with it. If it wasn't for the fact that he was a buddy of the Chief Constable...

Rafferty found a pleasant smile for his informant. 'Thank you, Gilbert. You've been most helpful. I expect the Chief Constable will send you a letter of thanks. You could frame it.'

Gilbert snorted. 'Likely story. Seems to me all the likes of me get from the police is nasty 'sinuations.'

'I wonder why?' Rafferty walked away, leaving a disgruntled Gilbert muttering obscenities behind him.

***

The pub was busy with its lunch-time crowd when Rafferty and Llewellyn walked in. Rafferty caught the landlord's eye and beckoned him over.

'Police. Sorry to trouble you again. We have information that Linda Wilks might have been in here last Friday night. The night she was murdered.'

The landlord frowned. 'Who told you that?'

Rafferty's confidence began to evaporate a little. 'Never mind. Just think about it. She was a local girl. You must have known her by sight. Surely you remember seeing her that Friday?'

'I can't say as I do,' he replied. 'It was a very busy night. Darts final and the bar was packed with supporters from The Horse and Groom in the village. Run off my feet I was.'

'She was in the private bar, not the public.'

'No. she wasn't,' the landlord contradicted. 'She might have been in the public bar, but, as I said, there was such a crush, it would have been easy to miss her.'

'Perhaps some of your regulars could help?' Llewellyn suggested.

Unfortunately, it appeared that the regulars had celebrated themselves senseless after their team had won the darts final, neither their evidence nor their memories could be relied upon.

'Sorry, Inspector.' The landlord was apologetic. 'It was a bit of a wild night, I'm afraid. We were all a bit sozzled. It's a good ten years since we won the trophy.' He glanced up at the silver cup proudly displayed above the bar.

Rafferty sighed. 'This other girl—the one who was in the pub, the one in the private bar? Perhaps you can describe her?'

He nodded. 'Reminded me of the sister-in-law a bit. She was a real classy looking piece, and she had long dark hair, whereas Linda tended to fade into the wallpaper a bit. Now, let me see.' He glanced again at the darts trophy as though seeking inspiration. 'She was about twenty or thereabouts, I reckon.

Stylishly dressed. Nicely-spoken, too. She stood out, see? Not our usual sort of customer at all.'

Although, as the girl hadn't been Linda Wilks, he didn't think it would be relevant to the case, Rafferty's curiosity was piqued. 'Anything else you remember about her?'

'I could tell from her accent she wasn't from around these parts,' the landlord went on conversationally. 'I remember thinking it a bit odd that she should come into my pub, as it's so out of the way.' The landlord fingered his double chin. 'I seem to remember seeing her in here a week or two ago, as well, now I think about it. I began to hope we were going to be taken over by some yuppie types. I'd have been able to put my prices up.'

Rafferty wasn't interested in the landlord's lost hopes. 'Those are the only times you'd seen the girl?'

'Reckon so.'

'The second time she came in, I understand she wasn't alone?' Llewellyn put in.

The man's eyes were bright with gossip. 'That's right. She was at first, but later, near closing time, she was drinking with a chap called Smythe from the hospital. Know him?'

Rafferty nodded. 'They didn't leave together?'

The landlord shrugged. 'Don't know. When I came round for the glasses, they'd both gone.' He grinned. 'I was pretty gone myself by that time.'

Rafferty nodded his thanks, and they left. So much for Gilbert's confidences, he thought. The porter had been careful not to positively identify the girl as Linda; Rafferty suspected that he had known damn well that Smythe had been with another girl altogether that night. After all, it would seem, from what he'd said, that his single glance had been one long, riveted stare.

Although Gilbert had merely told him about the incident and encouraged him to put two and two together and make five, he intended to have a few words with Gilbert when next he saw him. Still, it wouldn't do any harm to talk to Smythe. He'd already lied to them about being at the hospital the entire night. It was possible he'd told other lies as well. Linda Wilks could easily have been in the pub that night, unnoticed by the landlord. He'd said himself she tended to fade into the wallpaper

Why shouldn't Smythe know her, even if not by her real name? He could have used her services. He could even have been the medical type who had rung her up that evening. Perhaps he had booked her services for when he returned to the hospital from the pub and had tipped her the ink as he'd left.

Rafferty brightened. 'Come on,' he said to Llewellyn. 'Let's go back to the station and call Dally. He might have some results at last.' There was no point in going off half-cocked, he told himself. He wanted more substantial proof against Smythe than the fact that he had been in the pub, drinking when he should have been on duty and had lied about his whereabouts at the time of the murder.

Back at the station, Rafferty put his feet up on his office desk and took the telephone from Llewellyn. 'What happened to you, Sam?' he asked. 'I expected the results of the PM. before now.'

'We don't always get what we expect in this life, Rafferty,' Sam Dally replied laconically. 'Surely your mammy told you that?'

'My mammy told me a lot of things, Sam—not all of them very wise. But then, a woman who regards all doctors as gods can't be entirely relied upon.' Sam snorted disgustedly at the other end, but Rafferty carried on. 'Have you got any answers for me? Something that'll hold up in court preferably.'

'Beggars can't be choosers,' he was told. 'You'll have to make do with what I have got, and that's precious little—a few answers, but more questions. What would you like first?'

Rafferty sighed. 'Just give it to me as it comes.'

'Right. She died between 10.45 and midnight. From the blow to the back of the head, as I told you.'

According to Gilbert, Smythe had left the pub about 11.30 p m; ample time for him to meet Linda Wilks and take her back to the hospital. Ample time for murder. The timing was surely too coincidental for any other answer? Rafferty felt the excitement begin to build again. 'And had she had sex before she died?' Whatever other questions might remain unanswered from Sam's findings, Rafferty was confident that this wouldn't be one of them and Sam's firm 'no', muted some of his excitement. He had been relying on obtaining forensic evidence to confront Smythe with the murder. Uneasily, he wondered if it was possible he had been wrong about him? But he brightened again as he remembered that the coincidences connecting him to the girl's murder were pretty strong. The man had probably just lost his head. With a character like Smythe, the slightest suspicion of a sneer on the girl's part could be enough to push him over the brink. No doubt when he saw what his drunken frustration had done to her, his sexual desire had cooled quicker than the corpse.

'No sign of a struggle either,' Sam went on, happy to provide the rest of the questions he had promised earlier. 'Her body was untouched, there was no skin trapped under her nails. Someone just bopped her on the head, laddie, and then turned her over and set about removing her face. Odd sort of weapon, too. Not the usual blunt instrument. Could be some sort of garden tool. There were small traces of rust in the wounds. Obviously matey-boy didn't go to the expense of buying a new tool to bash her head in with.'

'Must have Scottish blood in him,' Rafferty murmured. But he wasn't really in the mood for their usual banter, and Dally was, anyway, impervious to insults.

'I've ordered further analysis. You'll get the results all in good time.'

In his good time he meant, Rafferty reflected glumly. Talk about Dally by name and dally by blooming nature.

Sam's evidence reminded Rafferty of something. Hadn't Mrs. Galvin mentioned that the patients were encouraged to help with the gardening? Perhaps they might have been allowed to carelessly leave their tools lying around? 'You mentioned that this weapon could be a garden tool. Can't you be more specific?'

'Could be a fork or a rake, something like that. But don't quote me on it, Rafferty. I'm not sure what it is.'

Rafferty frowned into the receiver. At least Dally had finally admitted it. So far, he was getting more questions than answers, as Sam had promised, and he didn't like it.

'Looks like you've got yourself an oddball, Rafferty. Someone who murders just for the fun of it.'

'You needn't sound so pleased about it.'

'Keeps me in employment,' observed the caring doctor, complacently. 'What do you reckon the motive could be?'

'The usual,' he replied, still thinking of Simon Smythe. 'He must have hit her harder than he thought and panicked. Still, it's strange that the girl didn't either put up some sort of a struggle or accommodate her attacker's sexual requirements. I mean, a need for violent sex is hardly likely to come as a surprise to a prostitute. Yet, according to you, she did neither. I don't know what to make of it, but I intend to find out.'

'And the best of British to you. Oh, and another thing,' Sam tutted to himself. 'You nearly made me forget, the way you go wittering on. She was pregnant. About two months gone.'

Chapter Ten

It seemed Smythe had had second thoughts about his lies, for when they got back to the hospital, they found a note pushed under the outside door to their office.

But arresting Smythe, even if he was the murderer, wasn't a prospect likely to fill Rafferty with triumph. If he had been a hunting man, Smythe was the kind of catch he'd have left for the dogs.

Still, he reflected, as he picked up the internal phone and dialled Smythe's number, it would be a relief to get his first murder case wrapped up. But there was no reply. 'Probably sitting up there in his office wetting himself,' Rafferty said. 'Let's go and see.'

Smythe's first floor office was small and rather cramped. The walls housed a display of achievements; his medical qualifications, and pictures of him at various stages of his school career, prep-school, and university and in a white coat outside some unknown teaching hospital. Each time, he was flanked by a man and woman; his parents presumably.

'You wanted to see us, Dr. Smythe?'

After passing his tongue over dry lips, Smythe nodded miserably. 'I suppose Gilbert's spoken to you?'

'You suppose right. You shouldn't have told us lies, Doctor. Did you really think we wouldn't find out the truth?'

'I meant to tell you, I'd gone into your office fully intending to, but I lost my nerve.' He licked his lips again. 'I thought you might be glad to pin it on me, especially as Dr. Melville-Briggs had offered you a bribe.'

'I didn't take the bribe,' Rafferty was quick to point out, annoyed that his morals should be questioned by Simon Smythe.

Smythe looked relieved at this. 'But I didn't know that,' he explained. 'I was called away just then. I'd been watching from my office window, and all I saw was his hand go in the pocket where he keeps his wallet and the confident expression he usually wears when he gets his own way. I was a gift, I thought. I was sure you wouldn't believe me if I told the truth. Once I'd told you the first lie, I had to go on. I didn't know what else to do. I found the body, you see, and I suppose I just panicked.'

His face looked bloodless, and his mouth opened and closed spasmodically, but no more words came out. Indeed, he seemed to have trouble breathing and appeared on the verge of collapse.

As Rafferty waited for Smythe to recover, he became aware of the steady tick of the clock on the wall. It was a sturdy looking thing, perhaps a survivor from the days when the house had been used as a private school. It had a paternalistic air; its large, round face reminiscent of a jolly schoolmaster. But Smythe didn't seem to find the deep, paternal voice of the clock any comfort. He sat staring down at the hands clenched in his lap, as though a thorough study of them would provide him with the answers he needed to convince them of his innocence.

With difficulty, Rafferty kept his features as rigid as Llewellyn's. Sitting either end of the desk as they were, he imagined they must look like a pair of particularly malevolent bookends.

The clock on the wall ticked away another thirty seconds, then, suddenly, Smythe slumped pitiably in his chair as though the weight of their suspicions was too much for him. 'I suppose you think I killed her?' Desperately, he searched their faces for signs of denial, seeing none, he slumped even lower, and his hands gripped the arms of his chair as though they were the only things that stood between him and disaster. 'I knew it. I knew everyone would think I did it. That's why I kept quiet. I've been such a fool. I didn't do it, you know.' He began to wring his bony hands. 'You must believe that I didn't do it. You must,' he repeated in a voice hoarse with fear and desperation.

He looked more like a frightened rabbit than a suspected brutal murderer, and Rafferty almost reached out a comforting hand, but then a picture of Linda Wilks's destroyed face flashed into his mind. For all that she had been a part-time hooker, she was the innocent victim in this, she the one deserving of sympathy. He would do well to remember it. 'You were the duty doctor that night. You told us yourself you were expected to stay on the premises. Why didn't you?' He leaned forward until his face was on a level with Smythe's. 'What happened when you brought her back here? Did she laugh at you? Is that why...?'

Smythe shook his head violently. 'No, no, you've got it all wrong. I didn't bring anyone back here. Not the dead girl nor anyone else.'

'You abandoned your responsibilities to go to the pub. Why? Did you have an appointment with Linda Wilks for later?'

Smythe shook his head again. 'I only went out for a drink. I didn't expect to meet anyone.'

'Don't take me for a fool, Dr. Smythe. I know enough medical men to know that they are always careful to keep a ready supply of drink to hand. Where did you keep your Dutch courage? In your desk or the filing cabinet?'

'In the desk.' He raised his shoulders and then let them fall again. 'I'd run out. That's why I went to the pub.

'You don't understand,' he told Rafferty, when silence greeted this. 'You don't know what it's like.' He looked down at his clenched fists, loosening and tightening them spasmodically, as though unaware of their movement. 'I hate it here.'

'Then why don't you leave?'

But even as he asked the question, Rafferty realised that for a man like Smythe, it wasn't that easy. He was hardly the type to impress a selection panel.

'Don't you think I've tried?' The nervous aggression returned briefly, but as though he realised it would gain him no sympathy, he sank back in his chair and his voice quietened. 'It's not that easy. I wanted to be a vet, you know?' He grimaced. 'I've never been very good with people, but my parents had set their hearts on my becoming a doctor. I didn't have the guts to disappoint them. They'd sacrificed so much to give me a decent education. I went into psychiatry because I felt the patients would be less threatening, I hoped I might be able to help them. I was wrong, of course. They've no confidence in me.'

He shrugged despairingly. 'I've no confidence in myself, so why should they have any? Not that Melville-Briggs's open contempt does me any favours, either.'

'If he thinks so little of you, why does he keep you on?' asked Llewellyn, coolly logical as usual.

Smythe laughed bitterly. 'Because he gets me cheap, Sergeant. He doesn't let me near his private patients, of course, but I'm good enough for the NHS patients the Health

Authority can't accommodate.' His eyes watered self-pityingly. 'Sometimes I think I'm destined to remain here forever as his whipping-boy. That's why, sometimes, I need to escape, so I go up to the pub. It's not far. It's warm, friendly, and unlikely to appeal to Melville-Briggs. And, for a time, I'm able to forget what a mess I've made of my life. I don't do it often,' he defended himself. 'Only—only, when...'

Only when you've booked a tart and her services, Rafferty added silently to himself, and needed something more than thin blood in your veins. Smythe's attempt at self-justification collapsed and he became vindictive.

'Just because I was unlucky enough to find the body, doesn't make me a murderer. There's one or two others who could have done it. Dr. Whittaker at The Holbrook Clinic, for instance. From what I heard, Melville-Briggs made Whittaker as mad as blazes last Friday night. And he left the dinner early, looking murderous by all accounts. Whittaker would have done anything to get back at him. Then there's Allward the Charge Nurse. He gets up to a few tricks at night, I can tell you. Have you checked their alibis?'

'But they weren't in the pub with a dark-haired girl that night,' Rafferty reminded him, deliberately ignoring the fact that Smythe had been with another girl, a stranger. 'You were.'

'But I bet none of them in the pub claimed that the girl I'd been with was the one who'd been murdered,' Smythe retorted.

'No,' Rafferty conceded. 'But neither did they confirm that Linda hadn't been in the bar that night.' He fully intended to have the other drinkers in the bar questioned, but from what the landlord had said, their testimonies wouldn't be any more reliable and, for the moment, he discounted the witnesses' inability to tie Smythe in with the victim. Linda Wilks might or might not have been in the pub that night, but she was certainly dead, the likely time of death tied in with the time Smythe had left the pub, which was just a few hundred yards down the road from the hospital.

'The girl was murdered in the hospital grounds, not near the pub,' Smythe defended himself. 'Anyone could have killed her.'

'Hardly. Not everyone has a key to that side-gate,' Rafferty reminded him quickly, though Gilbert had done his best in that direction.

'Charge Nurse Allward has. He could have brought the girl into the grounds. He's done it before.'

'Why didn't you report him, then?' Rafferty demanded bluntly. Had Staff Nurse Estoce suspected something similar?

Smythe shrugged. 'Why should I? I don't feel I owe Melville-Briggs any loyalty. But neither do I feel my contract includes being a patsy for his convenience, which is why I'm telling you these things now. It would suit him just fine if I was charged with the murder. I'm only on a short-term contract.

He'd make out that I was some sort of locum doctor and not actually one of his staff. He'd manage to wriggle out of any possible contamination somehow.' His mouth turned down petulantly. 'He's good at that.'

'If what you say is true, how often did Allward invite girls into the hospital at night?'

'Often enough. Who's to say that he didn't do it last Friday night? There are plenty of empty rooms at the moment with so many of the patients away. It would be an ideal time for him to get up to mischief, especially with Melville-Briggs absent for the night. What could be easier than for him to set up a little rendezvous and sneak away for half an hour during a meal break?'

'Like you, you mean?' Smythe scowled unhappily at the reminder. 'Do you know for a fact that Allward invited a girl here that night?' Rafferty persisted.

'No.' Smythe's reply was sullen. 'Why don't you ask him yourself?'

'I intend to, Doctor. After I've finished questioning you, that is.'

How on earth had Smythe's parents managed to convince themselves that he was doctor material? It was plain to him that the man wasn't suited to the job. The tragedy was he would probably have made a good vet.

Rafferty looked again at the photographs on the wall. His parents didn't look wealthy, but the pride of achievement shone from their faces; an achievement paid for by the hapless Smythe in years of degradation and humiliation, trapped in the wrong career.

Realising he was again on the verge of feeling a misplaced sympathy, Rafferty sighed and invited Smythe to continue. 'You said you had gone up to the pub for a drink?'

Smythe nodded. 'I only meant to go out for half an hour or so, but I—I got chatting to a girl. She was so pretty. It's ridiculous, I know, that I should think...girls have never bothered much with me, but I began to hope...' He broke off and swallowed hard in evident distress. 'She was waiting for someone,' he resumed. 'It wasn't me.' He wiped his face with the sleeve of his white coat and then looked down at his hands again. 'That's why I—'

'Why you met up with Linda and killed her?' Hadn't hurt pride and frustration long been sufficient motives for some men to kill?

'No! I told you—'

'You'd had a lot to drink—we know that, so you needn't trouble to deny it,' he added, as Smythe continued to shake his head. 'You persuaded her back here. Then, when she refused sex, you hit her.' He still couldn't understand why even a part-time prostitute would refuse sex, but presumably they, too, had their preferences. He didn't quite understand either why he should bludgeon her face to a bloody pulp yet leave her body untouched. If Linda Wilks had been killed in a frenzy of frustrated anger, there would have been blows to her body as well, but there hadn't been. He had been struck at the time by the fact that the body had been unmarked. Struck by it and then promptly forgotten about it, until Dally had remarked on it. Now, the strangeness of it struck him afresh. It hinted that the girl had been killed by someone in control, coolly, deliberately. Not Smythe's type at all. Altogether, it posed too many unanswered questions for Rafferty's peace of mind.

'Why won't you listen?' Smythe spread out his hands as though beseeching for alms. 'I had an argument, I admit it, but not with the dead girl. It was another girl entirely; surely you learned that much at the pub? I wanted her to come back for a drink. It was quite safe; I knew Melville-Briggs would be out at a dinner all night. He does the same thing several times a year.'

'So while the cat was away, you decided to play?'

'Why not?' he demanded truculently. 'I told you, I wouldn't be the only one. Melville-Briggs might think he owns me, body and soul, but he doesn't. I'm my own man.'

This defiant declaration was pathetic after what had gone before, but at least it seemed to give him some satisfaction, for now he calmed down a little. 'Anyway, she wouldn't come. She kept insisting that her friend would arrive soon, but when he didn't, she left. I left soon after. On my own.'

'Did she mention whether this friend was male or female?' Llewellyn asked.

Smythe shook his head sadly, as though at last accepting that his case was hopeless. 'I just assumed it was a man. Really pretty girls are always with a man or expecting one. They don't usually hang about waiting for a girlfriend. Only a plain girl would do that, and she'd latch onto an attractive, more popular girlfriend, hoping she'd fix her up with a man, too. Must be one of Mother Nature's more hit and miss methods of ensuring the continuation of the population, but it seems to work.'

It wasn't something that Rafferty had ever noticed, but Llewellyn was nodding his head sagely. Perhaps he'd made a study of the phenomenon in his psychology classes at university.

'She seemed nervous, strung up, and wanted me to buy her another drink. I'd already bought her several and she'd obviously had a few before I arrived. I imagine I filled the waiting time for her.'

His voice had a tinge of bitterness, of hurt pride that it was his destiny to be used as a convenient stop-gap till something better turned up. Rafferty could see how that would enrage a man, any man, but particularly a man of low self-esteem like

Smythe. It was probably the last straw after a day filled with problems which he had found hard to cope with.

Smythe went on. 'But it was already late. I was starting to get worried that I'd be missed, or that the police might come past and decide to find out why there were still so many vehicles in the car park—can you imagine Dr. Melville-Briggs's reaction if I was arrested in such circumstances?'

Rafferty could, and again, the unwanted sympathy came seeping slyly back. If he was unfortunate enough to be a man like Smythe, working for a bully like Melville-Briggs, he suspected he, too, might require liquid solace.

'She'd told me earlier that she had a Citroen in the car park. I was in time to see it roar off towards town.' He sniffed away a trickle of mucus. 'I was pretty fed up myself by then and I nearly went back to the pub. But I knew it was possible that Dr. Melville-Briggs might take it into his head to telephone and check up on me—he did that sometimes.' He glanced unhappily at the photo of the respectable couple on the wall. 'My parents would be terribly upset if I got the sack from here.' He sniffed again and went on. 'I'd bought a bottle of whisky from the landlord, so I decided to do what I'd originally intended, and come back to the hospital for another drink.'

'What time was this?'

'About 11.30, perhaps a little later. I'm not sure.' He began to look less hunted, as though, like an animal, he sensed that

Rafferty's determined pursuit of him was wavering. He had sufficient wit to make the most of it. 'It was dark. I hadn't had much to eat all day and I'd drunk more than usual. I fell over and broke my glasses just up the road from the pub.' A strained smile broke free from the tense set of his face. 'Amazingly, I didn't break the bottle.' The smile faded. 'After that, I was like a blind man stumbling along.'

'Your glasses weren't broken when I saw you,' Rafferty reminded him, frustrated himself now that his suspicions seemed to have led him to a dead end. They could have been broken in a struggle. But there'd been no trace of optical glass under or around the body, and according to Sam Dally, no struggle either.

Smythe's fingers touched the frames of his spectacles. 'These are a spare pair. With eyesight like mine, it's essential to have another pair for emergencies.' Rafferty nodded. It was plausible. Dropping his hand back in his lap, Smythe continued. 'Luckily, I saw the car before I got close enough to the hospital to be recognised, and I pulled my collar up and—'

'What car?' Llewellyn put in sharply.

'Do you know the make? Did you see who was in it? Would you recognise them again?' demanded Rafferty.

Smythe jumped at the torrent of questions and selected one at random. 'I don't know. I never recognise makes. Besides, I was too far away to see clearly. It had been parked close into the hospital wall, a little way from the side-gate. Almost as soon as I saw it, it began to reverse onto that piece of waste ground opposite the hospital and was driven off towards town. I kept my head down. The driver might have been someone from the hospital and I was scared I'd be recognised. All I wanted was to get back to my office before someone discovered I was missing.'

'You recognised the Citroen, though, didn't you?' Llewellyn put in quickly.

'Yes, but that was only because she'd told me what it was, and she was the only person to have left the bar. Besides, the lights from the pub car park caught the name as she sped off.'

'But you'd broken your glasses,' Rafferty pointed out.

'That was after.'

He hadn't managed to shake him. But as he no longer thought Smythe was the murderer, he hadn't expected to. 'Do you remember the colour of this car at all?'

'It was a lightish shade, and I remember there was the shape of only one person in it, no passenger.'

'What happened next?'

'I had a bit of trouble with the lock on the gate. I unlocked it, or thought I did, but it wouldn't budge. I tried again, and it opened.'

'Perhaps you'd forgotten to lock it when you came out?' Llewellyn suggested, glancing at Rafferty.

Smythe shook his head. 'I don't think so. I didn't forget to lock it behind me when I came back, even though I was far from sober. I hadn't gone more than a few paces into the grounds when I fell over again. Only this time it was a body I fell over. The feet were right across my path and tripped me up. I remember touching the toes as I scrambled up. I thought at first it was just a funny-shaped branch, but the moon came out just then, and as I got up, I could see her face quite clearly. It had all been smashed most horribly.'

Rafferty had to strain to hear; Smythe's voice was now the merest whisper, and his eyes stared straight ahead, as though he was reliving the moment, its horror clearly etched in his face. He shuddered and, taking a deep breath, tried to collect himself. 'She was still warm. She could only have died a short time before.'

'You're sure she was dead?'

The pathetic dignity returned as Smythe met Rafferty's eyes. 'I know you don't think me much of a doctor, Inspector, but I can still recognise a dead body when I fall over one. Believe me when I tell you she was quite, quite dead.'

And Rafferty could recognise the truth when he heard it. 'Go on,' he encouraged dispiritedly.

'Someone—her killer, I suppose, had removed all her clothes. Anyway, I couldn't see them anywhere.'

'What did you do next?'

'I left her there.' With obvious reluctance, he met Rafferty's eyes. 'I know it was a despicable thing to do, but I couldn't help her. She was already dead.' He lowered his gaze. 'I—I wasn't thinking clearly. I was drunk, distraught.'

'Oh, I would say you were thinking clearly enough, Doctor,' he remarked, and watched, unsurprised, as the dull red flush of shame stained Smythe's pale cheeks. But, even after listening to the ready excuses for the inexcusable, Rafferty could still feel sorry for him. It wasn't reasonable to expect more ethical conduct from someone so browbeaten as poor Smythe. Confronted by the problem of confessing his dereliction of duty, together with his proximity to a newly-dead body, it was no wonder he had put self-preservation first.

It was interesting about the car. They hadn't found any tracks, but then the weather had been very dry recently; unseasonably warm and muggy. There were no shops or houses just there to explain its presence. Only the hospital and the pub a good two hundred yards closer to the main road. There'd have been no reason for any of the customers to go that way, certainly not by car, as the road petered out into a dead end.

Of course, it was always possible that one of the staff had been dropped off at the illicit side entrance. But he didn't think so. The night staff came on duty several hours earlier, and how many other people could have been prowling around the hospital at that time of night? It was possibly a courting couple, but Smythe had mentioned only seeing one person in the car, and however blurred his vision, he was unlikely to make a mistake about that. Once the car began to move away, two separate shapes would have become visible, not just one, even to a person with Smythe's poor eyesight.

He'd get the house-to-house team on to it directly. He'd also have to put out an appeal for this other girl that the landlord and Gilbert had described, see if she came forward. And perhaps it was time he indulged himself with interviewing Melville-Briggs? Perhaps he could shed some light on who the other girl in the pub might be.

The fact that several points of Smythe's story checked out, made the story about the car more credible. Smythe wasn't streetwise enough to blend truth and falsehood in order to give a cohesive strength to his story. He was the type who would tell either the whole truth or a complete pack of lies. And he'd tried the lies. As they already knew some of his story was true, Rafferty was the more inclined to believe the rest was also.

If only he hadn't broken his damned glasses, he might have been able to tell them who had been in the car. It might well have been the murderer.

Smythe's head was still bent like a penitent as though he was awaiting Rafferty's absolution. His pink scalp showed through the thinning blonde hair; it looked soft, pleading, and vulnerable. Rafferty sighed. He believed Smythe's story, but he might as well tidy up the loose ends before he ploughed on with the investigation. 'What were you wearing that night?' he asked.

'What—?' Comprehension dawned. 'This suit.'

It was a plain, lightish blue with a rather distinctive stripe of darker blue. If, as he had said, he had fallen over the girl's feet, it would explain the lack of blood. If he had attacked the girl with the ferocity which her injuries suggested, the suit would surely have blood on it; a lot of blood. If he was telling the truth and this was the suit he had worn, of course. Perhaps Gilbert or the landlord would remember it?

'I'll have to ask you for the suit, Doctor, and your shoes and the other clothes you were wearing that night.' He paused, and then demanded, 'I suppose you know you've committed an offence? Several offences.'

Smythe nodded miserably, then his watery eyes gazed pleadingly at Rafferty. 'I suppose it'll all have to come out? My career... I was hoping... You couldn't...?'

Rafferty stared at him incredulously. Even now, Smythe still clung to the pathetic remnants of his professional dignity. The realisation temporarily cured him of compassion, and he observed bluntly. 'If I were you, Doctor, I'd be more concerned that someone in the pub remembers that you were wearing that suit, rather than another one that you could have since destroyed. Otherwise...'

He let the awful warning hang in the air for a few seconds before he turned to Llewellyn. 'Take him home and let him get changed, then take him to the station for a signed statement and a session with the identikit man. See if he can come up with a face for the girl in the pub.'

Watching Llewellyn take Smythe away, Rafferty reflected that, as Alice had said, this case was getting curiouser and curiouser. Perhaps, as well as speaking to Dr. Melville-Briggs, they'd do well to see Senior Charge Nurse Allward again.

Chapter Eleven

Charge Nurse Allward was a cool customer all right, Rafferty decided. Allward sat cross-legged and perfectly at his ease in their cramped little office, his glossy looks managing to make the room look even shabbier than normal.

'What made you decide to become a nurse, Mr Allward?' Rafferty asked suddenly, as Allward settled, hoping to ruffle his smooth feathers by an unexpected beginning to the interview. 'It's hardly the automatic career to appeal to a man like yourself, I would have thought.'

Allward smiled. 'You overestimate my talents, Inspector. But, to answer your question; nursing's as good a career as any, and even with Health Service cuts, it seemed a reasonably secure profession to enter. Why do you ask?'

'Just curious.' In fact, he was damned curious. Allward struck him as a type who would be more at home in a city office wielding a computer and three phones than a bedpan in a psychiatric hospital, even if it was a private one. Did he hope for a mention in a few of the older patients' wills? He was the type to appeal to old ladies.

'You're on permanent night duty here, aren't you?'

A hint of wariness entered Allward's eyes as he nodded. 'Is there any particular reason for that?'

Allward raised his elegant shoulders in a shrug. 'I see less of Dr. Melville-Briggs that way.'

Rafferty shot another dart at him in an attempt to shake his composure. 'It wasn't the opportunity for illicit rompo that appealed to you, then?' To his annoyance, Allward merely laughed, with what appeared to be genuine amusement.

'Have you been listening to gossip, Inspector?' he enquired dryly, seemingly not at all shaken by Rafferty's tactics.

'I listen to anything, Sir,' Rafferty replied tightly. 'If it's relevant to the case.'

'I wonder if I can guess who's been telling tales.' Allward's gaze rested thoughtfully on Rafferty. 'Simon Smythe looked even more hangdog than usual when I saw him earlier. And he had a policeman in tow.' His voice softened, became more intense. 'Been in here, had he? Did a bit of snitching?'

Rafferty said nothing, and Allward continued. 'After Gilbert shared the gossip, the rest of the staff has got Smythe jailed already. Especially Melville-Briggs. He looked positively smug when he heard Smythe had been carted off by the police. I expect he'll be in to congratulate you when he gets back from his conference, though I suspect his gratification is a little premature. If you thought you'd got your man, you'd hardly be questioning me again, would you?'

He didn't wait for a response from Rafferty. Instead, with a faint sigh, he said, 'I suppose Smythe couldn't wait to tell you all about my nocturnal activities? But I'm only following the boss's example, Inspector. Old Melville-do as I say and not as I do-Briggs. Still,' he mused, as though determined to demonstrate his lack of concern. 'I can hardly blame Simple Simon for not covering up for me.' He gave Rafferty another smile, but this time the charm failed to conceal his spite. 'Especially as he would appear to be a few answers short of an alibi himself.'

Rafferty ignored this. 'And what about your alibi, Mr Allward? Aren't you a few answers short as well?' He consulted his notes. 'According to your last statement, you were fifteen minutes late back from your early tea-break.'

'I've already explained about that.'

'So you have. What a shame no-one but a senile old man can vouch for you.'

Allward's eyes narrowed, but, outwardly at least, he retained his composure. 'Even if I had been with a girl, it's hardly a crime, Inspector.'

Rafferty wanted to see Allward's assurance crumble, that way he might get some more interesting answers. 'No,' he remarked slowly, 'but murder is.'

'Are you accusing me, Inspector?' Allward quirked an enquiring eyebrow. 'Should I have my solicitor present? You instigated this interview because you've discovered that I like a little diversion during the long nights. So what if I do? It doesn't make me a murderer.'

'No. But it does make you that much more interesting to suspicious policemen. I want to hear your statement again.'

Allward heaved a long-suffering sigh and repeated what he had already told them on the occasion of their previous interview. He'd had his tea-break at 11.15 p.m. and had returned at 11.45 pm, having been delayed by a patient for a quarter of an hour. 'I've told you all this before, Inspector,' Allward sounded wearied by the repetition. 'I was tending to one of the patients, as I said, not having fun and games with a local working girl.'

'So you said. Old Mr Tompkinson, wasn't it?' The patient with the convenient memory. Whose room was also handily situated near the back entrance to the bedroom block, to which Allward would have a key. He could easily have slipped out. How convenient that it had been Mr Tompkinson whom he claimed to have been tending. They'd already discovered that the old man was very suggestible. Had Allward told the patient that he'd woken from a bad dream on Friday night as a cover, sure that the patient would be too fuddled to contradict him?

'I believe you said he was a particular favourite of yours?'

'What of it?' Allward replied smartly. 'I didn't realise the time of death had been pinned down to one of my breaks.'

'All the staff are being asked to account for their movements, Sir,' Llewellyn remarked politely.

'Where do you take these breaks?' Rafferty questioned. 'In the staff lounge?'

'Sometimes,' came the guarded reply.

'And on Friday night—were you in the staff lounge then?'

'No.' A defensive tone had entered Allward's voice. Rafferty was pleased that he had at last managed to rattle the man. 'I put my feet up in one of the empty rooms in the male bedroom block. I was tired and wanted forty winks.'

Llewellyn raised his eyebrows at this. 'Surely sleeping on duty is against the hospital's rules?'

Allward gave a cynical laugh. 'You'd be surprised what goes on in hospitals at night, Sergeant; drinks parties, gambling clubs, a fair amount of naughties. Don't tell me it's not the same at cop-shops? It's difficult to believe that the "boys in blue" don't get a kick out of watching confiscated porno movies. I thought it was how you earned the nickname.'

'We're not here to discuss what the police have to do to prove an offence has been committed, Sir,' Llewellyn replied stiffly. 'I believe we were discussing what you were doing?'

'I've already told you. I was in one of the spare bedrooms.'

'Alone?'

'Unfortunately, yes.'

'Yet, surely with Melville-Briggs safely out of the way, you had an ideal opportunity?' Rafferty remarked. 'What stopped you from providing yourself with a little entertainment?'

Allward's eyes met Rafferty's boldly. 'I just didn't feel like it, that's all. We can't all be super-studs like the old man, you know. Of course, the rest of us don't have our virility stimulated by the thought of profit in the way that he does. I should imagine it's a great aphrodisiac.'

'The dead girl was a prostitute. A psychiatric hospital at night is not the obvious choice for a pleasant stroll. Not the likeliest place to pick up a john. Presumably she was expecting to see someone on Friday night. Have you any idea who?'

'No.' Allward was beginning to sound a little sullen, as though he was no longer finding the interview quite so amusing.

'Perhaps she was part of a midnight sewing bee?' Rafferty suggested sardonically. Allward said nothing, and reluctantly, Rafferty let him go, but remarked to Llewellyn when Allward had gone. 'I think we've found the "medical man" Linda's father mentioned telephoned.' He snorted. 'Probably told Linda he was a doctor.' He scowled as he recalled another task he had yet to organise. 'Remind me I need to get the Wilks's family's phone records checked. Maybe we can get a handle on this "medical man".'

Llewellyn nodded and jotted a few words in his notebook.

'Some of the other staff must be aware of what Allward gets up to at night, Staff Nurse Estoce, for instance. I think, with a little encouragement, she might forget that touching loyalty for long enough to drop him in it.'

Llewellyn looked doubtful. 'He's good-looking, confident, hardly the type to turn to a prostitute. And he's not the sort to lose his head—Smythe yes, but not him.'

'He might have been between girlfriends. Perhaps he rang Linda to fill a temporary gap. She said herself that the medical type who rang her was one of her men friends—a regular? And even if he hadn't used her services before, it seems likely he'd have heard of her on the hospital grapevine.'

'But what if there wasn't a phone call at all?' Llewellyn threw in. 'Sidney Wilks isn't completely above suspicion himself, remember? He could have invented that phone call to avert suspicion from himself. Of the two, I favour him.'

Rafferty shook his head. 'Even if Wilks did lie, it doesn't alter the fact that she must have known someone at the hospital to have come here in the first place. Otherwise why come? I want Allward's clothes checked by forensic, just like Smythe's,' he added decisively. 'He's too clever to refuse, and of course, if he did it, he'll have got rid of the ones he was wearing by now, but it'll rattle him and that's what I want.'

***

Simon Smythe had been telling the truth after all, and they would have to cross him off their list of suspects. Although the pub landlord had been unable to confirm what he had been wearing, forensic had discovered a few tiny splatters of Linda Wilks' blood on the bottom of his trousers, presumably picked up from the grass around the body which indicated that he had merely fallen over her body rather than killed her. There were signs that he'd tried to remove the stains, but minute traces had still clung to the fibres.

Smythe might be many things, but he wasn't a murderer. The only things he was guilty of being was a coward and a bit of a dummy, and they carried with them a punishment far longer and more severe than most courts would give out; a real life sentence, in fact.

Allward's clothes, too, were free of suspicious stains, though in his case, that proved nothing, merely that he was smarter than the younger doctor and not nearly so likely to incriminate himself.

So Rafferty was back to square one. Some questions had been answered only to find another crop springing up in their place. For instance, why had the killer gone to the trouble, not only of removing all Linda Wilks' clothes, but also of taking them away with him? 'Maybe the clothes the victim was wearing were an important clue,' he suggested to Llewellyn. Perhaps, Rafferty pondered, in some desperation, they were dealing with a necrophiliac—a tidy necrophiliac, who also collected the clothes of his victims. Perhaps he had gone out to his car for something before he began his vile practices, had seen Smythe coming up the road, recognised him, knew his "fun" was cancelled, and drove off?

Rafferty sighed. Perhaps he was being fanciful again. It couldn't have been easy to strip the body. He'd have expected bruises from rough handling, but there had been none. Had the murderer cut the clothes off the girl? If so, it pointed to premeditation, and that indicated that whoever had phoned her, had also killed her. If there had been a phone call at all.

Rafferty scowled. Why hadn't they checked with Mrs. Wilks? By now, if her husband had been lying about that call, he'd have had ample time to browbeat his wife into supporting his story. Still, it was worth a try. Perhaps, he thought, if they could ask the question when her husband was at work, they'd be able to winkle the truth out of her.

He got Llewellyn to organise the checking of the Wilks's phone records, and when he'd set that in motion, asked, 'Did the murderer fear the victim would be more easily traced through her clothes?' He couldn't imagine why. From what the parents had said, they'd been pretty nondescript; the sort lots of young girls wore. 'What other reason could he have had for taking them?' he asked Llewellyn, that fount of all knowledge.

'Perhaps he reads crime fiction or watches crime dramas on the television and was worried about the possibility that he'd left DNA evidence on them.'

Rafferty drummed his fingers on the table. 'Maybe. If only we could be sure what the girl was doing there; who she'd come to see. I still fancy Allward.'

'We haven't seen Dr. Whittaker at The Holbrook Clinic, yet, Sir,' Llewellyn reminded him. 'Unless we want to upset Dr. Melville-Briggs—'

'God forbid.' Images of the Chief Constable and his doctor buddy merged uncomfortably in Rafferty's mind. 'We'll see him this afternoon. I want to speak to his lady friend first, though, Gwendoline Parry. Let's have her in.'

***

Rafferty settled Miss Parry, the Hospital Administrator as comfortably as the rickety chairs would allow. He was surprised by a feeling of recognition. He felt he had met her before somewhere, and then it came to him. Big-boned, and with the rather old-fashioned bun hairstyle and practical short nails, she reminded Rafferty of one of his former school teachers, a Miss Robinson, who had fallen in love late in life, with the new French master. She had been an intense woman and had fallen hard. He remembered with a trace of shame how he and the rest of the school had sniggered over the affair, how they had mimicked the adoring eyes of Miss Robinson at assembly. She must, like Miss Parry, have been in her early forties: "Miss Robinson's last chance", the affair had been dubbed. The man had let her down, he recalled, and she had left the school soon after.

He wondered whether Miss Parry had found her last chance in Dr Whittaker, and if she was prepared to fight for it. According to Gilbert, she had a widowed, invalid mother, at home so would be unlikely to have many more such opportunities.

'I understand you've just returned from a few days leave, Miss Parry?'

Gwendoline Parry nodded.

'Do anything nice?' Rafferty enquired casually, aware that a few interested, non-threatening questions relaxed an interviewee. But this time, his technique failed abysmally.

For some reason Gwendoline Parry's fair skin flushed a delicate rose, though she replied calmly enough. 'I had some work I wanted to get on with at home, Inspector.'

'Doing a spot of DIY, were you?' he asked, reminded of the necessity to soon do something about the depressing yuppified magnolia walls of his own flat. He fancied something cheery like sunshine yellow or terracotta.

'No. As it happens I was typing up some research notes.'

'Surely Dr. Melville-Briggs doesn't expect you to do extra work when you're on holiday?' he queried sympathetically. Though Rafferty wouldn't put it past him.

Gwendoline Parry smiled faintly. 'No. Luckily, Sir Anthony isn't in need of my amateur typing skills. He has a perfectly competent secretary in Mrs. Galvin.'

Rafferty had a good idea who was in need of some free assistance. He couldn't imagine Simon Smythe went in for a lot in the way of research; he had as much on his plate as he could handle already.

But Gilbert's tongue had proved obligingly indiscreet on various topics; not least who was sweet on whom, and Miss Parry's love and loyalty didn't rest with Sir Anthony.

However, for the moment, he didn't pursue the question. 'You've heard about the murder, of course?'

She gave a grimace of distaste. 'How could I not? The papers were full of it. Still are.'

Rafferty felt guilty, as he remembered his reassurance of Linda's mother, but there had been no way he could have kept Linda's double life out of the papers. 'You understand that we have to check up on everyone's movements for Friday night?'

She nodded. 'Of course. As for myself, I was at *The George* in Hamborne from 7.30 p.m. till 2.00 a.m., Inspector.'

'The doctors' do? I didn't know administrators got an invite.'

'They don't. I was a guest of Dr. Nathanial Whittaker. He runs the Holbrook Clinic,' she explained. 'It's a few miles from here. Perhaps you've heard of him?'

Rafferty nodded again. Between Sam Dally and Gilbert, he knew all about Dr. Nathanial Whittaker: owner of a rival private mental hospital, he was a truly dedicated doctor, but a driven one. His father had been a brilliant surgeon until struck down with Alzheimer's disease when Whittaker had been a teenager. The boy had adored his father, and the cruel, undignified end of the man had apparently made a deep impression on him. He had abandoned his long-planned career as a surgeon, and decided instead, after his general medical training, to specialise in the psychiatric field, studying Alzheimer's, its causes and treatments.

Once trained, he had dedicated his life to finding a cure for Alzheimer's. The research had taken its toll on his health, his marriage, and his money, and the Holbrook Clinic nowadays barely kept its head above water. His wife had left him six months ago, and he'd been pretty cut up about it, according to Sam. The house had been sold – there had been no children of the marriage – and he'd ploughed his share into his hospital, where it was being swallowed up with the same dispatch as the rest of his money.

By a curious irony, Whittaker might be a dedicated and respected psychiatrist, but, according to Sam Dally, as a researcher, he was singularly inept. For all the long hours he devoted to the work, he lacked the plodding patience and meticulous attention to detail necessary, which explained both his lack of success and his inability to attract funding. Whatever money he made from his hospital was ploughed into his research work. Inevitably, his patients and their relatives had gradually turned to more comfortable establishments, where their ailments, real or imagined, were given that number one priority they felt they deserved.

As Gilbert had so graphically put it, *"Not even a lunatic would pay good money for group therapy on couch-grass when he could have gymnasiums and Jacuzzis just up the road."*

He was right of course. Whittaker had presumably done his best to keep the standards of his hospital to a certain level, but then, according to Sam, when his wife had left him, things had begun to slide downhill. Whittaker had turned more and more to his research work, burying himself in it almost.

Rafferty wondered how long the relationship between the doctor and Gwendoline Parry had been going on. He'd forgotten to ask Gilbert. Now, he signalled to Llewellyn to take over the questioning.

'What time did you leave *The George*, Miss Parry?'

'I stayed till it ended, Sergeant.'

'I see. But Dr. Whittaker didn't?'

She shook her head faintly, as though unwilling to confirm the matter, but, aware that there were plenty of other witnesses who would, she elaborated. 'He left around 10.30.'

'You didn't mind?'

Miss Parry raised her eyebrows. 'Why should I mind?'

'Most women would expect to be escorted home after being invited out, particularly at that time of night.'

'I am an adult, Sergeant. Dr. Whittaker knew I was perfectly capable of ordering a taxi.'

The sharp retort failed to conceal the fact that she had minded, and Rafferty's opinion of his sergeant's interview technique went up a notch. Who'd have thought that seemingly dedicated bachelor would appreciate that most women would mind? Perhaps there was more to this psychology lark than he'd thought?

It had been a very swish do, by all accounts, probably looked forward to for weeks; he vividly remembered his late wife, Angie's, reaction when he had had to leave her at some social function or other. He couldn't believe the elegant, if slightly repressed, Miss Parry, would be anything but extremely put out in similar circumstances. She would surely find it even more humiliating that her boss should witness it. Particularly as there was no love lost between the two doctors.

Rafferty wondered if Miss Parry and Whittaker had had a row. If so, no-one had so far mentioned it.

But that could be because the one between Melville-Briggs and Whittaker had been much more spectacular—fisticuffs, no less. Still, it would be worth making a few enquiries.

Now, with a sensitivity that surprised Rafferty, the Welshman abandoned this interesting sidelight, and returned to the main beam of the interview.

'We believe that the victim entered the grounds of the hospital by the side gate, Miss Parry. As you probably know, Mr Gilbert, the lodge-porter, took it upon himself to give out unofficial keys to this door. I believe you have one?' She nodded. 'May I see it?'

Surprisingly, for such a neat-looking lady, her handbag was a large affair, and she rummaged through it for some time with a worried look, before admitting defeat. 'I'm sorry, but my keys don't appear to be here.'

Rafferty's interest was sparked by this admission. 'You're sure? Perhaps you'd better check again, Miss Parry.'

She tipped everything out on the scarred table; pens, tissues, purse, make-up bag, diary, notebook, more tissues, a stray lipstick, and finally a small set of keys. Rafferty pounced on them.

'They're the keys to my office and the filing cabinets, Inspector,' she explained. 'I've always kept them separate from the main ring.'

'So when did you last see the other set?'

She frowned. 'I'm not sure.'

'Perhaps it'll help if I ask when you last used them. Would it have been last Friday? I believe you worked that day?'

Her lips pursed, and with a degree of reluctance, as though realising there was no way she could conceal the fact, she agreed that that had been the last time she had seen them. 'I had to work late, so I arranged for Dr. Whittaker to pick me up at the side gate as it's more convenient for the Hamborne road. I had to use the key to get out.'

Rafferty flicked a finger at her large handbag. 'And did you take that with you to the dance?'

'No. I had a small clutch bag. As I said, I had to work late, and knew I would have no time to go home and change. I left this bag locked in Nathanial's car. Luckily, I remembered it, and managed to catch him in the car park before he drove off.'

So, Rafferty mused, Nathanial Whittaker had had the opportunity to help himself to the keys. Did Miss Parry suspect as much? Was that why she looked anxious? Whittaker would have known she would be on leave till early the following week and therefore unlikely to miss the keys till then. 'How did you get in without your key when you returned from leave?'

'I generally use the main entrance. I have a car, so I mightn't have known the keys were missing for some time.'

'Perhaps they fell out of your bag into the car, and Dr. Whittaker found them?' he suggested gently.

'He did call round the next day. Perhaps—?'

Rafferty frowned uncomprehendingly. 'Didn't he say?'

She flushed again. 'I didn't open the door. I was busy working, as I told you. I didn't want to stop, and risk being delayed for hours. I live with my widowed mother, Inspector, but she was out on Saturday morning. I thought it might have been one of her friends, and they tend to linger. The flat is so designed that it's impossible to see who's at the door.'

'It might as easily have been Dr. Whittaker come to return your keys,' Rafferty remarked, trying to catch her out. She didn't fall for it. Now, she seemed subtly to withdraw from him, as though his attempted trick had somehow disappointed her.

'I only saw that it was Dr. Whittaker when I went to the window overlooking the car park. But as I was unaware that I'd lost the keys, Inspector, I wasn't to know that he'd call round.'

Touché. 'So you weren't.' Rafferty gave her a rueful smile. 'What a memory I've got.'

She gave no answering smile. It was apparent to Rafferty that she was very preoccupied about something. Could Whittaker have engineered an argument between them, so he could sneak off and keep an appointment with Linda Wilks? He'd had the opportunity to get the key to that side gate; had he, fired by his fight with Melville-Briggs, decided to make old Tony the butt of scandal-mongers for a change? Did

Gwendoline Parry suspect something similar? Was she trying to protect him from the consequences of his own folly?

Perhaps it was about time they saw Dr. Whittaker. He might have some serious explaining to do or he might not. He could have turned up at Miss Parry's the next day simply to kiss and make up, not to return the keys before she'd noticed they'd gone. Either way, he'd been unlucky.

Chapter Twelve

The Holbrook Clinic was crying out for money, that much was obvious, as Rafferty and Llewellyn drove through the open gates. The grounds were a lot smaller than at the Elmhurst Sanatorium, but they were badly neglected. Couch-grass pushed through the gravel of the drive, and the only plants were hardy shrubs that were capable of looking after themselves. As Gilbert had said, there were no gymnasiums or Jacuzzis here.

The Victorian buildings, too, had a shabby air of rather faded grandeur, and, like the minor gentry from that era, attempts were made to keep up appearances; like the freshly-painted black metal gates and the smartly-uniformed gate-porter—surface shows that cost little. But the further one penetrated, the harder the pretence was to keep up, and no attempt had been made to repoint the red brickwork or paint the many windows. It looked like the county asylum it had once been, and still sported the grandiose turreted style the Victorians had favoured for such institutions.

A passing nurse escorted them to the doctor's office. They introduced themselves, and with an air of distraction, Dr. Whittaker gestured at the two uncomfortable looking chairs in front of his desk.

Rafferty wondered if they were chosen specially to deter visitors from staying too long and interrupting his work. They would do the job admirably, he reflected as he sat down. The stiff, presumably horsehair padding, didn't give an inch.

Studying the doctor, Rafferty realised that, in his youth, Nathanial Whittaker must have been very good-looking, with his thin and elegant features and soulful dark eyes. He was still a fine-looking man, but now he had a careworn air, the thick dark hair was greying rapidly; it was quite long, and when it fell over his forehead, he pushed it back with long and impatient fingers; surgeon's fingers. Rafferty wondered if he regretted his youthful vow, because his research work over twenty years and more had achieved little. Perhaps it was as Sam had said, and his lack of success in the research field was because his work was driven by the grief of a personal loss rather than by a true vocation.

'You'll have heard about the murder at The Elmhurst Sanatorium, Doctor?' Rafferty began hastily, as, having sat them down, Whittaker seemed to promptly forget them. His gaze drifted down to his papers and he looked set to become immersed.

'What?' He raised his head, frowning slightly as though he had forgotten why they were there. With a sigh, he shut the file and sat more upright, looking from Rafferty to Llewellyn and back again, before he nodded. 'Yes, yes. A couple of the staff mentioned it.' He glanced at Rafferty with an air of bewilderment. 'But I don't quite understand why...?'

'Just routine, Doctor,' Rafferty reassured him. 'You didn't know the victim yourself, I take it?'

'Me? No. I didn't know her.' Rather naively, he added, 'She was never a patient of mine,' as though he couldn't imagine any other circumstances in which he might know a woman other than the wife who had left him, and the faithful Miss Parry.

'I understand you were at *The George* on Friday night?'

Dr. Whittaker nodded again. 'Yes. I didn't want to go; there's too much work to do here to waste time attending such self-congratulatory nonsense, but I knew it was too good an opportunity to miss. I hoped someone might put in a good word for me about research funds.'

His face darkened, and his sensitive features were distorted by an expression of such intense hatred, that Rafferty was taken aback. 'It was a waste of time, of course. Any chance I had was ruined before I got there. Anthony Melville-Briggs saw to that, as usual. I suppose you heard all about the fight I had with him?'

Rafferty nodded faintly and waited for further enlightenment. It wasn't long in coming.

'He made sure if there were any research funds up for grabs, he'd get them. He's too clever to ever accuse outright, but I knew it was him all right. Sly innuendo and locker-room jokes are more his style. Impossible to fight against, of course. That was another reason for going to that convention. I knew I was isolated. Unfortunately, socialising's important in my line, as it is in most professions, but I couldn't face much of it, knowing he'd be there, full of urbane charm and social ease, doing his best to make me look foolish.'

He fiddled with the cover of the file, the pens and other paraphernalia on his desk, his fingers never still for a moment. It was a wonder he didn't wear himself out, Rafferty reflected.

'I was in one of the toilet cubicles at *The George* when I heard the latest gossip doing the rounds. Now he's implying I go in for late abortions here as a useful side-line and use the foetuses for research. That I keep them wired up to machines to keep them alive, so I would have a steady supply of cells for my work.

'I was blazing. I found him, intending to have it out with him, once and for all, but he just laughed. And the madder I grew, the more contemptuous he became. In the end, I threw a punch at him. Of course I missed. His friends dragged me away. I left soon after. That would be about 10.30 p.m., I suppose.'

Rafferty and Llewellyn exchanged glances. Surely the man couldn't be that naive? Didn't he realise that he had just provided them with an excellent motive for murder? Had he killed Linda Wilks hoping to incriminate Melville-Briggs? At the very least, he could be sure that Sir Anthony would get some very damaging publicity, even if he wasn't suspected of the murder. Or was he being disingenuous? Aware that there was no way the argument could be concealed, had he hoped to cast doubt on such suspicions by his very openness?

The murder victim had been pregnant, although only two months along. He pondered the possibility of getting Superintendent Bradley to agree the funding for a DNA check on the foetus, and the same again for the most likely suspects. But he knew, even before he considered the possibility, that it would be a last resort for the budget-conscious Bradley. Even if he agreed, he'd make it plain that such a request only brought Rafferty's own detective abilities into question. Rafferty, for the moment at least, put that one on the back burner.

Her father had mentioned that Linda had received a phone call around 10.30 p.m. that evening from a man. If he'd been telling the truth, could it have been Whittaker phoning from the foyer of *The George* asking to meet her? He reminded himself to get Llewellyn to hurry along the checking of the Wilks's telephone calls that evening. Even Bradley was unlikely to question the need for that.

Linda Wilks's diary had been less help in tracing her clients than he'd hoped. She'd used a code; a crude, school-girlish thing, but it might have been as cryptic as *The Times* crossword for all the success they'd had with it. He returned to Whittaker's complaint. 'You're a psychiatrist, not a surgeon. Why should anyone believe...?'

'Any butcher can do abortions, Inspector.'

'But surely late abortions are dangerous?'

Whittaker's dark eyes looked sadly into his. 'Don't you know? Apart from my other evil habits, I'm supposed to offer these late abortions to desperate women—drug addicts, the homeless, the dregs of society; the implication being that I wouldn't worry if they died.'

He stopped fiddling with his desk furniture and looked Rafferty in the eye. 'Melville-Briggs knew very well that I've tended to cater for the poorer, more wretched elements of society, especially since my wife—' He broke off for a moment, and a shudder seemed to pass through him before he began again, his expression anguished.

'He always managed to add a certain measure of truth to his lies.' With a sigh, he glanced down at his fingers where they clutched at the file. Slowly, he straightened them out, but almost at once they involuntarily tightened their grip again. 'The evidence was all circumstantial, but people would wonder if there might be some truth in the rest.'

Rafferty was wondering about that himself, and he looked at Whittaker with new interest.

Whittaker laughed mirthlessly, and Rafferty guessed his unfortunately open face had betrayed his thoughts.

'There's no need to look at me like that, Inspector. It's not true. You can search the place if you like. Besides', his mouth turned down. 'Even if I'd contemplated such research, I wouldn't have the money for it. Do you know how much such equipment would cost? He could afford it, of course. The work I do is far more valuable, yet he's the one who gets the funding. And for what? That stupid study of the drug-addictive personality, while I'm starved of funds for vital research. I could tell them the type of people who become drug-addicts; it's the weak, the stupid, the desperate and the gullible. I sympathise with them; I treat them, after all. But their illnesses are self-inflicted. I don't know if you're aware of this, em, Inspector, but my late father had Alzheimer's disease. He—'

Rafferty nodded. 'I heard about your father, Doctor. I sympathise. My grandmother went the same way. It's a terrible thing to have to watch a loved one go like that.'

Whittaker gave him a grim nod. 'A man like my father could have had many useful years ahead of him—valuable years of helping others, saving lives, easing suffering. Instead, he was condemned to an undignified and degrading end. When I see how easily Melville-Briggs gets research funds, I despair.'

'But there's plenty of research going on in that field now. Aren't they finding some interesting results with—?' Human foetuses, he had been about to say before he thought better of it.

Whittaker nodded. 'But that's other people's research. Not mine. I want to contribute something. Something important. It would make up for a lot.'

'Does it matter who finds the cure as long as it's found?' Rafferty asked gently.

'It matters to me, Inspector.'

From Whittaker's taut face, it mattered very much. Melville-Briggs's accusation against him was beginning to look as though it might have a little more substance than Rafferty had originally thought. This man might just stop at nothing to nobble a rival; particularly one whom he had good reason to hate.

Rafferty cleared his throat. 'Er, to get back to the night of the murder, Sir. You said you left *The George* early?'

'Yes. If I'd stayed and got drunk, which is what I felt like doing, I'd have probably murdered the bastard.' He stopped abruptly, as if he had just realised what he'd said.

Rafferty wondered if he'd murdered Linda Wilks instead, leaving her body on his enemy's doorstep; an apt revenge for Melville-Briggs, that user of women. 'Where did you go, Doctor, when you left *The George?*'

'I came back here and continued with my work. Better than hitting the bottle, I thought.'

'Did anyone see you once you left *The George?*'

'I don't believe so.' Whittaker raised his head as though he had suddenly wondered why he was being questioned about his movements. 'Why do you ask?'

Rafferty stared at him, once again wondering if Whittaker could really be that naive. Circumstances were again building a case around Nathanial Whittaker; and this time, not simply for questionable professional activities, but for murder.

Melville-Briggs had forcefully implied that Whittaker was capable of the most desperate measures in order to get back at him. Rafferty had assumed that Sir Anthony suffered from paranoia. Now he wasn't so sure. 'A young woman has been murdered, Doctor,' Rafferty reminded him softly. 'We need to question everyone, however remotely connected.'

'And you suspect me?' Nathanial Whittaker gave an incredulous laugh. 'God,' he demanded roughly of the ceiling, 'what else can that bastard do to me?'

Rafferty shuffled on the hard chair, his own suspicions making him uncomfortable. Whittaker's wife had left him, his work, to which he had devoted a lifetime, was not going well, and he had to suffer the derision and public success of a man he regarded with contempt. Whittaker was a man frustrated in both personally and professionally. Had that frustration and resentment led him to murder?

Linda Wilks had been one of society's dregs, as described by Melville-Briggs. And she had been pregnant. Put the two together and you had the ideal victim for Whittaker if he chose to make use of her. Had Whittaker been the medical man who had phoned her? Had she met him and sought his help to get rid of the baby? Perhaps, through contacts at the Elmhurst Sanatorium, she had heard about the rumours that Dr. Melville-Briggs had spread about his work and mentioned them. Even if he hadn't met her with the firm intention of killing her, it was possible this had brought back the fury raised earlier that evening. Had he struck out at her in a blind rage? Had he, with a dead body on his hands, done some quick thinking and mutilated her? He had access to a key to the gate, so would have no trouble gaining entrance to the hospital grounds.

But if the murder had happened like that, it smacked more of premeditation than sudden rage, for he'd have had to obtain the keys before he met her, knowing full well why he would need them. If he'd merely made the appointment with Linda for sexual gratification, he would hardly choose to meet her on the enemy's doorstep. Rafferty could imagine the play old Tony would make of that if Whittaker was caught with a prostitute.

Rafferty began thinking about his relationship with Gwen Parry as he gazed at the now bent greying head. It appeared very one-sided. She typed up his research notes and made herself available on the occasions when he required an escort, but to Rafferty it seemed Whittaker made nothing more of her than a convenience, and she was apparently happy to let him. A strange relationship.

Whittaker had left *The George* early, and alone, and had seen no-one. And he had a big grudge against Melville-Briggs. Means, motive and opportunity, as the crime writers put it. Now Rafferty gave the nod to Llewellyn to take up the questioning.

'Dr. Whittaker?' The still handsome head rose, and bleak eyes gazed back at him. 'I'm sorry that this has been a painful experience for you, Sir,' murmured Llewellyn softly, with every evidence of sincerity. 'But it is necessary, I hope you understand that?' Whittaker nodded. 'I believe you escorted Miss Gwendoline Parry to the dinner at *The George*?'

Again Whittaker just nodded. It was almost as though he had lost interest in the conversation. But Llewellyn's next words regained his attention.

'I understand you called round to Miss Parry's home on the Saturday morning after the murder?'

Nathanial Whittaker stared at him. 'How did you know that?'

'You were seen,' Llewellyn replied, without elaborating. 'Did you often call at Miss Parry's home?'

'No. Not—not often.'

'What sort of relationship do you and Miss Parry have?'

'Relationship?' He looked puzzled for a moment, as though he had never thought about it before. Then he shrugged, and said, 'We're—friends, I suppose you'd call it.'

'Not lovers?' Rafferty put in.

The suggestion seemed to horrify him. 'Certainly not.' Whittaker blinked rapidly. 'I fail to see—'

'You're both adults, both free,' Rafferty went on. 'There's nothing to stop you.'

'My relationship with Miss Parry wasn't like that, I assure you. We were friends, nothing more.' He frowned. 'Surely Miss Parry hasn't given you the impression that she was any more to me? I thought she understood. My work...' His voice trailed off, and he looked embarrassed.

Poor Miss Parry thought Rafferty. It was obvious that Nathanial Whittaker's intentions towards here were only too honourable, if a little selfish. Had she been hoping his intentions would grow a little more dishonourable? A little more passionate? He had abandoned her at the dinner, seemingly without a thought, which indicated that his feelings about her were just as he had described. He had neglected his wife, who had apparently been quite a looker, a wife, whom everyone that Rafferty had spoken to, had claimed Whittaker loved, as much as he was capable of loving anyone. Had Gwen Parry really believed she would fare better at his hands? Like

Miss Robinson, Rafferty's old school teacher, she was doomed to bitter disappointment. Research used up all his passion. It was apparent that he would have none left for the Gwen Parry's of this world.

Llewellyn continued his questioning. 'Perhaps you'd like to tell us why you called round that particular morning?'

The question seemed to trouble him. He gazed around the office as though seeking an answer in the dark and dusty corners. 'I—Miss Parry was typing up some research notes of mine. I—I wanted to see how she was getting on.'

'But she could hardly have made a start on them by then, surely? I understood that she intended to spend the whole of the weekend on them? Had taken a day's leave to finish the job.'

'Had she?' Dr. Whittaker looked startled, then annoyed, as though this latest evidence of Gwendoline Parry's devotion was altogether too much.

'So why did you go round there?' repeated Llewellyn doggedly, when Whittaker made no attempt to answer his question.

Whittaker became agitated at his persistence. 'Why are you asking me all these questions? Does it matter why I went round to Miss Parry's house? What has that got to do with this murder?'

'That's what I'm trying to establish, Doctor,' replied Llewellyn. 'You see, Miss Parry's hospital keys have gone missing. Naturally, we need to find out what happened to them. Did you see them, by any chance?'

'Me?' Whittaker's fingers stilled. It was as though he had finally realised the precariousness of his position and was worried about betraying any anxiety. Ironically, the unnatural stillness achieved the opposite of what he intended.

'Miss Parry wondered if they could have fallen out of her bag into the boot of your car. We thought that might have been the reason you had called round to her place.'

Whittaker slumped back in his chair, as though he no longer had the strength to fight off their suspicions, as if he no longer even cared. 'There's no need to be so delicate, Sergeant. What you really want to know is if I stole them in order to gain entrance to the Elmhurst Sanatorium. Isn't this what all these questions are about?'

Llewellyn didn't deny it. 'And did you?

'No. I did not.' Whittaker's lips thinned to a mulish line.

They'd got all they were going to get out of him today, that was clear. Rafferty stood up. 'You understand, Doctor, that we'll have to speak to you again?' Whittaker nodded mutely.

As they left, Rafferty looked back. Whittaker was still sitting at his desk, but now his papers were ignored, and he stared into the middle distance with haunted eyes. Rafferty shook his head sadly. In many ways, he could sympathise with Nathanial Whittaker; both their marriages had failed because their work and their wives were incompatible. But Whittaker wasn't tormented by guilt; his wife was still living, unlike Angie, who although dead now for two years, was in some ways still with him, still reaching out from beyond the grave to wound him.

Into his mind flashed a vivid picture of his wife as she lay dying in the hospital. It should have been a time when mutual regrets softened the resentments, but even in death, Angie hadn't been gentle. She had used her remaining breath to ensure the time of her dying lingered painfully in Rafferty's memory. He should be happy now, she had told him, now she would no longer be able to come between him and his precious job. What wife could make a greater sacrifice? It seemed she had been determined to make her mark on him in death far more effectively than she had managed in life.

Because he had wished death on her during one of their rows—had actually said that he had wished her dead, so when she had received a death sentence from the cancer, she had accused him of causing it, as a kind of wish-fulfilment.

'"*Heav'n hath no rage, like love to hatred turn'd,*'" Llewellyn murmured philosophically from behind the wheel as they drove back to the station.

'God, are you off again?' Rafferty scowled.

'"*Heav'n hath no rage, like love to hatred turn'd*,"' Llewellyn repeated, but before he could continue, Rafferty, getting his sergeant's drift, voiced the rest of the quotation for him.

'"*Nor hell a fury, like a woman scorn'd.*"'

'William Congreve,' Llewellyn added, sotto voce.

'Is that what you think?'

'I was just wondering if Miss Parry finally realised, after Dr Whittaker abandoned her on Friday night, that she meant nothing to him. I wondered if she could have lied about losing her keys. Whether, rather than trying to shield him, she's been deliberately trying to lead our suspicions to him as a punishment for not desiring her.'

'You're a deep one, aren't you?'

Llewellyn shrugged wordlessly.

'Perhaps she killed the girl herself,' Rafferty threw in a suggestion of his own for good measure. He didn't want Llewellyn getting above himself in the ideas department. 'And got back at Melville-Briggs *and* Whittaker, both of whom probably used her in different ways. After all, she was hardly a prominent guest at *The George*, and unlikely to be missed.'

'But she had no transport,' Llewellyn objected. 'She'd hardly take a taxi from *The George* to the hospital, tell the driver to wait while she killed the girl, and then calmly get the taxi driver to take her back as if nothing had happened. Apart from any other consideration, she'd have been covered in blood.'

'Valid points, granted. But, I think we ought to investigate Miss Parry's alibi a little deeper. She picked up her car from the hospital sometime over the weekend. Why not that night? She could have overheard Whittaker arranging the meeting with Linda and been overcome with jealous rage. She could have paid the taxi off at a reasonable distance from the hospital and walked, then murdered Linda, and driven away in her own car.'

He sighed. 'But perhaps, just in case, we ought to check out the cab firms as well? Check too, to see if anyone at the hospital noticed her car missing from the car park on Saturday morning.'

Llewellyn nodded, and asked, 'So you think it's a case of "*Dux femina fact*"?'

'What?' Rafferty scowled again.

Llewellyn sighed. 'Or "*Cherchez la femme*", if you prefer.'

Rafferty preferred plain English and said so.

Chapter Thirteen

By the next day, they'd managed to turn up nothing on the cab firms, and the hospital staff were extremely vague about precisely when Miss Parry had picked up her car.

But that was about par for the course, Rafferty reflected wearily. Even the telephone call that evening to the Wilks's home had been from a public phone, which, to Rafferty, seemed suspicious. Who, in these days of mobiles, used a public phone? Someone with a need to hide their tracks, seemed the obvious solution. But there was little point now, after so many hours had passed, in getting a team there to check for prints.

None of the staff, or those patients whom they'd so far spoken to, had admitted to knowing Linda, either. Nor, at the hospital or anywhere else, had anyone identified the girl in the pub from Smythe's photo fit—at least, they hadn't identified her to Rafferty, whatever they might have suspected privately, and he wasn't hopeful that anyone would.

That was why, when the telephone rang, he anticipated only further failures, especially when he heard Llewellyn's voice on the other end.

But incredibly, for once, the Welshman had a result for him. It brought about a complete revival of Rafferty's optimism. At last, someone from the hospital had recognised the photo-fit of the girl in the pub.

'Keep her there,' Rafferty ordered ebulliently. 'I'm on my way.'

'But Sir, I think I should warn—'

'Not now, Llewellyn. Whatever it is will keep. I'll get there as fast as I can.' Rafferty grinned, dropped the phone, and made for the door. No doubt Llewellyn was worried about his precious car and imagining the squeal of brakes and the smell of burning rubber as Rafferty tore through the distance separating them. Well, he'd have to bear it as best he could. This might be the breakthrough they'd been looking for, and he wasn't going to waste any more precious time pandering to Llewellyn's mechanical sensitivities.

God knew they needed a breakthrough, because ironically, although they were overloaded with suspects, they had no firm evidence against any of them. The latest news might make all the difference.

***

Rafferty strode through the empty passages and pushed open the door of their temporary office. He stopped short when he saw the woman with Llewellyn and shot his sergeant a reproachful glance. Was this the witness he'd placed such hope in?

She must be eighty if she was a day, he guessed. Dim, rheumy blue eyes, peered vaguely out at him from a mass of wrinkles, and her head nodded continually on her thin neck. It seemed likely she'd have difficulty remembering her own name, much less anyone else's.

Rafferty's eyes swivelled to the right, and he frowned. Nurse Wright sat silently by the door, while her charge was interviewed, as though she didn't trust them not to browbeat the old lady. She needn't think she was going to listen in, Rafferty vowed. Her behaviour over the missing note had already irritated him, and he wasn't inclined to conduct the interview with her listening in.

'Please wait outside, Nurse,' he said sharply. 'Llewellyn, escort Nurse Wright to that little waiting room we've arranged, and then come back. Sergeant Llewellyn will call you when we're finished, Nurse.'

Nurse Wright opened her mouth as if to protest, but after one look at Rafferty's implacable expression, she shut it again. She stopped only long enough to direct a dirty look in his direction, before she flounced out.

When Llewellyn returned, he nodded at Rafferty to confirm the nurse was safely ensconced on the other side of the bolted door.

Turning to the old lady, Rafferty swallowed his disappointment, and smiled as Llewellyn introduced them.

She inclined her head in a gesture meant to be gracious, but there was more of pathos than regality in the movement, and it touched a nerve of memory in Rafferty that ensured his voice was gentle. 'It's very good of you to come and see us, Mrs. Devine.'

'That's quite all right, young man. Only I do hope it won't take long. Only, you see, my daughter's coming to see me today. She always comes to tea on a Friday,' she told him. 'Four o'clock prompt. Never misses. And I do want to make sure everything's perfect.' With a glance at the door, she confided in a loud whisper, 'It isn't always, you know.'

'Please don't worry, Mrs. Devine. This will only take a few minutes.' He pulled a chair up and sat beside her. 'Now, perhaps you could start by telling me when you saw her last?'

The question seemed to trouble her a great deal. The smile faded to be replaced by a worried look, as though she had been found out in some deception. Her head shook more agitatedly than before, and her eyes filled with the easy tears of the very old.

'Take your time, Ma'am.' Moved by compassion, Rafferty spoke in comforting tones, as Llewellyn, clearly embarrassed, shuffled his feet. The old lady's behaviour seemed to make the Welshman uncomfortable, but Rafferty was used to the very old.

Hadn't his grandparents ended their lives in the cramped Rafferty home? Many a time as a teenager, he had spoon-fed his grandmother her meals, wiping the dribbled food and saliva with a cloth; many a time, too, he'd comforted her when she'd wet her bed and cried befuddled tears from an indistinct feeling of shame.

Then his tenderness had sprung from a wealth of fond memories of childhood, when his Gran had gamely bowled to his fantasy Colin Cowdrey batting. She hadn't been half a bad bowler either, he remembered.

It was those fond memories that now served to remind him that Mrs. Devine, too, was maybe somebody's loved granny, and patiently, he attempted to rekindle her recollection. 'Perhaps it was here in Elmhurst?' he suggested gently.

Llewellyn tried to overcome his own discomfort. 'You said you met her in London,' he prompted, in the loud tones some people use to the aged, as if they are all hard of hearing.

Rafferty could see comprehension and something like relief fight their way through Mrs. Devine's clouded brain, and he stifled a grin as she directed a look of scorn at Llewellyn.

'I didn't think you meant *her*,' she informed him tartly.

For a few seconds, intelligence gleamed out of the rheumy eyes; the nodding head stilled, and Rafferty caught a glimpse of the woman she must have been, before old age had caged her sharp mind in a fog. He bet she'd been a bit of a tartar; the sort unwilling to suffer fools at all, never mind gladly. As Llewellyn had just discovered.

'I thought you were talking about my daughter.' She gave Rafferty a coy glance. 'Are you married, young man?'

'No Ma'am.' Not any more, thank God, he thought.

'Then you must come and take tea with us. With my daughter and myself. You'll like her. She's such a thoughtful girl.'

'That's kind of you, Mrs. Devine. Perhaps another time, when I'm not so busy?' He took the photo-fit from Llewellyn. 'I understand you recognised the girl in this picture?'

Mrs. Devine's nose wrinkled faintly. 'Oh her. That's Miranda...Miranda...I can't recall her other name. I used to see her regularly at Dr. Melville-Briggs's London consulting-rooms, before, before—' She broke off.

Before her family had had her put away, Rafferty concluded.

Her expression was anxious, as though she realised, deep within her, that there had been a time when she had been very different. The realisation clearly upset her, and although, not surprisingly, she was reluctant to bring past and remembered reality into her present unhappy situation, somehow, she gathered a tattered dignity about her and went on, quite lucidly.

'I had a weekly appointment, and she saw Dr. Melville-Briggs after me, which I thought a little strange, as I always asked for the last appointment, and by the time my consultations finished, the staff had left. I suffer from giddiness and used to retire to the ladies' room till I felt more composed. Often, I'd find this Miranda lurking in there, quite furtively, as though she didn't want anyone to see her. Very odd it was.' Mrs Devine seemed lost in the memory, and it was several seconds before she continued her tale.

'She wasn't a very pleasant young woman. On the few occasions I tried to engage her in conversation, she was unpleasant, really quite rude, in fact. So unnecessary.' She looked distressed for a moment, as though the memory was particularly unwelcome and etched forever in her mind. 'I recall her eyes glittering at me quite furiously as though I had no right to be there.' She handed the picture back with a look of distaste and, rising unsteadily to her feet, made for the door.

'Just a moment, Mrs. Devine. Llewellyn, ask Nurse Wright to come back, please.'

Nurse Wright returned just in time to hear Mrs. Devine repeat her invitation to Rafferty. For some reason it made the nurse smirk.

'I'll expect you for tea with my daughter next Friday then, young man. At four o'clock. Anyone will direct you.'

'I'll look forward to it, Mrs. Devine.'

The nurse hovered in the doorway as though torn between Rafferty and her charge. Rafferty won. 'You don't want to believe everything Mrs. Devine says, you know,' she advised sharply. 'She wanders in her mind.'

Rafferty's mind did a little wandering too, to the interesting question of why she should seek to convince him that the old lady was unreliable as a witness. 'Her mind seemed sharp enough to me,' he remarked quietly.

The nurse gave a derisive smile. 'You think so? She invited you to take tea with her daughter, Inspector, but I wouldn't bother turning up next week if I were you. She hasn't seen her daughter once in the nine months that I've worked here. The visits are as much fantasy as whatever she dragged you over here to listen to. She's probably seen you about the hospital and wanted to look you over to decide if you were suitable husband material for her daughter. Match-making is one of her obsessions, unfortunately.' Nurse Wright grimaced. 'I suppose she'll be ringing up caterers next to arrange the wedding. She did that last year when one of the doctors took her fancy. We had the devil of a job convincing the firm that the wedding was all in her mind. So you see, you can take whatever she told you with a large pinch of salt.'

'I'll bear it in mind,' he told her dryly, reluctant to let the nurse have the satisfaction of the last word. 'Though she seemed lucid enough to me. The bit about the daughter was wishful thinking – dreaming – we all do it. But the other part seemed real enough. She didn't particularly want to remember—' He grinned teasingly at the nurse's avid look, 'What she told us. You see the difference?'

She gave him a withering look as though to say, "Not another amateur psychologist?" Then she shrugged and remarked tartly. 'Believe what you like, Inspector. Only I still wouldn't bother turning up for tea next week. She'll have forgotten all about you, and it, by four o'clock today, never mind next Friday.'

'Perhaps. But if Mrs. Devine remembers anything else, I want you to tell me.'

The nurse looked as if she would like to tell him what he could do with his wants. Her attitude angered him. 'One girl has been murdered,' he reminded her bluntly. 'Information can be dangerous. It's better passed on to the police. I'd like you to remember that.'

'But you've arrested Simon Smythe for the murder. I hardly think—'

'I don't know who's told you that. Dr. Smythe has not been charged with murder,' he told her with quiet satisfaction. 'Neither has anyone else—yet.'

Nurse Wright's mouth dropped open in a perfect "O" of surprise. 'But Gilbert told me he saw him being driven off to the police-station. He hasn't come back to the hospital since, and Gilbert said—'

'Never mind what Gilbert said,' Rafferty snapped. 'You might tell Gilbert that I said if he's not careful he might just find himself involved in a suit for slander. With you added to the ticket for good measure.'

The nurse nodded quickly and shut the door behind her, no doubt eager to pass on the latest news about Smythe.

Rafferty went over their latest information. Smartly-dressed and nicely-spoken, was how the landlord had described the girl in the pub, something of a looker, too, he understood. Smythe had suggested she had been waiting for someone. Mrs Devine had identified Smythe's identikit picture as this Miranda; could she be the same girl who had given Nurse Wright the note for Melville-Briggs? Annoyed, he realised he should have shown the nurse the photo that he'd shown Mrs Devine, but the woman had irritated him so much that he'd never thought of it.

But the girl in the pub certainly sounded the type who might appeal to the doctor, and it seemed she'd made a point of seeing him very privately. If she was this Miranda, presumably she had been hanging around the scruffy neighbourhood pub waiting for him, not realising that he was out on the town. It seemed an unlikely venue for the self-important Sir Anthony. Even if he'd been available, Rafferty couldn't imagine him being willing to rub shoulders with the celebrating darts players.

He dispatched Llewellyn to find Nurse Wright and show her the photo. Not that he really had much in the way of expectation from that quarter. After that, he had orders to carry on to the nick to get more copies made of the photo-fit, and then go on to Dr. Melville-Briggs's London consulting-rooms to interview the staff there. Surely, if anyone had occasionally stayed late, they might have seen this Miranda? If Mrs. Devine's mind had really been as clear about the identification as it had seemed, and they were one and the same girl.

If Rafferty could locate this Miranda, she might turn out to be a valuable witness. It was surprising that she hadn't already come forward voluntarily; it wasn't as if the case hadn't received enough publicity, as the tabloids had seized on the story like sensation-starved cannibals. It was possible, of course, that she was trying to protect someone; and that someone could only be Melville-Briggs. The man seemed to bring out such an instinct in too many women for Rafferty's liking. Perhaps, when Llewellyn returned from London, he would rattle the doctor's cage a little?

***

Rafferty looked at his watch for the third time in as many minutes. Damn Llewellyn. It was eleven o'clock; he should be back by now. The Welshman had rung yesterday afternoon to say he would have to spend the night in town. Some of the staff at Sir Anthony's London consulting-rooms had left quite recently, and he was having trouble tracking them down. But there surely couldn't be that many people employed in one doctor's rooms?

Not for the first time in his career, Rafferty cursed his impetuosity. It was rather a pity that he'd given way to the satisfaction of telling Nurse Wright that Smythe hadn't been arrested for murder. She wouldn't have known any different if he'd kept quiet, as Smythe was off duty for a few days and wouldn't have been expected at the hospital anyway.

The element of surprise might have been useful when he saw Sir Anthony. Still, he mused, it was still possible he didn't know, as he was attending a conference in the Midlands and wasn't expected back till lunchtime today. Unless someone rang him with the news—an image of the pert Nurse Wright came into his mind, and he frowned.

Rafferty had agreed that Llewellyn should kill two birds with one stone as it were, by going to see the Melville-Briggs's son at his business—not that it seemed likely that the effete Timothy, as so graphically described by Gilbert, would be likely to have any doings with a prostitute, leastways, not a female one. But they might as well check it out. Though if Llewellyn was wasting time chatting about vintage cars at that garage...

This was the only positive lead they had—slight though it might be, and Rafferty didn't want to tackle Melville-Briggs till

Llewellyn got back, only too aware how easily the supercilious doctor made his hackles rise.

The frustration only increased his impatience. For, otherwise, their investigations had scored a big fat zero. They had yet to find the murder weapon or Linda Wilks's clothes, and in spite of the press coverage, no-one but Smythe had seen the car parked outside the hospital. Added to that, the house-to-house had yielded nothing in the way of more information, and no-one calling herself Miranda had so far come forward.

Too late, he realised he should have gone to London himself. It would have been better than hanging around waiting for Llewellyn to dig the dirt—if he was even capable of something so grubby. Though surely, even Llewellyn realised that they needed answers, and needed them quickly.

Pressure was building from every angle – press, public, and hospital staff – especially its leading light. Once Melville-Briggs discovered that Smythe wasn't going to be charged with the crime—if he didn't already know, courtesy of Nurse Wright—he would be sure to make his displeasure felt.

Melville-Briggs had made it clear, right from the start, that he wanted a quick and convenient solution. Rafferty wondered if his only reason was concern about what the bad publicity would do to the hospital and its profits.

Had the girl in the pub really been this Miranda come down to see him? It seemed possible as, apart from Mrs. Devine, no-one else admitted to knowing the girl before that evening. Not that Melville-Briggs had either, of course—yet.

Miranda was a loose end and he didn't like loose ends. He consulted his watch again, with the same result as before; its hands seemed to be crawling.

***

Llewellyn had finally returned, but he was minus any good news, which didn't altogether surprise Rafferty. Timothy Melville-Briggs was out of the running—not that he'd ever really been in. And, needless to say, no-one at Sir Anthony's London consulting-rooms had recognised the girl in the photo-fit picture.

Still, Rafferty consoled himself, that didn't necessarily prove anything. Perhaps she and the aging Lothario had been up to after hours' naughties—hadn't Mrs. Devine said the girl had always had a very late appointment, after the staff had gone home?

It seemed the likeliest explanation given this Miranda's behaviour. After all, it was improbable that the doctor would confine his amorous activities to Elmhurst. Although Rafferty was disappointed not to have something more on Melville-Briggs, he was still determined to tackle him. Perhaps he would yet be able to bluff him into some revelation.

He decided he and Llewellyn would wait for him in his office. In the unlikely chance that Nurse Wright hadn't already revealed Smythe's non-arrest.

Sir Anthony hadn't yet returned, though he was expected imminently, but at least Mrs. Galvin made them tea while they waited. Picking up his cup, Rafferty asked, 'Have you worked for Dr. Melville-Briggs long?'

'Three years.'

He gave a low whistle. 'Really? That long? You surprise me.'

She looked steadily at him. 'I fail to see why.'

'Human nature intrigues me,' he explained. 'What people do and why they do it. I find they often have the oddest reasons for their actions.'

'I'm afraid you'll discover nothing to intrigue you about mine,' she replied. 'I work here because I need the money.'

'Surely you could get much better paying work in London?'

She shrugged. 'Perhaps. But I have other considerations to bear in mind, like suitable housing. My husband is an invalid, Inspector. He was paralysed over two years ago. I doubt if we could afford to buy a house in London in any case. Even if we could, we'd need to persuade the local council to equip a house with the necessary aids As I found here, it can be a lengthy business. And with councils all over the country cutting costs to the bone...' She gave a hopeless shrug. 'As you can appreciate, commuting is out of the question, given my husband's condition.'

'I'm sorry to hear about your husband. How did it happen?'

'A car accident,' she replied briefly.

It was obvious that she didn't want to talk about it. Like Melville-Briggs's unfortunate junior doctor Simon Smythe, here was another member of his staff unlikely to find another suitable job. She was trapped as surely as Smythe and would have little choice but to continue to hold onto her position here. No doubt Melville-Briggs made full use of his knowledge of her circumstances.

She'd already made her statement; not that it amounted to much, beyond saying she was at home all evening with her husband on the night of the murder. It hadn't been corroborated yet; in her case, he had thought it would be just a formality. But when he recalled Melville-Briggs' apparent pursuit of any attractive woman, he thought again. And when he mentioned the necessity of this corroboration, her reaction surprised him.

'Surely that's not necessary?' Her voice suddenly sharp, she added, 'You don't imagine that I—that a woman would attack a young girl in such a brutal fashion, Inspector? Especially as the papers said she was a prostitute.'

In his experience, anything was possible, and Sam Dally had said a woman could have murdered the girl. Mary Galvin came over as a woman of strong passions behind that calm exterior—certainly capable of killing if the motive was strong enough.

Mary Galvin might be slim, but the skinniest murderers generally managed to find the required strength if the motive was strong enough. And if she had been one of Melville-Briggs's discarded mistresses, sexual jealousy would be as good a motive as any and better than most.

The women in this case struck Rafferty as particularly strong-minded, and wasn't it true that the gentler sex were often less squeamish than mere males when it came to disposing of a barrier to happiness? Doubtless, when they were alone, he'd have to listen to Llewellyn maundering on about that "deadlier than the male" stuff. In Latin.

'We have to check out everyone who had a key to that side gate,' he told her. 'It doesn't mean that we suspect you of anything. Your husband—'

'I've already told you that he's a cripple, Inspector,' she retorted, even more sharply than before. 'The only time he leaves his wheelchair is to go to bed. Surely you don't suspect that he murdered the girl?'

Her agitation interested him. He was about to question her further when the intercom on the desk buzzed.

'Saved by the bell,' he murmured. But Mary Galvin's reaction to his questions was turning out to be something of a mystery. He wouldn't be happy till he got to the bottom of it.

Her hand pressed the appropriate button, and Anthony Melville-Briggs's smooth tones caressed their ears. 'I'm back. Any messages?'

After passing on the messages, Mary Galvin added, 'The police are here, Sir Anthony. Inspector Rafferty and Sergeant Llewellyn. They'd like to see you.'

'Of course. I've been expecting them.'

The smug voice practically purred, and an anticipatory tingle tickled Rafferty's spine. It seemed he might have been lucky, and old Tony hadn't yet heard the latest on Smythe. The beginnings of a grin added to what Llewellyn would probably call a triumvirate of pleasure. Four syllables. God, he was getting good at this wordy lark. He'd be spouting Latin next. Or perhaps that *was* Latin? Just don't ask Llewellyn, Rafferty reminded himself. Or you'll get a lecture. In Greek, probably.

'Show them in at once,' Sir Anthony commanded. 'We mustn't keep such diligent officers waiting.'

'Seconded,' Rafferty muttered. 'Lead me to the Pleasure Dome.'

'And Mrs Galvin, I don't want to be disturbed, so keep back all calls. Oh, and, I'm sure they'd like some coffee. 'Got that wrong. Rafferty paused only to mouth: 'Tea, please', at Mrs Galvin before he made for the doctor's office.

Chapter Fourteen

Sir Anthony positively beamed as they entered his office. 'I understand you've got some good news for me? I must say, I never thought...'

Diplomatically, he bit off whatever he had been going to say, but Rafferty guessed it would have been less than complimentary.

'Ahem, do sit down. 'It's a great relief that you've discovered the culprit,' Melville-Briggs went on. 'And so promptly. It's obvious that Smythe was the man, of course. He's just the type to need to turn to prostitutes for sexual gratification.'

Melville-Briggs appeared to have forgotten his slanderous accusations against Nathanial Whittaker, Rafferty noted, as the doctor continued smoothly. 'And although I appreciate your courtesy in keeping me personally informed, surely you should be at the station, interrogating him?'

Rafferty was grateful that his impetuosity in telling Nurse Wright the true position vis-à-vis Smythe hadn't met its deserved reward, and he intended to get maximum enjoyment out of the situation. It wasn't often he got the chance to be one up on someone like Melville-Briggs.

He allowed his face to register surprise, and his voice to assume a lightly ironic, teasing tone, out of sheer devilment. 'I'm afraid you're a bit out of date, Sir Anthony. I assumed you'd have heard.'

'Heard?' Sir Anthony's face stopped beaming. 'Heard what? What are you talking about, Rafferty?'

'I didn't arrest Dr Smythe. He was merely helping us with our inquiries. I imagine he'll be at home. If you want him.'

'What?' Sir Anthony leaned forward over the desk as though he was about to psychoanalyse him. 'Have you gone mad?'

'I don't believe so, Sir. Smythe was just unfortunate enough to be in the wrong place at the wrong time, that's all. He hasn't murdered anyone as far as I'm aware.'

Melville-Briggs opened his mouth again, but the telephone buzzed before he could say anything. He snatched at it and practically snarled, 'I thought I told you not to put through any calls? Do I have to—?'

Mrs. Galvin must have said something soothing; something that jangled of cash, because instead of continuing to carp, he just said peremptorily, 'Oh, very well. Put her through.'

To Rafferty's amusement, when Sir Anthony next spoke there was no trace of irritation in his voice. It was apparent that when it came to well-heeled clients, he could be quite charming; a veritable fount of patience and solicitude.

'My dear Lady Harriet, how very nice to hear from you again. How was your holiday? Good. Good. So nice at this time of year, I've always found. No, no. Nothing at all to be alarmed about, I assure you. We all know how the press exaggerate... No, no, just some foolish girl who managed to get into the grounds. Probably turn out to be a lovers' tiff, nothing more. In fact—' He broke off, and it was apparent that he'd been interrupted once again. It seemed that Lady Harriet was rather more astute than Melville-Briggs had thought. She seemed to find his explanation less than satisfactory, for he was forced to go on in this placatory vein for several minutes.

Although Rafferty still listened to the one-sided conversation, getting more of a kick out of it than his thankfully sleeping conscience would normally allow, he let his gaze wander round the room.

Not for Melville-Briggs the interview conducted in a drab and comfortless basement. Oh, how the other half live... The good doctor had decreed early in the case that if they wanted to see him, they would have to come to him.

Rafferty concluded that he'd been so insistent because he had believed the splendour of his own office would the better impress on him that he was a man of wealth and influence— something Rafferty would rather forget. It was strange that a practising trick-cyclist didn't realise that, to Rafferty, the opulent office acted more as a red rag to a bull than a reminder that respectful deference was the required response.

The spacious first-floor room had presumably once been the drawing-room. It still had the original encircling cornice and panelled wainscot. The polished wood floor was covered with an Oriental carpet in rich golds and blues and, either side of the marble fireplace, two matching mahogany bookcases, the height of the ceiling, contained expensively-bound medical text-books. Enormous gilt mirrors decorated the walls and, whichever way he turned, Rafferty could see himself and Llewellyn reflected, over and over again. His own bemused expression so disconcerted him that he swivelled his head away, but not before noting that his thick auburn hair was badly in need of a cut.

Rafferty was put out to discover, that beside his well-groomed sergeant, he looked a bit of a scruff. The discovery disconcerted him even more, and determinedly, he concentrated his gaze on the window-facing wall behind the doctor's desk.

A veritable photographer's gallery of framed prints were on display there, and he let his eyes take in the coloured photographs of the doctor with various members of the royal family, and others, where he posed with white-coated and presumably distinguished medical men. Perhaps, Rafferty reflected, he should be grateful Sir Anthony didn't have a large, colour picture of himself posed with the Chief Constable. Now that would have had good intimidation value.

An even more impressive array of medical qualifications was grouped together in the centre of the display. Rafferty squinted as he tried, without success, to read them. Surely, they couldn't all be proper qualifications? Perhaps Melville-Briggs had bought some of the certificates as he'd tried to buy him? You could buy anything on the internet. Or so Llewellyn, his personal geek, had often told him. A man like Sir Anthony thought the entire world was for sale. Sadly, much of it was.

As he thought of Simon Smythe's pitiful collection of honours and memories, Rafferty felt a gush of fellow feeling. Unlike Sir Anthony, the poor sap couldn't even buy himself a much-needed bottle of whisky without the world tumbling about his ears.

He brought his full attention back to Sir Anthony's dulcet tones. By the time he had finished, even Rafferty was beginning to believe that the facts of the murder were just an exaggeration on the part of the gutter press.

However, this happy illusion lasted no longer than it took Melville-Briggs to wish the lady a pleasant adieu and place the phone on the desk with an exaggerated care; almost as if it was the lady herself. Or, more likely, her wallet. Reality then again took over from the delights of make-believe.

The telephone conversation had given Sir Anthony time to get his disappointment in perspective. He sat back in his chair and drummed his fingers testily on his desk.

The desk didn't suit the elegant proportions and restrained plaster-work of the room, Rafferty noted, unreasonably pleased that, beneath the surface sophistication, Sir Anthony's tastes reflected his lowly Brummie origins.

Like Melville-Briggs, the desk was large and showy; seven feet long, its top was covered with maroon leather, and around the edge, the mahogany was inlaid with a flamboyant quantity of what looked like gold-leaf. It was almost as though Melville-Briggs had determined to thrust his own forceful personality on the otherwise elegant room.

Behind the desk, Sir Anthony sat in a high-backed, throne-like chair, from which he could look down on lesser mortals. Perhaps his more anxious patients approved of such an arrangement; they probably found such dominance comforting.

Rafferty didn't; it merely made him keener to prick the ego on the throne. He set about it with a barely restrained gusto. 'Of course,' he remarked, 'in view of the news about Smythe, you'll understand that it's necessary to interview everyone again? Perhaps, Sir Anthony, you'd like to enlarge on your previous statement about your movements on the night of the murder?'

'Enlarge on my previous statement?' Melville-Briggs's glowered. 'What game are you playing, Rafferty? You've let a perfectly good suspect go. Now you're plunging round desperately trying to find a replacement. Well, I'm not it. And if you try to make me one, I'll create the biggest stink on either side of the Atlantic since Watergate.'

'Surely that wouldn't do the reputation of the hospital any good, Sir?' Rafferty remarked in a pseudo-comforting voice. 'Besides, it's hardly necessary. Can't we be civilised about this?'

'It's not very civilised to come in here and accuse—'

'No-one's accusing you of anything, Sir,' Llewellyn put in politely, with a pained glance at Rafferty. 'It's just that—'

Melville-Briggs ignored him and concentrated on the organ grinder.

Due deference and recognition at last, was Rafferty's cynical thought. Bit late for that, old son.

'I didn't even know the girl.'

'That may be so, Sir,' Rafferty remarked, glad he'd managed to disturb Sir Anthony's equilibrium, 'but without investigating, we can hardly be sure of that. After all, it's common knowledge that you have many women friends. The victim, as far as we know, could have been one of them. You must see,' he added with an air of sweet reason, 'the necessity of investigating the possibility.'

'As I was at *The George* all night, it would appear the possibility is more of an impossibility,' he barked. 'I have a fool-proof alibi, Rafferty. You won't succeed in breaking it.'

'I expect you're right, Sir. But even fool-proof alibis have to be closely scrutinised.'

Melville-Briggs laid his hands flat on the desk and leant forward. 'If you doubt my word' – by the tone of voice, it was apparent that he thought the idea absurd – 'you can ask your own pathologist, Dr. Samuel Dally. He was there.'

'I see. He was with you the entire night, was he, Sir?' Rafferty didn't bother to edit out the sarcasm, even though he knew it was unwise; if Melville-Briggs's alibi really was as sound as he claimed, he would pay for it. We must find our pleasures where we may, he thought, as he crossed his fingers under the desk's concealing magnificence.

'No, of course he wasn't with me all night.' Melville-Briggs's face was slowly becoming a marvellous match for the maroon leather of the desk. 'I don't like your tone, Rafferty. I don't like it at all.'

Rafferty didn't much care for his either. The man was too confident; a confidence that sprang either from innocence...or the knowledge that he had bought and paid for an alibi that couldn't be faulted. But surely even Melville-Briggs couldn't bribe half the medical men who had been at *The George* that night?

'I'm sorry about that, Sir,' he replied quietly. 'But if, as you say, you weren't with your wife, Dr. Dally, or anyone else all night, it would seem that your alibi isn't quite as strong as you implied. In a crowded room even a man of your eminence,' he gave the word an ironic stress, 'wouldn't be missed for half an hour or so.'

The thin lips settled into a sneer. 'Nathanial Whittaker would be far less likely to be missed than myself.' Sir Anthony's tone was icy as he returned to his earlier and too hastily-abandoned suspicions. 'As you've decided to swallow whatever lies Smythe's told you, you'd be better advised to ask him to account for his movements that night. Especially as he left early, looking murderous.'

'We already have, Sir.'

'And?'

'As with all the rest of the possible suspects, we're continuing our enquiries. Mr Whittaker will be interviewed again, just as you are being.' Silently he added, but for the moment, we're trying to find out your possible motives for murdering the girl. 'I hope you'll bear with me, while I run through a possibility or two?'

Sir Anthony waved his hand irritably in the air, as though to say, "Do what you like", and subsided heavily in his chair.

Rafferty picked his next words carefully. He selected the ones most likely to push the doctor into unwise disclosures.

'Let's say you were having an affair with the murder victim. We're just surmising here, Sir,' he quickly added before either Melville-Briggs, or the ever-more pained-looking Llewellyn, could get a word in. 'Perhaps you were afraid Lady Evelyn might find out about it and you feared she would divorce you? Perhaps you felt you risked losing all this?' His arm took in the splendours of the room and the grounds beyond it.

Melville-Briggs gave a derisive snort. 'Do you really believe that I was having an affair with this wretched little tart? And that after having my wicked way with her, I tossed her aside, and she threatened to tell my wife? Is that the best that your bourgeois little mind can conjure up, Rafferty?'

Rafferty gave his best Sphinx-like impression at Melville-Briggs's derision. Beside him, he heard Llewellyn give a heavy sigh, as if keen to establish some kind of Apartheid between himself and his superior's lack of finesse. Rafferty shot him a furious glance.

Sir Anthony held out his hands in a gesture of innocence. 'My hands are clean, Rafferty.' He gazed down at them from his throne-like chair. They were strong hands, expertly manicured, rich and smooth like the rest of him. 'Everyone knows that my wife and I live virtually separate lives and have done for some years. It's no secret. It suits us both rather well. My wife has the Hall and her church committees. I—I have another hobby, as you have discovered. Women. But not cheap tarts, Rafferty. My tastes run to something a little more up-market.'

Frustrated that his words hadn't had the desired effect, and that Llewellyn would be sure to rub it in, in bloody Latin, Rafferty was, for the moment, content merely to listen, while frantically scurrying about in his head to resurrect his argument. And to gather several apt put-downs for his oh-so-superior, sergeant.

'My wife knows and accepts that I have certain...needs; needs which she no longer wishes to satisfy. But we still manage to live fairly amicably. Besides, apart from anything else, I know my wife would never divorce me. Perhaps you weren't aware of it, Rafferty, but the Melvilles are an old Catholic family. There's never been a divorce in my wife's family, and my wife is not the sort of woman to end a centuries'-old tradition.' He leaned back in his throne-like chair, effortless superiority well to the fore once more. 'So you see, even if I had known the dead girl, I knew "all this", as you call it, was perfectly safe.' Sir Anthony picked up a slim manila file from his in-tray, as though to indicate that the audience was over. 'Now, if I might be allowed to get on with my work?'

Rafferty ignored the hint and remained seated.

After a wait of thirty seconds, Sir Anthony raised his head and fixed him with a haughty glare. 'Was there something else, Rafferty?'

The way Sir Anthony ignored his rank and called him by his surname riled Rafferty; it had done all along. He might have been the butler, dismissed once he'd brought the after dinner port. The quick temper of his Irish forbears was aroused and demanded some retaliation. He tried to keep his voice as bland as Melville-Briggs's better efforts, but not altogether certain he'd succeeded, he ploughed on regardless. 'I'm sorry you should be so antagonistic, Sir. I would have thought a man in your position would recognise his duty to help the police.'

Melville-Briggs fixed Rafferty with a chilling stare, and, for a few brief moments, the real man behind the cultivated urbanity showed through. 'A man in my position recognises only one thing, Rafferty—the importance of staying there.'

Rafferty blinked, and it was as if he'd imagined the real Sir Anthony, as pomposity returned.

'I find it offensive to have my good name besmirched, my professional colleagues questioned about my movements; it invites speculation and gossip of the crudest kind.'

'Most people would find murder more offensive, Sir,' he said reflectively, as he remembered the victim's bludgeoned face and her family's distress and destroyed respectability. 'Or don't you think a common tart has a right to justice from the law?'

Melville-Briggs waved the suggestion aside.

'We can't be sure that another young woman won't meet the same fate.' Sickened by this dismissal of the poor young victim, and the way her unfortunate choices and sad end had affected her family, Rafferty decided to play his wild card. He took the photo-fit picture of the girl in the pub from his pocket and threw it on the desk. 'Miranda, for instance.'

Perhaps he only imagined Melville-Briggs's loss of colour. His adversary recovered quickly and called his bluff.

'Miranda?' he questioned softly. 'Miranda who?'

Rafferty cursed under his breath. But he was determined not to let on that he didn't know.

The doctor's bold bluff-calling might just be a fishing expedition to test the extent of his knowledge, Rafferty knew. It would be a mistake to let on that both his information and his semi-senile informant were far from reliable.

Rafferty took out his own Olivier skills and dusted them off. 'Let me get this straight, Sir—just for the record, you understand. Are you saying that you know nobody who bears any resemblance to this girl? Nobody by the name of Miranda?' He allowed a note of faint surprise to enter his voice as he tried to imply that he had information to the contrary. 'It's not a very common name.'

'I cannot recollect anyone of that name who resembles this girl,' the doctor replied briskly. 'Perhaps you would like me to make a few inquiries amongst my colleagues?'

'That won't be necessary, thank you, Sir. Our own inquiries are proceeding very satisfactorily. Very satisfactorily indeed,' Rafferty repeated, with an air as confident as only an Olivier-manqué could make it.

This time even Melville-Briggs couldn't entirely conceal his dismay.

Rafferty assumed an even more omniscient air and decided he could risk exaggerating the extent of their knowledge. 'We have reason to believe this Miranda had connections with your London clinic, Sir.

'We also have reason to believe she was in this area on the night of the murder and expected to meet someone. Odd that, because, so far, we haven't found anyone locally who admits to knowing her. Perhaps she had intended meeting the dead girl? Or perhaps not. But it's strange that she hasn't chosen to come forward.' He let his eyes meet the doctor's. 'I imagine Nurse Wright told you about the young woman who gave her a note for you?'

'I believe she did mention something of the sort,' Melville-Briggs blustered, clearly struggling for an appearance of untroubled calm. 'But as she threw the note away, I've no idea who the girl might have been.' He adopted the expansive, man of the world air again, and, with a throwaway gesture, said, blandly, 'I have a large circle of friends and acquaintances, Rafferty, a lot of them young women, as your investigations have no doubt revealed. The girl could have been any one of them.'

'Don't you think it strange that she hasn't come forward?'

The doctor shrugged. 'That's easily explained. I move in very successful, well-travelled circles, Rafferty.' Melville-Briggs's very pores seemed to exude smugness.

Rafferty felt class-hatred of the rich, the powerful, the effortlessly well-connected, rise from his own pores. With difficulty, he subdued them as Melville-Briggs continued.

'This woman could have been out of the country at the time news of the murder broke. It's possible that she isn't even aware that you're looking for her, yet you seem determined to make it look suspicious and—'

'It's just that I wondered why she didn't telephone first if she wanted to see you, Sir. Instead of turning up out of the blue.'

'I've no idea. But you know what impulsive creatures women can be, Rafferty. They don't always stop to think.'

Rafferty smiled. In a men-together sort of way. As, from the side of his vision, he took in Llewellyn's firmly-Liberal affront. Just as well the doctor hadn't met any of the Rafferty family women. Fluffy wasn't in it...

Melville-Briggs's, sexist response irritated him—wouldn't Llewellyn be pleased about that? But with a Ma who commanded respect, and three bolshie sisters, Rafferty had learned it was wise not to besmirch the female of the species; like the Black Widow spider, they tended to bite. Still, he couldn't resist a little sexual insinuation in his response. 'If your friend is abroad, I expect she'll turn up shortly. Then we'll find out the truth, won't we, Sir?'

Melville-Briggs turned an interesting assortment of colours; several of which might be termed eau de fucking temper.

Rafferty leaned forward. 'Now. Just for the record, you understand?' In a casual aside, he asked: 'You're taking this down, Llewellyn?' As if his superior Welsh sergeant would do anything else; the man was an automaton. He didn't look for or acknowledge Llewellyn's response, but ploughed on. 'Are you quite sure you knew neither the murdered girl, Linda Wilks, nor this Miranda?'

After a telling, momentary hesitation, Melville-Briggs stated firmly, 'Quite sure.' With a scowl, he declared, 'Now, I have work to do—if there's nothing else?'

Sir Anthony's voice was tightly controlled, and Rafferty felt disappointment seep into his soul. Now what? He hadn't succeeded in rattling him. He'd played his wild card and had nothing left to throw.

But even if he had nothing in his hand but duds, he could still finish the game with dignity. 'Not at the moment, Sir,' he conceded. 'But when we have, we'll know where to find you.'

Balked of victory, Rafferty perked up as he remembered that even the most cast-iron alibis had been known to be broken,: and by him. Still, he would give a great deal to see the effortlessly-superior Melville-Briggs humbled.

But, he reminded himself; salvaging his bruised pride wasn't the object of the exercise; that was to find out who had murdered that poor, carelessly-loved young woman, Linda Wilks. The young girl with her dreams of film stardom shattered.

After he had sketched an ironic bow at the pointedly bent head, Rafferty and Llewellyn took their leave.

'Well?' Rafferty, by now weary of the Olivier-pose and its unnatural demands, burst out when they were safely the other side of the bear's den. 'You were watching him. What do you think?'

'What do I think?' I think you're courting trouble. Sir. And the Superintendent's displeasure.'

Rafferty shrugged. 'We both know that's a given. What else, man? Nitty-gritty time.'

'His alibi seems sound enough, Sir.' Llewellyn pursed his lips thoughtfully and directed a reproving glance at Rafferty. 'But we already knew that, that's why I don't understand why you pushed him so hard. He doesn't even seem to have any motive. Or at least, none that we've been able to discern.

'Besides, he doesn't seem to me to be a man who'd soil his own hands with murder. He'd more likely pay someone else to do his dirty work for him.'

Llewellyn's eyes darkened, and his expression became enigmatic. 'I know you don't like him, Sir, but rest assured, whatever his sins, he'll pay for them eventually.' He paused, again, and went into quotation mode. Rafferty groaned. *"Every guilty person is his own hangman,"* according to Seneca.'

'Well, that's a comforting thought. Would improve our clear-up rate no end.'

Although he was impressed by his sergeant's summing-up of Melville-Briggs, he wasn't in the mood to compliment him; Llewellyn so often seemed to act as though he was the superior officer that it stuck in his craw.

It didn't help that his own behaviour during the interview had been a bit over the top; which was something he could be sure Llewellyn would remind him about in his own sweet time.

And, if old Seneca was right, and if he recalled one of Llewellyn's previous wiseacre quotations correctly: retribution was sure to follow. 'It's a pity your mate, Seneca, won't be about with his reassuring platitudes when matey-boy in there starts complaining to the brass about me,' he observed sourly.

Sensibly, Llewellyn made no attempt at commiseration.

What would be the point? Rafferty mused dispiritedly, when they both knew that Superintendent Bradley, a gruff, no-

nonsense, professional-Yorkshireman, with gimlet eyes firmly fixed on that greasy ladder, hadn't got where he was by treating his junior officers with kid-gloves when they threatened his comfortable niche.

Rafferty concluded that not only could he soon expect a flea in his ear, but that all the flea's friends and relations would come along for the ride. And, although he had the nous to keep the rest of his opinions to himself, it was obvious that Llewellyn would think it served him right.

Chapter Fifteen

So the old man wanted results did he? Rafferty slammed his way into his office. It would serve Superintendent bloody Bradley right if he got ones he least wanted, gift wrapped.

As he had anticipated, retribution had been very swift. And he didn't need two guesses as to who had stirred the shit. Even though he'd been warned off treading too heavily on those particular corns, he, for one, would enjoy tying Melville-Briggs up in presentation red ribbon, even if he got reduced to the rank of sergeant for his trouble.

Disgruntled that Llewellyn seemed to number a knack for disappearing when the flak was flying among his other talents, Rafferty slumped dejectedly in his chair. The trouble was he had too many possible suspects. Sidney Wilks, for instance, was turning out to be a very interesting possibility, as he'd tried to explain to the superintendent, in an attempt to halt Bradley's Vesuvius-like eruption. It didn't help that Wilks had been the Welsh Wizard's preferred choice, rather than his own.

According to Tina, the absent Streatham flat-mate whom he'd finally tracked down, Sidney Wilks wasn't the solid citizen his privet hedge proclaimed, but had used his respectability as a shield for something far from seemly. Linda had confided that her father had regularly abused her sexually as a child. Was it true, though? And if so, had Daphne Wilks known?

Rafferty's nose twitched, once – an infallible guide – and he nodded slowly. Wilks was capable of such an act. And Daphne Wilks? Wasn't it true that those who denied knowledge of such a dreadful act denied it most strongly to themselves?

He viewed the coming interview with distaste but consoled himself with the unkind thought that Llewellyn would relish it even less than he did.

***

The nets were twitched discreetly aside and as quickly twitched back before Mrs. Wilks opened the door, flattening herself against the wall out of sight, and as soon as Rafferty and Llewellyn were safely gathered into the hall, she slid the door shut again. The whole operation had taken only moments.

'Is your husband home, Mrs. Wilks?' Rafferty asked as she let them through to the flowery claustrophobia of the living room. He knew very well that he wasn't. It had seemed sensible to question his wife without risking any promptings from Wilks. However, hoping to get under her guard, he kept up the pretence.

'Sidney?' Her eyes were wary as they darted from Rafferty to Llewellyn and back again. 'Why do you want to see Sidney?' she demanded. 'What's he supposed to have done?'

'I didn't say he'd done anything. I just want to speak to him. Is he here?' She shook her head. When do you expect him?'

She shrugged. 'He didn't say when he'd be back. He's gone up to the Hall, the home of that doctor who owns the hospital where my girl was killed.'

Rafferty frowned. 'Gone up to the Hall? Why's that?'

'He does the occasional bit of work up there. Can turn his hand to most things, my Sidney.'

'I see.' He gave her a careful scrutiny. 'Close, were they, your husband and Linda?' he asked quietly.

Daphne Wilks stiffened. 'I don't know what you mean.'

Rafferty met Llewellyn's bleak gaze at the defensive answer. 'Look Mrs. Wilks, there's no nice way to put this, but was your husband *unnaturally* close to your daughter?'

Mrs. Wilks took a step back. 'Who told you that?' she demanded. 'It's a wicked lie,' she asserted. 'A wicked lie.'

Rafferty took her arm. 'Come and sit down. Getting yourself all upset won't help matters. Suppose you tell us all about it?'

After dabbing at her eyes with a delicate lace-edged handkerchief, Mrs. Wilks proceeded to screw it into a ball. She stared down at her lap and began to speak, forcing out the words as though each one might choke her. 'He was always cuddling her, as fathers do, there was nothing in it, but Linda got it into her head he'd done something wrong and told me he—did things to her.' She raised her head and stared at them defiantly. 'I gave her a smack for telling such wicked lies and I heard no more about it after that.'

'You didn't believe her, then?' asked Llewellyn gravely.

'Of course not!' In spite of her denial, her eyes avoided the Welshman's. 'Little madam was always making up tales. Liked to imagine herself important, you know how kids do?' She gave a sniff. 'As if my Sidney would do such a thing. He's a respectable man and she's shamed him, shamed us both.'

Rafferty sighed. 'Did Linda accuse her father of doing these things at any particular time?'

Daphne Wilks looked defiantly at him. 'Crafty she was. Told me he went up to her room when I was at work. I used to help out at that hospital part-time in the evenings.'

Interesting, thought Rafferty. Here was yet another hospital connection. 'So your husband and Linda would often be alone here?' he questioned.

Unable to disagree, she burst out, 'But he didn't do anything, I've told you. She made it up to get back at him.'

'Why should she want to get back at him?' asked Llewellyn.

Daphne Wilks sighed and began to pull at the lace of her hankie. 'He was always a bit strict as a father, my Sidney. *"Spare the rod and spoil the child"*, he used to say. Linda was a naughty child and used to get spanked regularly.'

'Did you never punish her yourself?' Llewellyn questioned. 'Surely, it's more usual for a mother to punish a daughter?'

'Oh no, Sidney always said that disciplining Linda was his duty. Said I'd be too soft. He used to take her into the dining-room and shut the door. He told me he didn't want to upset me. Mind, the spankings worked. She'd always be good for a long spell afterwards.'

'Did you never think she might be telling the truth about what her father did to her?' Rafferty demanded, unable to conceal his repugnance at her giving the nod, as it were, to her own daughter's abuse.

Her face flushed an ugly red as she briefly met his gaze, mumbling, 'No, of course not,' before looking away again.

It was hopeless; she would never admit the truth, not even to herself. Rafferty stood up, now wanting only to get out and sensing that Llewellyn felt the same way. But, before they went, he had one or two more questions for her. 'About that phone call on the night your daughter died.'

Daphne Wilks looked wary again. 'What about it?'

'Who answered the phone?'

'My husband.'

'Did he say he recognised the voice? Did he say if they'd rung before?'

The unexpected questions seemed to bewilder her. 'Why should he? We were both far too upset to think about such a thing.' She frowned suddenly. 'Do you think the caller might be the one who killed her?'

The possibility seemed to cheer her immensely, Rafferty noticed. Perhaps she had also suspected her husband of killing Linda?

'Do you know, it never occurred to me before, but I suppose that's a possibility. Why didn't I consider it before? Such wickedness to ring up and invite her to her own murder.' Mrs. Wilks looked at them indignantly, as if they'd been the ones to issue the invitation. 'Because that's what he did, you know. I remember; it rang three times before Sidney answered it. Just like the three cock crows in the bible.' With a stunned look, she stared at them. 'It was a bad omen.'

At least, it seemed to confirm that there had been such a phone call. Rafferty didn't think her that accomplished an actress, no matter how much her husband might have primed her. Surprisingly, she seemed to want to talk now she'd somehow satisfied herself that her husband was in the clear, and it was a good ten minutes later before they managed to make it to the door of the living room.

'Perhaps you'll tell your husband we called?' Rafferty suggested. 'And that we'll be back.' She gave them a defiant look, as though to challenge them to make her change her story. 'We'll see ourselves out.'

Once outside, Rafferty rubbed a hand over his face as though to wipe off the feeling of disgust. 'She knew what her husband was doing all right. Linda wasn't lying. Poor little bitch. Who could she turn to if her own mother wouldn't believe her? I wonder if she brought it up during their row. Accused her father of pushing her into prostitution? It's possible. Perhaps she told him she wasn't going to keep quiet about what he'd done to her any longer?'

Llewellyn nodded. 'He'd have been terrified of discovery. He could have followed her, waited for her to open the hospital's side gate, and pushed through after her. He was working on his car. It's quite likely he still had one of the tools in his hand, so he would have had a weapon.'

Rafferty shook his head. 'You're the car buff. Do you know of any mechanic's tools similar to a rake or a fork?' Llewellyn admitted he didn't. 'Even if he had such a tool, I still don't see him doing it,' said Rafferty slowly. 'If the attack had been done in a mindless and frenzied passion, her body would have received blows as well as her face, and it didn't. And another thing,' he continued, well into his stride now, even though he argued against himself with some reluctance. 'If her father were the murderer, surely, he would have removed her fingerprints? After all, he had just discovered she was a prostitute; for all he knew, she had been picked up for soliciting at some time. Do you think a man who could cold-bloodedly remove her face would then be so careless as to risk the possibility of her fingerprints being on record? He'd want to remove all chance of any association between them being traced. He couldn't be sure that Linda hadn't revealed what he'd done to her to one of her girlfriends. He'd want her to disappear; an unidentifiable body would ensure it. "She's moved to London", he'd say to his neighbours when they asked after her.

Besides, they'd have to get Wilkes DNA, to prove it, and Rafferty couldn't see him submitting to such a thing willingly.

'No,' he added slowly, 'I think we have to look elsewhere for our killer. Someone who didn't know about Linda's double life; someone who had no reason to think she had a record; someone who thought we'd discover their identity once we knew the girl's. But we haven't, dammit.' He brought his fist down with a thump on the roof of the car and Llewellyn winced. 'Why?' he demanded. 'Where are we going wrong?'

Llewellyn didn't answer, but he still looked doubtful when they got in the car. The trouble with his sergeant, thought Rafferty, was that his knowledge of psychology was all text-book stuff, whereas his own was practical. And, whatever Llewellyn might think, he found it hard to believe that a man who relieved his sexual frustrations on his young daughter rather than an adult and possibly demanding mistress, would be bold enough to kill. Of course, he could be wrong.

***

Cautiously, conscious of the superintendent's strictures, Rafferty continued his digging into Melville-Briggs's alibi. But, to his frustration, it seemed ever more impregnable. Although it wasn't substantiated for the entire night, so far, they had been unable to discover any long period when he wasn't vouched for by someone. He had appeared to stay with the same cronies for most of the evening, punctuated only by very short breaks in order to rid himself of an excess of good wine and after dinner port and brandy.

As though to drive the fact of the impenetrable alibi more forcefully home, Sam Dally, their own police surgeon-cum-pathologist, was a prominent witness—one amongst many unfortunately, all eminently respectable professionals, who were prepared to swear on their Hippocratic Oaths that the good doctor hadn't left *The George* all night.

Rafferty's prediction that the press coverage of the crime would create more fear in the town than the actual murder, was becoming horribly true. As they drove through Elmhurst, he could see the huddled groups of women on street corners, and Rafferty, sensitive about his continuing failure, remembered the hostile editorial in the local rag, *The Elmhurst Echo*. Unhappily, he wondered if the worst aspect of the crime wasn't what it did to the living. What had been a small and – for this part of England at least – a remarkably close-knit community, had been split apart in a matter of days. Where before there had been trust, there was now overt suspicion. Any man who had been absent from home on the night of the crime was the subject of doubt and speculation; husbands, brothers, sons— everyone looked sideways at his neighbour.

All this made Rafferty more harassed by the hour, and the feeling that he was getting nowhere fast, didn't help. He supposed Simon Smythe must be feeling the strain even more acutely than himself, especially as Melville-Briggs had sacked him, thereby increasing his neighbours' suspicions. No smoke without fire was the generally accepted reaction to his sacking.

The stupid police mightn't be able to prove he did it, but the general feeling was that his boss must have good reasons for getting rid of him. Poor Simple Simon. Poor Rafferty, too, he reflected, for the pressure on him to solve the crime, combined with the lack of any conclusive lead, put him in danger of losing his previously sunny disposition. Much more of this, he thought, and there would be little to choose between him and Llewellyn.

When they reached their headquarters, Rafferty slouched along to his second-floor office and flung himself in his chair. He was barely aware of Llewellyn as he followed him in and sat unobtrusively at his own desk.

Rafferty gazed through the window disconsolately. It was too much to hope that someone, anyone, had noticed old MB sneak out of *The George* with a large claw-hammer clutched in his lily-white hand. He'd even begun to dream about arresting the smug bastard.

Phlegmatically, he straightened up, and pulled the pile of doctors' statements towards him. There must be something he'd missed. If he went through them just one more time...

Rafferty sensed Llewellyn's disapproving eye. However, the Welshman made no comment, and Rafferty did his best to ignore him, aware that his sergeant's nose was getting more pinched and his lips thinner and more bloodless with each turning page.

Finally, he could stand the silent reproach no longer. He slammed the file shut and demanded, 'All right! If you've got something to say, say it. Don't just sit there looking like a slapped arse. You think that I'm out to get the bastard because he's well-heeled, successful and I don't happen to like him, don't you?'

Llewellyn looked down his nose at this ungrammatical outburst. 'Aren't you perhaps a trifle obsessive about the gentleman, Sir?' he queried. 'There are other suspects.'

'Yes – no – I don't know!' Glowering, Rafferty slumped back in his chair, aware that Llewellyn was right. But only up to a point. It wasn't just for those reasons that he felt an overwhelming desire to follow his mother's advice and slap the cuffs on the doctor. Melville-Briggs was a wrong 'un. Instinctively Rafferty knew it. All right, so far, it seemed, he wasn't into murder. But he had something going; Rafferty's nose told him so, even as he recognised that he wouldn't get the controlled, enigmatic Welshman to take notice of such a thing as intuition.

To Rafferty's way of thinking, a man who cheated on his wife cheated in other ways. And Dr. Melville-Briggs didn't just cheat on his wife. He cheated on his mistresses as well. Rafferty was prepared to concede that a man in Melville-Briggs's position might require the occasional diversion, but, from what they had discovered so far, the doctor's diversions occupied enough of his time to look more like a second career. They'd traced eight ex-mistresses so far, thanks to the indefatigable Gilbert's appetite for other people's dirty linen, and Rafferty, sure there'd be more, was disappointed to confirm that Mrs. Galvin, the cool, self-contained and efficient secretary, was one of them.

Somehow, he'd thought she'd have been more discerning. But, as he'd be the first to admit after his own disastrous marriage, he was no judge of women. According to Gilbert, she'd been making permanent noises and it had only been her husband's accident that had ended it.

Rafferty wondered if Gilbert had a soft spot for Mary Galvin. He'd been reluctant to dish the dirt on her, and the information had been prised from him only with difficulty.

Andrew Galvin had been paralysed from the waist down, and she had been driving. Was it only duty and a guilty conscience that had persuaded her to return to her husband? Or the realisation that her lover was too self-centred to ever allow anyone to put his so convenient marriage at risk? Was her love for the doctor of the obsessive variety that would make no bones about murdering a rival?

Mary Galvin had given an Elmhurst address. She and her husband lived alone. She had had the opportunity to kill the girl, and she didn't strike him as the sort of woman who fell in love either quickly or easily. Did that quiet exterior conceal a jealous rage? As mistress succeeded mistress, had that rage finally erupted in an orgy of violence? Had Linda Wilks been the victim of that fury; unlucky in death as she had been in life?

Rafferty couldn't begin to imagine what appeal the smooth, unctuous Sir Anthony could possibly have for any woman. Yet he seemed to have them eating out of his hands—the accommodating wife; the outwardly unassuming and apparently loyal secretary; the massed ranks of discarded mistresses, as well as the hopeful future ones, like Nurse Wright. For the life of him, Rafferty couldn't see what they got out of it. But then he was a simple man; given to sudden bursts of passion and hot temper that passed as swiftly as they came—how could he ever hope to understand the complicated morals of more sophisticated souls?

GERALDINE EVANS

Was the doctor some sort of esoteric gigolo? Did he, rather than flex his muscles, flex his bedside manner instead? And had he flexed it once too often? And if so, how the hell did he prove it?

He looked thoughtfully at Llewellyn. 'You're an educated chap, Taff. Tell me—what would happen to a doctor who forgot to keep his bedside manner this side of the sheets?'

'He'd get struck off the Medical Register, of course,' Llewellyn replied guardedly, apparently not pleased to discover that Rafferty's mind was still on the same tack.

Rafferty nodded happily. That was what he'd thought. If Melville-Briggs lost his right to practise medicine, he lost everything of value to him.

Llewellyn sighed softly and looked wearily at his chief. 'You're not still suggesting he's the culprit?'

Stung by the implied criticism of his professionalism and miffed by Llewellyn's desire to use nothing but logic to solve the case, Rafferty raised eyes innocent of such intent to Llewellyn's. 'Would I?' he queried softly. 'That sweet, kindly, white-haired old man? Shame on you, Taff. The very idea.'

Rafferty was amused by his own whimsy and Llewellyn's determinedly pursed lips. Who'd have thought the coolly logical Llewellyn would have the knack of restoring his good temper? Perhaps he'd keep him after all. He had his good points, even if they only extended to providing bait for his own barbed wit.

Rafferty was an instinctive copper, and every one of his instincts told him that he was heading in the right direction— even if the path at present seemed to have as many twists and turns as the way through a maze. A maze had a heart and he was convinced that Dr. Melville-Briggs lurked at the centre of this particular leafy conundrum.

It was just a matter of turning up each path till it proved to be a dead-end, eliminating it from the route plan and trying the next. He couldn't expect Llewellyn to be willing to follow him on the often circuitous journey necessary to reach the goal. After all, Rafferty told himself complacently, he lacked the necessary nose, and all the degrees in the world wouldn't provide him with one. It was hardly his fault that murderers didn't go by the police book any more than Rafferty did.

Yet, he was forced to admit to himself, there had been occasions when Llewellyn had come up with a discerning judgement that had left him floundering. For all his annoying traits, from his intellectual superiority to his deflating morality, Rafferty recognised that there was a tantalising depth to his sergeant that was intriguing. Perhaps his judgement had been a bit rash? He'd let his Welsh terrier have another bite at the bone. 'It's worth following up, Dafyd,' he remarked reasonably. 'Such a scandal could have cost him a lucrative career. Don't you think he'd consider it worth a murder, when, as far as he's concerned, the murder of someone like Linda would be a very little murder?'

Of course, Llewellyn immediately made him regret his generous impulse. 'But Linda Wilks wasn't one of his patients,' he pointed out reasonably. 'She was no threat to him. Besides, he's got that alibi, Sir,' Llewellyn reminded him unkindly. 'I fail to see that it matters with whom he was having an affair.'

As though determined to rub it in, he continued in the same negative vein. 'Besides, we've found no evidence that he even knew the victim. I find it extremely unlikely that he did know her. She's hardly his usual type.' He delicately refrained from remarking on the unlikelihood of Melville-Briggs ever having to pay for sex, but his point was clear enough even for Rafferty.

'Besides,' Llewellyn continued, after a short pause, 'He's not the type to commit murder himself. He's what I call a mean sinner, the kind who may be involved, but who hides behind somebody else. There's an old Czech proverb which goes, "*It isn't the thief who is hanged, but the one who was caught stealing*".'

Trust his sergeant to trot out an appropriate quote, Rafferty thought with a grimace. He comforted himself with the thought that Llewellyn couldn't be so smart after all, if his wisdom consisted solely of borrowing dead men's words.

In spite, or because of, Llewellyn's proselytising, Rafferty perversely persisted in his argument. 'All those professional men at *The George* had drunk their fill and more. Why should their evidence under such circumstances be any more reliable than that of any other drunks?

'All right,' he went on hurriedly, as Llewellyn looked set to interrupt, no doubt with more borrowed philosophy, 'I'll grant you, that as she wasn't his patient, any liaison with her wouldn't be enough to get him struck off for misconduct. But surely there are other forms of misconduct which the wise doctor avoids? Consorting with a prostitute, for instance? Linda might have thought he was a suitable subject for blackmail. He was wealthy and successful, unlikely to miss a few grand; the sort of man vulnerable to such smears. And she mightn't have known that Lady Evelyn knew and turned a blind eye to his affairs.'

If only it wasn't for that seemingly rock-solid alibi! Even his finely honed instincts had so far found no way round that, especially when the other doctors at the dinner seemed determined to minimise their varying states of drunken incompetence in their statements.

Still, even if none of the doctors present that evening had expressed the slightest doubt that they were telling the truth, it was only the truth as they saw it, not what they actually knew to be the truth. There was a difference.

'It's by chasing every snippet of information and gossip, however unlikely, that murderers get caught,' he insisted to his sceptical sergeant. 'Many a time I've known a little judicious juice-gathering dissolve the most impressive alibi. It's a matter of first gathering the fruit – the gossip and titbits, then sorting the pips from the pap, and what remains is pure juice – the truth, rich, ripe and damning.'

'What happens when the fruit has already been squeezed dry, Sir?' Llewellyn asked, with a hint of frost.

'We go out and gather some more. That's what.'

Llewellyn sniffed and, looking as if he'd thoroughly got the pip, he replied flatly, 'A second harvest, you mean?'

'That's exactly what I mean.'

The Welshman didn't look enthusiastic—but then he never did. But he'd have to lump it, resolved Rafferty. This was his case and he would solve it his way, even if he had to drag a dubious and critical Llewellyn along behind him through the entire labyrinth.

Chapter Sixteen

Rafferty's optimism didn't last long. Far from being any nearer the centre of the maze, he hadn't even managed to find the entrance. There had been no second harvest, either, and certainly no sign of an orange grove of juicy clues ripe for the plucking.

The feeling that he'd missed something; something so obvious that he was incapable of seeing it, persisted. It didn't help that Llewellyn intimated that his blindness was caused by his growing obsession with proving Melville-Briggs's guilt. Could he be right? Was he letting his antagonism to Melville-Briggs warp his judgement? It wouldn't be the first time, of course. Luckily Llewellyn didn't know that.

His sergeant had only joined the Essex force from the Welsh borders some two months earlier, just before Rafferty's own promotion. His quiet disposition didn't encourage the other officers to swap gossip, so no-one seemed to have told him why Rafferty had been passed over for promotion before. Although that time, too, he had been convinced he was right, it was impossible to forget that in the end, his single-minded pursuit of another high-powered suspect in a brutal child-assault case had nearly caused his suspension. If Bradley had been in post, he'd have no qualms about it.

Could he be heading down the same road again? Then, as now, he had taken an overwhelming dislike to one of the suspects in the case – a man of too similar a type to Melville-Briggs for Rafferty's comfort – and he had gone charging after him with his head down, like a rogue bull elephant. Yet, in the end, the man had been proved innocent. Rather, Rafferty amended, he'd had nothing to do with that particular crime, whatever else he might have been guilty of.

That case had made him several enemies amongst his fellow officers – the ones who relied for promotion on a network of well-placed contacts – important people whispering discreetly in the right ear. And his suspect had been important, very important. They hadn't appreciated Rafferty's lack of subtlety, especially when the suspect had started shouting very loudly and very bitterly about the entire investigation and all the officers involved in it.

That hadn't gone down at all well, and some of his fellow officers were long on memory and short on forgiveness. One in particular, Rick Brown, wouldn't hesitate to do Rafferty down if he got the chance. Luckily, he'd been seconded up north on a case that looked like lasting some time yet. Rafferty hoped he stayed there—at least until this case was over.

Although he knew he must accept that Melville-Briggs couldn't have killed the girl, it didn't make him like the man any more. The way he openly sneered, not only at him but also at the wretched victim, angered Rafferty. Her short life and ugly death resurrected a deeply buried and previously unsuspected chivalrous aspect of his character, and he resolved to find her killer, no matter how many obstacles barred his way to the truth. He conceded he made a poor knight – he couldn't even ride a horse – but he was the only champion Linda Wilks was likely to get, and he meant to do his best by her.

It was quite late, he was feeling tired and a little sad— combinations that often caused him to wax philosophical. They did so now as he thought about Linda and her parents. 'Funny thing, marriage,' he mused, more or less to himself. 'The strangest couples get together, promise to love, honour, etc, and before the honeymoon's over, they realise they've made a horrible mistake. Why are so many people incapable of seeing the obvious before they make it legal?'

'Impetus,' replied Llewellyn.

'What?'

'Impetus,' Llewellyn repeated solemnly. 'The thing gathers a momentum of its own. Like a runaway car, beyond control. People start going out together; they continue going out together, either because no stronger force stops them, or because at a certain time in their lives they're convenient for each other in some way. Before they know it, they're married with a child on the way. Even nowadays, in spite of the permissive society, most people are conventional and do what's expected of them. Most women want the white wedding and the orange-blossom. Of course, marriage is now big business; once the date's set and huge amounts of money are spent on wedding finery and rings and caterers, couples find themselves on a roller-coaster ride to the altar. It takes more courage than most people possess to stamp hard on the brakes at that stage. Little wonder there's so much divorce.'

This was a side to his sergeant that Rafferty had never seen before and he was intrigued. 'You seem to know a lot about it.' He'd momentarily forgotten that Llewellyn had studied philosophy and psychology at university. 'I know you're not married. Did you stamp on the brakes to make sure you stayed that way?'

'Me? No Sir. I've never got close enough to matrimony to require brakes.'

'Very wise,' said Rafferty dryly. 'So what was it? Did all that observation of other people's marriages put you off?'

Llewellyn shrugged, and began to look decidedly uncomfortable, as though wishing he'd never started this conversation. 'Women take the order out of life,' he told Rafferty with a defensiveness that sparked his curiosity. 'Lipstick on the cups, shoes all over the hall, fripperies everywhere. And they're always expecting you to keep them amused, or else they're trying to change your ways.' Rafferty could see that, for Llewellyn, all that might be a problem. 'Then they tend to want children. Messy things, children.'

Strangely, Llewellyn's words lacked conviction. It was almost as though he hid his real desires behind a strongly worded support for their opposite.

Rafferty wondered whether – like the plain virgin – his rejection of matrimony was more to conceal the fact that he'd never met anyone who wanted to marry him. Dafyd Llewellyn certainly wouldn't be to everyone's taste.

'You want to try the older woman, Dafyd,' Rafferty advised. 'Someone who'd appreciate neatness after years of tidying up after husband and kids. A nice divorcée, for instance.' Llewellyn's nostrils quivered with distaste and Rafferty held up his hand. 'I know—messy things divorces, right?' Llewellyn nodded. 'Widow then,' Rafferty went on in his self-appointed role of agony uncle.

Llewellyn didn't look any more enthusiastic about a nice little widow than he had about a divorcée, and Rafferty wondered why he was bothering. Must be his mother's influence, he decided. Still, Llewellyn seemed lonely. It would do him the world of good to get married; a little disorder in his life might just be the making of him.

Rafferty stood up and remarked with grim humour, 'Now's your chance to observe another odd couple— Mr and Mrs Galvin. It might be a good idea to take your psychology degree out and dust it off.' As they headed for the car park, he mused, 'I wonder whether they're another couple who were overtaken by impetus?'

They left the car just past the side gate of the hospital and walked from there. Teams of police frogmen were visible across the fields, as they searched the river for the murder weapon and Linda Wilks's clothes. Their movements were slow, and it was clear they were having no success.

The Galvins' lonely, flint-built cottage looked unkempt, and but for the thin stream of smoke from the chimney, which was quickly whipped away by the still sharp winds off the North Sea, Rafferty would have thought it was empty. It wore an air of neglect, as though the heart had gone out of it. Apart from the top floors of the hospital visible over the high walls of the grounds, there wasn't another house within sight. The fields gave way to the marshland, desolate and silent, apart from the continual crying of the birds—curlews and warblers and moorhens, taking off and landing, taking off and landing again, to pluck fat moist worms from the squelching mud.

The gate creaked noisily behind them as they walked up the overgrown path to the Galvins' cottage, and although he couldn't make out the words, Rafferty caught the tail-end of a hastily cut-off argument.

He lifted the knocker, let it fall, and pinned a friendly smile on his face as Mary Galvin opened the door. 'You remember I said I'd call?'

She nodded. It was plain she'd been weeping; her eyes were red and sore-looking as though the tears had been particularly bitter.

After taking their coats, she led them into a small sitting-room-cum-kitchen. The room had a half-finished look; one side of the kitchen had modern fitted cupboards and looked quite sleek and stylish, while the other half had an old stained stone sink and a cheap red drop-front kitchen cabinet, the sort his mother had thrown out years ago. An attempt had been made to strip the many different layers of paint off this, but patches had clung, stubbornly resistant to the paint stripper, and had been left as though the effort required to finish the job was too much.

Rafferty turned as he heard the wheelchair behind him and introduced himself and Llewellyn. Andrew Galvin seemed a surly individual. He barely managed a nod, before he brought the chair to a halt and gazed at them with a brooding, unblinking stare.

During the course of the case, Rafferty had come to expect hostility, but this was something else again, and he found himself meeting Galvin stare for stare, feeling that it was somehow important not to betray any pity. Although Galvin's legs, under the thick working trousers, might be withered, his arms and shoulders were powerful and strained against the denim shirt. A sprinkling of sawdust covered the material, and Rafferty could see a trail of it leading from a door at the far end of the living-room to the connecting garage, which was an obvious later addition.

'Well now,' Rafferty began, with a mock cheerfulness that did nothing to lessen the tense atmosphere. He unlocked his gaze from that of Galvin. The Galvins had the air of people waiting for the axe to fall. The house was very quiet; set amidst the fields as it was, the limited traffic on the road, several hundred yards away, passed unheard. He found the silence and isolation of the Galvins' house depressing. Coming from a large family, he was a sociable man, and liked to hear the sounds of the neighbours through the walls of his flat.

How did Andrew Galvin stand being alone here, day after day, while his wife was at work? But perhaps solitude was preferable to long uncomfortable silences, broken only by the next argument, to company that created strain without companionship. How many times had he felt that way about his own wife?

As he had expected, Mary Galvin's alibi was backed up by her husband, as his was by her. They had both been at home the entire evening of the murder. Whether they were telling the truth or not, Rafferty thought it would be impossible to shift them. They seemed to have decided to present a united front, yet he sensed it was an uneasy alliance and wondered if he might succeed in breaking it.

Apart from supporting his wife's version of events on the night of the murder, Andrew Galvin said little. He sat in his wheelchair, a sullen and withdrawn presence. He was still quite a handsome man, in spite of the lines of pain deeply engraved from nose to mouth. The full lips were compressed impatiently as though he was only waiting till the statements were noted down in Llewellyn's little book before he burst out with some furious comment.

Rafferty sensed the frustration and bitterness just beneath the surface, and he guessed Galvin had been a sensual man before the accident. Rafferty wondered how he would feel if he lost his mobility, his job, the love of his wife, and in their stead suffered continual pain and the knowledge that his wife was as bitterly unhappy as himself.

He had to admit he didn't know—he, at least, had a large family to cushion him should he need it. In this man's presence he felt suddenly ashamed that the death of his wife, Angie, hadn't caused him to grieve either long or deeply. It was only guilt that had caused him suffering. His family had realised his wife was little loss to him as a human being, for they'd left him to come to terms in his own way with the feelings of mingled self-reproach and relief her death had brought. If he'd truly loved her and mourned for her his family would never have been out of his flat, especially his Ma.

Yet Andrew Galvin had grieved; was still grieving. His wife's infidelity had obviously devastated him as much as a bereavement. Llewellyn's earlier remarks had made Rafferty oddly contemplative, and now he wondered if there had been anyone to comfort Andrew Galvin.

While he left Llewellyn to continue the interview, Rafferty let his eyes flicker casually around the room. There was no evidence of brothers or sisters, nephews or nieces; no photographs of any description. But even if there were such a family in the background, it was usually the woman who took the trouble to frame and display their pictures. And Mary Galvin struck him as unsentimental, not the sort to put such things on show, the sort of woman who would keep her deepest feelings locked away from prying eyes. It was strange that a man like Sir Anthony had been able to release them. Perhaps his psychiatric training had supplied him with a few tricks denied to lesser mortals.

After getting their statements out of the way, both the Galvins seemed to loosen a little of their stiff control.

Rafferty decided now was the time to get under their guard. 'I've some – rather delicate – questions for you, Mrs. Galvin. Perhaps you'd rather speak to me without your husband being present?'

To his surprise, she shook her head. Her back seemed to straighten a fraction more and she gave him a sad smile; the smile of a woman who knew she had already lost everything of importance.

'I think I know what you want to ask about, Inspector,' she remarked quietly. 'There's no need to be so circumspect on my account. I no longer have any secrets from my husband. Andrew already knows about Sir Anthony and me.' She raised her head and met Rafferty's eyes boldly. 'I'm sure you already know all this, Inspector, but you might as well have the true version rather than the more lurid gossip from the hospital grape-vine.

'I'd been having an affair with Sir Anthony for six months before the accident that paralysed Andrew. Oh, now I see him for what he is,' she exclaimed bitterly, 'but then he took the trouble to be as charming and considerate to me as he is to his rich patients. It was only later that I realised what a fool I'd been, thinking myself in love with a man who didn't exist. He played a part, you see and played it to perfection. It took Andrew's accident to show him in his true light. Even then, I didn't want to believe it. I thought his reluctance to leave his wife stemmed from concern for me, worry about my reputation.'

Her eyes didn't flinch from his, but now, the hatred was plain in her face. 'All the time, of course, his only concern was for the social position he enjoyed through his wife. Without her, he was only another doctor—not a terribly good one at that. She got him his first clients.' She laughed harshly. 'I used to think it was loyalty to him that kept them. But of course I was wrong.'

She didn't elaborate, but left Rafferty to come to his own conclusions. He could believe that it was loyalty to Lady Evelyn that brought his patients back time and again.

Rafferty wondered again if Mary Galvin could have killed the girl, her personality corroded by seeing her now hated ex-lover day after day and having to watch as he paraded his latest mistresses under her nose. Had she decided to hit him where she could do most damage—in his reputation? It would explain why the victim's body had escaped the blows. She didn't hate her ex-lover's latest mistresses; why should she? She knew they would be replaced in their turn, as she had been. But she was astute enough to realise that a 'Faceless Lady' would catch the imagination of the press and guarantee far more damaging publicity and that would surely be what she wanted.

Had she known the girl would be coming to the hospital that night? Had Sir Anthony delighted in telling her about his mistresses? Rafferty didn't find it hard to imagine that he would get pleasure from such casual cruelty. Had he intended to slip away from *The George* that night to meet Linda? And had she known about the assignation and decided to meet the girl herself and kill her?

Looking at her sitting calm and composed as she related the details of her affair, he felt her to be fully capable of it. The thought brought the realisation that if he wanted answers, he would have to get tough with her. She might yet regret that confident assertion that she had no secrets from her husband.

'You must have felt very angry when Sir Anthony told you the affair was over,' he remarked. 'I can imagine what a traumatic time it must have been for you; your husband crippled, your realisation that Sir Anthony didn't love you. A lot of women would brood over the unfairness of it all, maybe even want revenge. Is that what you wanted, Mrs. Galvin? How many lonely nights while your husband was in hospital did you scheme to get back at Melville-Briggs?'

'I didn't,' she protested. 'I—'

'How many mistresses did he parade under your nose before you snapped?' he demanded remorselessly. 'Was it one? Three? Six?'

'No, I tell you. It wasn't—'

'Come now, Mrs. Galvin. You can't expect me to believe that a woman passionate enough to have a love affair wouldn't also have enough passion to kill. I understand your husband was paralysed from the waist down in the accident. You must have felt very frustrated after Sir Anthony dumped you. Did you channel that frustration into planning murder? One that—'

'Stop it!'

Startled, Rafferty stared as Andrew Galvin raised himself from his wheelchair and launched himself at him. He tried to protect his head from the man's fists as they rained blows down on him.

'Leave her alone. Leave her alone, I tell you. Of course, she didn't kill that bastard. I know damn well she didn't because—'

Llewellyn had finally managed to drag him off. Galvin stood in the middle of the room, breathing heavily and swaying, before he turned and flung himself back in his chair. There was a stunned silence that lasted all of thirty seconds after Galvin's outburst.

Llewellyn was the first one to gather his wits. 'When did you discover you could walk, Mr. Galvin?' he asked quietly. 'Was it before the murder? Or after?'

Andrew Galvin's painfully rasping breath was now the only sound. As though satisfied that his outburst had caused sufficient shock, he wheeled his chair away from them and spat out a single word. 'Before.'

Rafferty shifted uncomfortably in his chair. The man's manner seemed to challenge them to arrest him. Why? Was he trying to protect his wife? Or was there a deeper reason? Andrew Galvin had been discounted from the murder investigation. The man couldn't walk, or so they had thought. Apart from the difficulty of manoeuvring his wheelchair through the undergrowth and trees planted at the perimeter of the hospital, there had been no sign of any tracks, no sign of vegetation flattened by the passing of such a vehicle. But if he could walk...

Although he might find the feat difficult, it wouldn't be impossible. Was that why Mary Galvin had kept up the pretence of his paralysis? Had she secretly suspected? He remembered that she'd become very defensive when he'd told her he would have to check her alibi with her husband. Did Andrew Galvin secretly want to punish her for her infidelity? And was being arrested for the murder of one of her ex-lover's mistresses the method he had hit on?

Bemused that so many possibilities should fall into his lap at once, Rafferty glanced at Mary Galvin. Her face was chalk-white and anguished. Her eyes, when they met his were pleading.

'Well, what are you waiting for?' Galvin demanded, when the silence had dragged on a little longer. 'Aren't you going to arrest me?'

'Why?' Rafferty asked. 'Did you kill the girl?'

The reply was slow in coming. 'No.'

'Then why should I arrest you?'

Andrew Galvin looked helplessly from Rafferty to his wife and back again. Then he shrugged, and slumped back in his chair, his expression defeated.

Rafferty took a deep breath and began to question Mary Galvin again. 'How long have you known your husband could walk?'

'Since just after the murder. I came home unexpectedly and found him in the shed. His chair was in here.'

'Did you suspect he might have killed the girl?'

Pain-filled eyes met his. 'I didn't know what to think. I only knew how much torment I'd caused him. How bitter he had become and...' Her voice trailed off before beginning again more firmly. 'I couldn't let him be suspected of murder as well. I owed him that much. It was bad enough that I'd caused the accident which paralysed him, but when he discovered about Sir Anthony and me—'

Her throat muscles worked up and down spasmodically and she gave a particularly joyless little laugh. 'I really thought Sir Anthony loved me, you know. I was—dazzled, I suppose. He showed me a lifestyle I'd never experienced before. Andrew and I were going through a rocky patch, and it was as if the scales had fallen from my eyes. That life didn't need to be so dull, so dreary. For the first time since I was a teenager, I began to have fun.'

Her face twisted as a spasm crossed it. 'I was stupid not to realise that all fun has to be paid for, and not by the Sir Anthony's of this world. You could say that, after Andrew's accident, the devil called in his debt. I knew then that he didn't love me at all, or if he did, it was only as a very poor second to his upper-crust life style.'

She was being brutally honest, stripping herself of pride in a way that was embarrassing to watch. Up to now, her husband had sat silently listening to her outpourings, but now he looked at his wife's tear-wet cheeks with a shocked expression.

'Did you really think the police would suspect I killed the girl in some fit of blind rage?'

She nodded once, her features taut with emotion.

'God!' He put his head in his hands and tugged at his hair as though he would wrench it out by the roots. 'How can you not have realised that if I'd wanted to kill anybody it would have been him?' He wheeled himself over to her and took her hands in his. 'Oh, I told myself I hated you; perhaps I did for a little while, but that was nothing beside all the grief I felt for what we had lost. I couldn't hate you. Not for long.'

She looked at him as if not quite certain she had heard aright. 'What are you saying, Andrew?'

His expression raw, he said simply, 'That I still love you.' His voice hoarse with the intensity of his emotions, he added, 'That I don't want you to leave me, now or ever.'

'Oh Andrew. My love.' With a sob, Mary Galvin flung herself into her husband's arms and they clung together with a kind of fierce desperation.

Quietly, Rafferty signalled to Llewellyn, and they let themselves out of the cottage. He wondered if it was possible that they had staged that touching little scene for his benefit. They'd certainly had plenty of time to plan it and he thought Mary Galvin's mind was sufficiently cool for the job.

But even if their emotional display had been genuine and not merely intended to divert suspicion from Andrew Galvin, it still didn't bring him any closer to making an arrest. Sourly, he reflected that the case would have caused him a damn sight less trouble if Melville-Briggs had been the one to be found murdered.

Chapter Seventeen

Rafferty had kept away from the hospital all the next day, so he wouldn't be tempted to interview Melville-Briggs again. Not that he had anything new to tackle him with, anyway. He didn't even have any solid proof that the, so far, elusive Miranda and the girl in the pub were one and the same. Even if the girl in the pub proved to be this Miranda, it added nothing to the investigation, rather it confused matters. Given Dr Melville-Briggs's womanising, there might be any number of unexplained females, however tenuously connected with the case, still to come out of the woodwork.

But even if a couple of battalions of women appeared, none of them would be Linda Wilks. Dr. Melville-Briggs hadn't murdered her, and he'd better accept it if he was ever to solve the case.

It wasn't as though he was short of other candidates for the crime; if anything, he had an over-abundance of them, and would have been happier if their numbers were less and the pointers to someone's – anyone's – guilt more conclusive. But as wishful thinking wasn't going to solve the murder, he decided to ring through to the station to see if, by some miracle, the killer had decided to come in to confess. His radio was on the blink, he'd left his mobile in his dank little office at the hospital, and when he finally went reluctantly to the grim box assigned to them, it was to find a message from his mother awaited him rather than a murderer's confession. She had been trying to contact him for several hours, apparently.

'You're sure she didn't say what she wanted?' he asked the desk sergeant.

'She said it was a private matter. You want to get round there, Sir. She sounded a bit breathless to me—agitated like. Didn't she have those heart palpitations last year? Anyway, she said you were to go as soon as you got the message.'

The heart palpitations had turned out to be nothing more than indigestion. Rafferty wondered briefly why she hadn't phoned one of his sisters, and then shrugged. He'd find out soon enough. He hoped it wasn't a ruse and that he wouldn't discover Maureen concealed in the cupboard under the stairs when he got there. She could be as crafty as any double-dealing diplomat, his Ma.

Still, she wasn't getting any younger, and she'd never summoned him off a job before. Perhaps this time she really was ill. He'd left Llewellyn holding the fort in the office, so he instructed, 'Tell my sergeant I'll ring him if it looks as though I'm going to be a while.'

Rafferty left his grim box and put his foot down all the way to his mother's house, but when he got there he found her sitting in her favourite chair by the window, watching the world go by, and looking a damn sight more hale-and-hearty than he felt himself. His eyes flickered suspiciously when he saw she was in her best navy-blue Crimplene dress and his ear cocked for the sound of footsteps emerging from the cupboard under the stairs.

'What's going on, Ma?' he demanded. He felt hot and cross, and not in the mood for any romantic games.

She stood up, arms akimbo, and he didn't need his policeman's nose to sniff trouble.

'What's going on?' she repeated caustically. 'Little enough from what I hear,' she went on. 'Where've you been? I've been ringing that station all morning.'

'My radio's on the blink so they couldn't get hold of me. Anyway, I'm here now. What's the problem?'

'The same one,' she told him flatly. 'Jack.'

Jailhouse Jack! He'd forgotten all about him. He must have been charged by now, Rafferty realised guiltily He'd probably be in the remand cells at the Harcombe nick – their local prisons being full to the brim with other ne'er-do-wells – awaiting trial about the stolen whisky.

'You said you'd see to it, Joseph, but you haven't. According to Deirdre, you haven't been near nor by. I was that ashamed when she told me. So much for my son, The Inspector,' she mocked. 'And to think I promised Deirdre she could rely on you. Do you want the poor thing left standing at the altar?'

'It won't come to that, Ma,' he muttered feebly. Worse luck.

'No?' Her voice was sharp with annoyance. 'It seems it will if you've got anything to do with it. I was going to go to the station myself and wait for you if you didn't turn up.'

'I'll see to it, Ma,' he vowed desperately. 'I'll see to it this afternoon, I promise.'

'Yes, well,' she sniffed. 'See that you do. I promised the poor girl,' she repeated. 'Would you make me go back on my word?'

His mother had always had the knack of making him feel like a guilty schoolboy, he reflected. Perhaps all mothers were the same, but his was expert at cutting him down to size. At the moment, he felt about twelve years old. He scowled, but that, of course, only encouraged her to rub salt into the wounds.

'Why couldn't you have been a builder like the rest of the family?' she demanded plaintively, 'then at least I might have been able to get hold of you when I wanted you. But oh no, you were set on becoming a policeman, wouldn't listen to your mother.'

She made it sound as though he had joined the police solely from a perverse desire to annoy her. Yet having a son in the police force had been almost entirely her idea. The free boots for his expensively large feet had held a strong appeal for a widow with five younger children to feed and clothe.

'Now look at you.' His mother was in full spate and unstoppable. 'Not only have you no time to ring your mother, but you're in charge of trying to catch a dangerous murderer at that loony bin. I don't like it, Joseph. I don't like it at all.'

He was getting progressively less keen on it himself as the case went on, but he wasn't prepared to admit it to his mother. 'There's more than me standing between chaos and the forces of law and order, Ma,' he remarked soothingly.

'That's as may be, Joseph' – Rafferty didn't fail to notice the second use of his full first moniker – 'but I'd feel much easier in my mind, if you must be a policeman, if you had a wife to look after you. A nice sensible girl. Like your Uncle Pat's girl, Maureen, for instance.'

Here we go again, Rafferty thought with a sigh. However, to his relief, having put across her feelings in her usual forceful fashion, she relented, and for once, didn't pursue the point.

'I don't suppose you've eaten?' Another guilty flush crossed his features. 'I thought not. The kettle's on.' She looked closely at him. 'How's your murder going, anyway? Any nearer to catching the wicked creature?'

'No,' he admitted flatly.

'Well, it's early days yet. Look at some of the cases you read about, drag on for weeks they do.'

Rafferty managed a weak smile. 'Thanks, Ma. You're a real Job's comforter. That's sure to keep the Superintendent sweet when next he wants a report on my progress.'

'Well, if he thinks he can do any better, let him try,'

That was the trouble, Rafferty reflected grimly. He just might. 'I ought to be going, Ma.'

'A few more minutes aren't going to make any difference.' she insisted. 'Let that Superintendent cool his heels for a bit. You might as well take your wedding present while you're here.' She pointed to a beautifully wrapped parcel sitting on an occasional table by the kitchen door.

'What is it?'

'A slow cooker.'

'How much do I owe you?'

'Ten pounds.'

'That's cheap, isn't it?' he asked suspiciously. 'It's not knocked-off, is it? Because, if it is—'

'Of course it's not,' exclaimed his mother vehemently. 'It's bankrupt stock. With so many businesses going to the wall these days, there's a lot of bargains about.'

Bargains—the very word made him uneasy. His Ma's love of "bargains" didn't stop at the January sales, unfortunately, and although, like most of the rest of the family, she was honest enough after her own lights, she saw nothing wrong in buying the occasional questionable item.

Everybody did it, she defended herself when he tried to remonstrate with her. But of course, with so many relatives working on building sites – which seemed to positively breed illicit items – she had more opportunities than most. Little had changed it seemed. Why should she pay over the odds, she had often demanded, just because her son was in the Police Force? And her on a widow's pension.

She knew how to turn the knife, his Ma. No wonder he'd been glad to leave home early and move into the section house. He could hardly have arrested his own mother for receiving, yet neither could he pretend to uphold the forces of law and order when his dinner was heated in a "hot" infra-red grill. He sighed. A policeman's lot in the Rafferty family was not a happy one.

An hour later he was finally able to escape, after finishing his tea and thick ham sandwiches, picking up his present and promising, once more, that he would see to Jack straightaway.

At least, by doing as he was bid in this it would give his mother one less excuse to persuade him into her parlour for matchmaking purposes and he might be able to get on with solving the murder in relative peace.

***

Rafferty popped his head round the door of his office. 'I'm back, but I've got to go out again. Some checking up to do,' he explained quickly, shutting the door behind him before

Llewellyn could offer to come with him. This was one task he wanted to see to by himself.

And once he'd got Jailhouse Jack sorted out, he would have to try to persuade Superintendent Bradley to sanction the funds for DNA tests on Linda Wilks's foetus and the male suspects in the case. He wasn't optimistic that he'd get Bradley to agree—he wasn't called "Long Pockets" for nothing.

He turned into the car park at the Harcombe police station, ready, if not wholly willing, to do his familial duty. But as he knew he'd never hear the end of it if he didn't at least make the attempt, he gritted his teeth and put a good face on it.

'Morning, Tom,' he greeted the desk sergeant with false bonhomie in an attempt to cover his awkwardness. 'I rang earlier about a fellow called Jack Delaney. The constable who answered the phone told me he'd been charged and was back in the cells on remand. I'd like a word with him.'

'Oh yes?' The sergeant eased his bulk off the counter and looked at Rafferty with interest. 'I didn't know you were involved in this case, Inspector. You know Brown's back from that case up north and has taken over the investigation?'

Rafferty hadn't, and now he swore silently. The desk sergeant whistled and obtained the services of the nearest constable to escort Rafferty down to the cells. 'Brown's in his office,' the sergeant told him slyly. 'You'll want to see him, of course. Out of courtesy, like.'

'Of course,' Rafferty muttered, trying to stop himself from glaring at his persecutor. In his late forties, the desk sergeant was only hanging on for his pension. He knew all about the little feud between Rafferty and Rick Brown, and, having long since given up on getting beyond the rank of sergeant, it amused him to pass the years till retirement fomenting trouble amongst his superiors, the "clever young buggers", as he called them. He wasn't partisan; he despised them all without particularity.

Affecting an air of unconcern, Rafferty said, 'I'll see chummy first,' and followed the constable down to the cells. Before he'd learned that Brown was in charge of the case, he'd still had a faint hope of emerging from the station with his pure policeman image virgo intacta. But once he discovered their distant family ties, Brown would plunder his most secret cranny with all the finesse of a mad rapist. Rafferty knew well enough that Rick Brown was still looking for an opportunity to get his own back, and here he was with no choice but to present it to him, gift-wrapped.

The constable unlocked the door of the cell and let Rafferty in, banging the door shut behind him. Luckily, Jack waited till then to express his joy at their reunion, leaping to his feet as relief chasing the worry from his face. 'Long time no see, Jar. Sure an' you're a sight for sore eyes. Are they lettin' me go then?'

'No. Not yet.'

The expression on Jack's face was that of one whose trust had been irretrievably shattered. 'But Deirdre said... I thought you'd come to get me out,' he reproached. 'What's goin' on?'

If it hadn't been for Jack's fiancée, Rafferty's cousin, Deirdre, a sensible girl who didn't deserve such a husband, he wouldn't have bothered his head about his gormless relative's fate. But he consoled himself with the thought that Jack was taking his bride back to Dublin with him after the wedding. It could be worse. 'Why don't you tell me all about it, 'he encouraged now, sitting companionable beside Jack on the thin mattress.

With a face as deceptively blameless as a choirboy's, Jack chorused in his peculiar high-pitched voice, 'They're fitting me up, Jar, I didn't do it, as God's me witness.'

'Let's save God for the real witness-box, shall we?' Rafferty suggested tightly, annoyed by Jack's use of his old childhood nickname. 'I'm sure he's got enough on his plate at the moment worrying about your nuptials. Right. Where and when is the crime of the century supposed to have taken place, and what were you doing at the time?'

'It was last Friday night, way over near Colchester. But I wasn't anywhere near there.'

Rafferty's drooping head jerked up at this. 'You mean the night of the murder?'

'Was that the same night?' Jack grinned, his troubles evidently forgotten. 'Well, well, you were kept busy then, one way and another. Poor old Jar. Still,' he added airily, 'if you will join the pigs you've only yourself to blame.'

Rafferty looked pityingly at him. The eejit didn't even have the nous to keep his usual insults to himself. Now he said flatly, 'If you want this particular pig to squeak in your defence, you'd better remember your manners.'

The tactlessness of his remark must even have penetrated Jack's thick skull, for he murmured, 'Sorry, Joseph,' in a suitably chastened manner. 'Slip of the tongue.'

'Try not to have any more,' Rafferty advised, 'or there's a good chance I might have a slip of the foot and slide right back out that door, leaving you this side of it. Wedding or no wedding. Now,' he leaned back against the scarred wall of the cell, 'why don't we make ourselves comfortable? Then you can tell me the rest.'

'I didn't do it, Joe, honest, I didn't. Admittedly, the money would have come in useful for the honeymoon, but I was casin' a joint out at Elmhurst that night.'

'And that's your defence, is it?' Rafferty sighed. 'It won't do. It won't do at all. Let's start again. You were out for a walk on a particularly fine spring night...'

Surprisingly, Jack caught his drift. 'Right. I was out for this walk, like, me and Deirdre, and—'

'Hold on, hold on. Let's get this straight. Do you usually take your fiancée out with you when you look over a likely prospect?' It seemed a strange thing to do, but then, with Jack, anything was possible, the dafter the better.

'It was only a general once-over,' Jack defended himself from the slur of unchivalrous behaviour. 'We'd been to the pub by the loony-bin. Deirdre knows the landlord and I fancied me chances of gettin' a late session.'

Rafferty's instincts went into overdrive at this. 'What time was this?' he demanded. 'What time did you leave the pub, I mean?'

Unnerved, Jack was, for a moment or two, incapable of getting his small vocabulary together, but at last he managed it. 'I dunno. About half eleven or thereabouts, I s'pose.' He pulled a face. 'Deirdre knocked the idea of afters on the head. Shame, as it was a good night, too. Anyhow, sure an' we was walkin' back up the road to where I'd left me car and—'

'You hadn't left it in the pub car park then?'

'Course not! Do you think I'm daft?' Rafferty forbore to comment. 'I'd had a few drinks, hadn't I? It was after hours and the landlord's late with his back-handers this month. Deirdre was worried the cops might pounce out of spite. You know how the bastards...' Jack's voice trailed away and a sheepish grin decorated his face. 'Sorry,' he mumbled. 'Anyway, the car was up the road, on the patch of waste-ground opposite the nut-house.'

Rafferty broke in. 'Why didn't you tell the police you'd been in the pub with a bar-full of witnesses when someone was ripping off the lorry?'

'I told you,' he explained patiently. 'It was after hours. I'd have got them all in shtook, wouldn't I?'

Apparently, Jack's capacity for making instant friends hadn't changed either. He thought the whole world was his bosom buddy.

'I'd a still been there meself, only Deirdre kept on at me till I agreed to leave.'

Rafferty reminded himself that he was related to this cretinous individual, even if only distantly, and counted to ten before he allowed himself to reply. 'I see. So in your opinion, it's better to go down for another five stretch than to nark on your new mates for after-hours drinking?'

It wasn't even as if they'd been that much over time, but perhaps his cousin had a point. Back-handers were a way of life, and some of the uniformed branch could be most unpleasant about any delay in receiving their dues.

Jack nodded, quite impervious to the sarcasm. 'That's right. I'll tell you somethin' else, an' all. Deirdre said I'd 'ad enough to drink – you know how women do – anyway, when I saw the bleedin' monk, I thought she might 'ave a point. Perhaps I ought to lay orf it for a bit. What do you think?'

'Monk? What monk was this then? Friar Tuck?' Rafferty was beginning to wonder if the low-wattage light bulb of his cousin's intelligence hadn't finally flickered out altogether.

'I dunno,' Jack answered in all seriousness. 'He 'ad his hood over 'is 'ead. I only saw 'im for a second. Gave me quite a turn, I can tell you. Thought I was gettin' them whatdoyoumacallits—the DTs'.

Rafferty decided to humour him. 'This monk,' he asked patiently, 'where did he go?'

'Into the nut-house.'

Rafferty didn't believe it. It couldn't be happening. Surely God wasn't so kind as to reward his good deed with such charity? Could it be, was it possibly—a lead?

He felt a taut shiver of awe run up his spine as he looked at Jack's vacant features. What was it the bible said? Something about the least of his creatures? Out of the mouths of babes and the simple-minded? Llewellyn would know, of course, but Rafferty had no intention of mentioning this little tête-à-tête.

Careful, Rafferty warned himself, as he felt the urge to grab hold of Jack and shake him. Don't spook the witness. Take it nice and slow. 'You didn't, by any chance happen to see a car parked outside the hospital gate as well did you, Jack?'

'A car?'

'You know, one of those painted jobs with a wheel on each corner,' he enlarged sarcastically, saintly patience quickly forgotten.

Jack's mouth dropped open. 'How did you know that? Bloody 'ell. You're smart and no mistake.'

Rafferty smiled smugly. 'I try. Any idea what make it was?'

'Can't remember.' Jack gave a sheepish shrug. 'I'd just come out of the pub, remember? One of those small sleek jobs though. I'm thinkin' of getting one meself,' he added.

Stealing one, more like, thought Rafferty. 'Get a glimpse of the license plate, did you?'

Jack shook his head again.

But it wouldn't have made any difference if he had. Rafferty had forgotten that eleven years of schooling had failed to teach Jack even the rudiments of the alphabet. Perhaps Deirdre would know.

'You've been lucky, Jack,' he told him, as he stood up and knocked on the cell door. 'I'll tell the inspector your story myself; it'll save Deirdre the trouble.'

If he'd known his cousin had been with his girlfriend that night, he could have saved himself the unpleasantness of sorting it out. Women, he generally found, didn't worry overmuch about the shamefulness of snitching. Practical creatures, women.

Still, he'd done himself a bit of good as well as Jack, so he shouldn't complain. 'You'll be out of here in an hour or two, I shouldn't wonder.' Ebullient, he nearly told Jack he could buy him a pint when he got out but stopped himself in time. That wouldn't be such a good idea, he realised. The fewer people who saw them together, the better he'd like it.

The constable let him out, and Rafferty walked thoughtfully back up the corridor. He stopped abruptly as his mind strove manfully to connect the tenuous strands of the case to the latest information. There was something, some glimmer of a connection. Was it, no wait a minute, could it be—? Something heavy lurched against his shoulder.

'Sorry Inspector.'

The constable grinned apologetically for his clumsiness and walked swiftly away as Rafferty scowled ferociously at his back. Whatever his mind had been reaching for was gone. A few seconds before he had felt puffed up, good deed for the day performed and smug with the self-righteousness of the properly rewarded. Now he felt horribly deflated.

Slowly, reluctantly, he walked towards Rick Brown's office. But at least he wouldn't have to admit to a delighted Brown that Jack was his relative. Just checking out a possible witness in a murder case, wasn't he? And he had a whole bar full of drinkers to back him up.

Chapter Eighteen

Rafferty had just got back from Harcombe police station when Llewellyn gave him the latest news: Anthony Melville-Briggs was dead.

It took him a few minutes' to take it in. Apparently, the doctor had wrapped his car around a tree at Wivenhoe, his body pierced through the heart by one of the lower branches, taking with him any faint remaining chances of charging him with murder.

Llewellyn had been right when he'd quoted that old bod's words. How had it gone? Something about every guilty person being his own hangman? Well, Rafferty concluded sombrely, it certainly looked as if Sir Anthony had been his own executioner, whether or not his sins had included murder.

He supposed it fell to him to break the news to Lady Evelyn—he checked with Llewellyn that uniformed hadn't already done so—they hadn't, and he told Llewellyn to give them a bell and let them know he'd take on the task.

To Llewellyn's undisguised relief, Rafferty told him to remain at the office. Rafferty picked up WPC Green on his way out and they drove to the Hall. The butler let them in, and after briefly stating they were there on official business, they followed his broad, black-clad figure into the winter parlour.

'Inspector.' Lady Evelyn seemed pleased to see him and he stared guiltily at her. 'What can I do for you? Have you come to see over the house? I'm sure I've got time, if you have.'

Rafferty shuffled his feet. 'No, Ma'am. Er— That is—' He broke off awkwardly. To fill in the gap while he remembered his carefully rehearsed words, he introduced his companion. Then, taking a deep breath, he said, 'I'm afraid I have some bad news for you, Ma'am.'

Lady Evelyn frowned. 'Bad news? What do you mean?'

'It's—your husband, Lady Evelyn. I'm sorry to have to tell you this. He's had an accident—it seems his car went out of control.'

'How—how bad?'

Rafferty shuffled his feet again.

'Please. Just—tell me.' Her voice was faint as she asked, 'Is he—is he dead, Inspector?'

'I'm afraid so, Ma'am.'

Lady Evelyn sank down slowly on to one of the chairs. As though looking for consolation, her eyes rested on the array of family photographs on her desk. Her lips tightened, and Rafferty hoped she was bringing her stiff upper lip into play. It would ease his discomfort if she did.

He was only able to offer her limited comfort. 'It—it would have been very quick,' he told her. 'He wouldn't have suffered.'

'I see.' She shuddered slightly, briefly closed her eyes as if offering up a prayer for the repose of her husband's soul, and then sat up straight in her chair. 'Thank you for coming to tell me. I understand how difficult it is to break such news.'

She seemed dazed, but apart from a faint white line around her tightened lips, she had taken the news with remarkable composure, much to Rafferty's relief. He had a quiet word with the butler, who alerted the staff. The housekeeper took charge, and she and one of the older female servants were soon plying their mistress with hot sweet tea. After quietly offering his condolences and having them as quietly accepted, Rafferty left the WPC behind with instructions that he'd send a car for her in a couple of hours and let himself out into the gathering dusk.

***

Strangely, Melville-Briggs's death seemed to act as a starter's pistol and, all at once, things began to move more swiftly.

When Rafferty got back to the station, it was to find that Staff Nurse Estoce had finally decided to tell them the truth about Charge Nurse Allward's habits on night duty—he had been the one who had rung Linda that night, as they had suspected.

When Linda had told him about the row with her parents, Allward promised her a bed for the night in exchange for a freebie. Staff Nurse Estoce had heard him on the phone arranging it. Yet, she was adamant that the girl hadn't turned up, and had assumed that she had changed her mind. She had thought no more about it till the next morning when Linda Wilks's body had been found.

But Rafferty didn't have time to dwell on this news because hard on the heels of the Staff Nurse's revelation came another breakthrough.

They had found Miranda, or rather, she had found them. She turned up at the station just after Nurse Estoce left and demanded to see Rafferty. She'd been hiding out in a cheap hotel in Wandsworth, apparently, and only now, with the news of Sir Anthony Melville-Briggs's death breaking in the media, had she felt safe enough to leave it.

As she sat down on the visitor's chair in front of Rafferty's desk, the light from the window shone full on her. Her eyes were dilated, a fine sheen of perspiration marred the pale skin, and as she fiddled with the collar of her expensive silk blouse, Rafferty noticed that her fingers were trembling.

'It—it began a year ago.' Haltingly, she began her story.

'What did?' Rafferty asked. Although he suspected he already knew, he was, determined to get everything laid out nice and clearly.

'The—affair between Tony Melville-Briggs and myself.'

So—she had been yet another mistress. Rafferty mightn't have admired the man, but he certainly had to applaud

Melville-Briggs's energy. 'I don't quite understand,' he rapped out sternly. 'What has that got to do with Linda Wilks's death? You said it was connected.'

Her eyes widened in surprise. 'Of course it's connected. It must be. Why else would he—?' She broke off, clearly not yet ready to reveal all of her story. She paused and began again. 'I was there the night the girl was murdered. It was meant to be me, don't you see?'

'Perhaps you could be a little more explicit, Miss Raglan,' Llewellyn suggested quietly.

She nodded. 'I'd learned a lot of things about his practice when I was with him—I wasn't the only woman to whom he was giving powerful drugs.' Her voice had a vicious bite to it as she went on. 'He turned us into junkies for his own profit. Before I met him, I was only into drugs in a small way, parties and so on, but that soon changed. He made sure of it. Mostly, as my habit increased, I was just grateful for a reliable source, but later, when I realised just what he'd done to me, I wanted revenge. And I knew the perfect way to get it.

'What would be more just than to make him pay for the habit he had created?' she asked them. 'I needed more drugs and I expected – demanded, that he supply them for nothing – or else. He just laughed at me, was convinced that I'd be so desperate to get the drugs he supplied that I'd be as cowed as the rest, only too glad to do what he said.

'But I'd already begun to try to kick the habit. I'd voluntarily reduced my intake; he didn't know that, of course. I still needed them.' She looked bleakly at them out of over-bright eyes. 'Perhaps I always will. Anyway, I was soon able to convince him that I meant what I said.'

She shuffled restlessly on her chair, opened her handbag and started to light a cigarette before changing her mind and crushing it out in the nearest handy receptacle, which happened to be Rafferty's mostly empty mug of tea. Which was just as well; with the No Smoking policy, she'd likely have set off the smoke alarm.

'He soon realised he'd badly misjudged me when I put my demands more plainly. I knew he couldn't refuse.' An expression of malicious spite hovered for a second on her vapid features. 'I threatened to go to the papers. I could have ruined him, you see. That's when the meeting at the hospital was arranged.'

Rafferty remembered Nathanial Whittaker's description of the character of drug addicts; the weak, the stupid, the desperate and the gullible, and in spite of Miranda Raglan's outwardly tough stance, Rafferty detected the rather foolish, insecure young woman concealed beneath the bravado.

Llewellyn broke into his thoughts. 'But he can't have killed her. He had an alibi. We've checked it out very thoroughly.'

'But it couldn't have been anyone else,' Miranda insisted, with a trace of hysteria. 'He was the only person who knew I was meant to be there; I'd arranged it with him myself.'

Whatever she thought, it was evident to Rafferty that someone had known. And he suspected that he knew who that someone was.

He fixed her with a grim stare. 'You were blackmailing him, you say. How did you—?'

Miranda turned up her dainty nose. 'Do you have to use that sordid word, Inspector?'

'A sordid word for a sordid deed, Miss Raglan,' Llewellyn told her reprovingly. 'Did you never think of going to the police instead of taking matters into your own hands?'

'The police?' she repeated scornfully. 'And what would they – you – have done? Arrested me, not him, most probably. I knew he had powerful friends, you see. He threatened me with them once.'

Rafferty felt the sympathy of a fellow-sufferer stirring and quickly stifled it. 'How did you meet him originally?'

'I'd heard on the grape-vine that he'd supply drugs that other doctors wouldn't, so I contacted him. He was happy to oblige. I used to see him at his London consulting rooms twice a week, after hours, when the staff had gone home.

'Gradually he began to supply me with stronger and stronger drugs. I didn't realise at first, because he was careful to make sure that to a layman's eye the tablets looked similar. It was only when my cravings began to get out of control that I began to suspect. By then I was a helpless addict. It was costing me a fortune. So you can imagine how grateful I was when he suggested I sleep with him to reduce the price.' She gave a bitter smile. 'I gather I was one of a select little band.'

Mrs. Devine had described Miranda as having "glittering" eyes—a typical description of a drug-addict's eyes. Why hadn't he made the connection before? But, of course, the fact that the doctor openly specialised in drug-related problems had put him off the scent. Didn't the old crime writers say that if you wanted to hide a letter, put it in the letter-rack with the rest of the mail?

Suddenly, he was glad he hadn't dismissed Mrs. Devine as a senile old woman whose information was useless. 'So you made an appointment to meet Dr. Melville-Briggs in his flat the night Linda Wilks was murdered?'

Miranda Raglan nodded.

'That was a risky thing to do,' Llewellyn commented. 'Didn't it occur to you that you might be in great danger?'

'Not then, only after. I was getting desperate.' She pulled a face. 'It's difficult to think straight when you're on drugs, Sergeant. You should try it sometime.'

Ignoring this piece of advice, he asked, 'How did you arrange the meeting?'

'After phoning him to let him know just what I expected, I told him to contact me with the details. He wrote me a note. Just the time and place.' She smiled, but her eyes were empty of humour. 'He knew he didn't have any choice. But, once it was arranged, I became nervous, so I arrived early, waylaid one of the nurses as she arrived for duty, and asked her to deliver a note to him. It said I'd changed my mind and I'd meet him in the pub up the road sometime before 11.30 p.m. But he never came. Obviously, that stupid nurse forgot all about the note and never gave it to him. And then I heard about that girl's murder. It was too much of a coincidence not to be connected with me. I went to ground while I thought through what to do.'

'What time did you get to the pub?'

She shrugged. 'About ten. I'd come down a few weeks before, just to look around, when the idea of making him pay first occurred to me, and I'd gone in the pub for lunch. I discovered then, that, as long as they had paying customers, they didn't bother to close.

'On the night of the murder, I waited there for an hour-and-a-half, being pestered by some appalling little man, but Tony didn't turn up. I learned why the next morning.' Her face took on an expression of distaste. 'That's when I booked into that scruffy hotel. God knows what the girl was doing wandering around the hospital at that time of night, but whatever she was doing there, I'm convinced Tony killed her, mistaking her for me in the darkness. From the pictures in the papers, we are superficially alike.'

'When did you make the appointment with Melville-Briggs?'

'The week before the girl died.'

Rafferty frowned. Couldn't she even be bothered to remember Linda Wilks's name? After all, the poor bitch had died for her.

But he wasn't here to make judgements, he reminded himself grimly. In some ways, Miranda Raglan, too, had been a victim. 'But he must have known when he arranged to see you that he'd be at a medical dinner at The George all night. Such important events are arranged weeks in advance. It seems likely he would check his diary before agreeing to meet you. It looks very much as though he made the appointment knowing he wouldn't be able to keep it.'

'Are you saying that he arranged for someone else to murder me? Some hired assassin?'

It was a possibility that Llewellyn had suggested. But somehow, with him, it struck a false note. Would Melville-Briggs be likely to place himself in jeopardy from another blackmailer? Even if a hired killer didn't blackmail him, how could he be sure that such a criminal wouldn't cop a plea in the future if arrested for another killing?

No, he was still convinced this was an inside job. But who thought enough of Sir Anthony to kill his troublesome mistress for him? His wife, who had long accepted his faithlessness and lived her own life? Simon Smythe who feared him? The Galvins, both of whom had reason to feel a bitter hatred towards him? There was no-one connected with the case that Melville-Briggs could persuade to do his dirty work. Even the obliging Gilbert, who wasn't beyond indulging in a little attempted blackmail himself if he thought he could get away with it, would shy away from murder. Besides, he had stayed in the pub till he had been chucked out at one in the morning, not that Melville-Briggs would be likely to trust his sly porter with the task, anyway.

Rafferty's phone rang. He snatched it up, said, 'Rafferty. What?' He listened for a while, growing increasingly incredulous.

His telephone conversation was interrupted when Timothy Smales popped his head around the door. 'I've got Mr Allward in Interview Room. 1, Sir. You said you wanted to speak to him. Shall I bring him up?'

Rafferty slammed the phone receiver back on its rest and shook his head. 'I haven't got time for him now. Let him stew for a bit.' Smales's head began to withdraw, and Rafferty said, 'Hang on a minute, Tim.'

Rafferty turned to Miranda Raglan, asked her to wait in reception.

She pouted a bit, but left, escorted by Tim Smales.

'As I said, Allward will have to wait. Him and Sidney Wilks both. That was Simon Smythe on the phone,' he told Llewellyn. 'Lady Evelyn must have got him temporarily reinstated. It was all a bit garbled, but it seems someone's attacked Gilbert, the lodge-porter.'

'Who?' Llewellyn asked.

Rafferty shrugged. 'God knows. Smythe hung up before I got an answer to that one.' With a worried frown, he asked, 'You don't think Gilbert saw something on the night of the murder, do you, and tried another spot of blackmail?'

'What could he have seen?' Llewellyn asked reasonably. 'He was in the pub when the murder happened. I hardly think the murderer would wait around after killing the girl.'

Neither did Rafferty.

'I imagine the answer's simple enough. Personally, I've been expecting something like this for several days.'

'Oh?' Rafferty's gaze narrowed. This was the first he'd heard of Llewellyn's suspicions. 'Being wise after the event, are we?'

Llewellyn shook his head. 'Not at all. I imagine one of the patients attacked Mr Gilbert. Murder unsettles the mind,' he explained. 'And it unsettles the troubled mind even more.'

'I bet it unsettled Gilbert's,' Rafferty remarked grimly. 'He's all right, though. At least, Smythe didn't seem too bothered about him. Of course, that's not altogether surprising, and knowing Gilbert, he's probably got all the pretty nurses giving him tea and sympathy right now.'

Rafferty picked up his emerald-green jacket and headed for the car park, Llewellyn on his heels. Llewellyn was probably right. Again. One of the patient's had probably taken a dislike to Gilbert's face. Understandable really.

The hospital was in uproar when they arrived. They'd barely got through the gates before the car was surrounded by a throng of shouting, gesticulating staff, Simon Smythe at its centre.

Smythe was trying to establish order, without any noticeable success. He emerged from the scrum surrounding him and a look of relief appeared on his face when he reached Rafferty. 'Thank God you've come, Inspector. It's one of the patients, Brian. He—'

'Where is he?'

'In the lodge. He's locked himself in and refuses to come out.'

'I take it you've got a hefty injection of sedative handy?'

Smythe nodded.

That was something. 'Come along then, Doctor.' Rafferty headed purposefully for the lodge, feeling like the Pied Piper of

Hamelin as Llewellyn, Smythe, and most of the still-depleted hospital staff, fell in behind.

At least Constable Hanks, left on duty at the gate, had shown some presence of mind. Armed with a dustbin lid, he'd stationed himself outside the lodge, while, from inside, came the sound of crashes and bangs. It seemed the patient was intent on demolishing everything within reach.

'Has he tried to come out?' he asked Hanks.

'Not so far, Sir. More interested in wrecking the place.'

'Damn near wrecked me 'ead,' complained Gilbert.

Up till now, Gilbert had kept quiet and Rafferty hadn't noticed him in the crowd. But as the shock began to wear off he became increasingly voluble. 'Gave me the fright of me life when I saw that religious nut, Brian, with that great lump of wood in 'is 'ands. Murder 'e 'ad in 'is eyes. Murder!'

'I was just about to try to establish what steps Gilbert took, Inspector,' Smythe interjected, in an obvious attempt to justify his less than professional panic.

'I'll tell you what steps I took,' exclaimed Gilbert vociferously. 'Bloody great big ones, of course. What do you expect me to have done?' he demanded. 'Reasoned wiv him? Ain't my job to reason wiv em, mate. I just let the buggers in and out. Reasoning's your job.'

Gilbert shot a worried look at Rafferty. 'You reckon 'e's the one as done fer the girl?' He went quite pale and ran his hand over his face as though to make sure he still had all the bits that belonged there.

For a moment, Gilbert's suspicions revived Rafferty's own earlier one that the misogynistic religious nut, Brian had somehow escaped the vigilance of Staff Nurse Estoce and committed the murder after all. Then common sense reasserted itself. He'd already checked and discarded that possibility. Besides, since when had such an easy and obvious solution fallen into his lap?

'No.' Gilbert answered his own question. 'It must 'ave been old smarmy-pants. Why else would 'e top 'imself?'

'Is that what everyone's saying?' Rafferty asked curiously. 'That he committed suicide?'

'Stands to reason, dunnit? He certainly looked as sick as a parrot when I last saw 'im, just before 'e made a concertina out of 'imself in the Carlton. Looked, I dunno—glazed, I s'pose. Almost as though 'e was drugged or something.'

Sir Anthony had prescribed himself some tranquillisers; the officer called to the scene had found them in his pocket when he'd looked for some identification. But the label said they were mild, only 2 mm, certainly not enough to bring a glazed look to his eyes, not unless he'd taken a handful of them.

Yet, according to Sam Dally, who'd performed the post mortem, he must have done. Perhaps, afraid that his many sins were soon to be revealed to a censorious world, he'd dosed himself up to deaden the pain of the impact when his car wrapped itself around the tree. 'Didn't you try to stop him?' he asked Gilbert.

'Me? And remind 'im that 'e 'adn't sacked me yet? Not bloody likely!'

'So he just got in his car and drove away?'

Gilbert nodded. 'Pretty fast too, considering the patients were milling about the place.'

'Powerful car, a Carlton,' commented Llewellyn, the car buff.

'Still, it was rather out of character,' commented Rafferty. 'I understand he was usually very careful of his patients.'

'Not one to risk endangering 'is investments,' agreed Gilbert. 'Not Sir Anthony.'

By now, the sound of destruction from inside the lodge had slowly petered out.

'Sounds like Brian's exhausted himself,' said Rafferty. 'Right, Gilbert. I'm sure you've got another key for that door. Let me have it please.'

Gilbert released a key-ring from his belt. He selected one and handed it over to Rafferty, with the comment, 'Mind you let me 'ave it back, now. I'm responsible fer it.'

Given his less than zealous guardianship of the other keys under his protection, Rafferty was sorely tempted to make a sharp retort. Instead, he wordlessly took the proffered key, crept up to the broken window of the gate lodge, and peered in.

Brian was taking a well-earned rest and was calmly sipping a piping hot brew from Gilbert's personal mug, which had somehow escaped the ravages suffered by the rest of the equipment. To Rafferty's relief, the patient's destructive storm seemed to have blown itself out.

He unlocked the door and stepped inside the lodge. Brian continued to calmly sip his tea, and Rafferty remarked quietly, 'I like the mug.'

Brian raised his eyes suspiciously. 'It's mine.'

'Oh? I wouldn't have thought the wording on it would appeal to you.'

'Why? Work is a four-letter word. The Lord's work. Why was that blasphemer Gilbert using it?'

As Rafferty shrugged noncommittally, Brian finished his tea and, with the help of a couple of the nurses, Smythe managed to sedate him. He went off between them as quietly as a lamb, still clutching Gilbert's mug, much to the porter's loudly-voiced indignation, and Rafferty and Llewellyn were left alone to survey the ruins of Gilbert's little castle.

Brian, with the surprising strength of the deranged, had made a thorough job of wrecking the place. The table was overturned, lists and rosters were torn to shreds, even the key-cabinet had been wrenched off the wall, the keys scattered all over the floor, some of them large and rather cumbersome.

They reminded Rafferty of something, and as he struggled to remember, suddenly, into his head popped a conversation he'd had some time ago, and all at once he knew who the killer was; a double murderer, for he was now convinced that Sir Anthony's death hadn't been suicide. He knew who and how— he even knew why. The means, motive and opportunity were all there. All that remained was to carry out the arrest.

Chapter Nineteen

The nursery school was quiet; it was 6.00 p.m. and the toddlers had long since gone home. Rafferty had had a word with the elderly caretaker who lived in the flat above, and he had gone off, quietly grumbling to himself. They waited in the ground-floor play-room. Large and airy, it was decorated with a jolly Disney cartoon mural, its colourful characters seemed mocking, and for once, Rafferty managed to look even more long-faced than his sergeant.

In the silence, they heard footsteps approaching down the linoleum-covered hall, but instead of the door to the nursery opening, the suddenly increased roar of the traffic told them that the front door had been opened. Seconds' later the roar slackened off again as the door shut with a soft click.

Rafferty and Llewellyn exchanged a questioning look that turned to alarm as the unmistakable whish-wishaw of air-brakes hurriedly applied was followed by a deathly silence. They rushed to the street door.

The body lay mangled under the front wheel of a huge Juggernaut. The driver was in his fifties. White-faced and shaking uncontrollably, he clutched the small silver crucifix around his neck as he told them in a dazed voice, 'Did it deliberately. Looked straight at me and made the Sign of the

Cross before stepping off the pavement.' He brought his sleeve across his suddenly wet eyes. 'I couldn't do anything.' Shock was clearly taking a hold for he kept repeating, over and over, like a stuck record, 'I couldn't do anything.'

Rafferty checked the pulse, but he guessed before he tried that he would find none. He told Llewellyn to ring for an ambulance, left the distraught driver to the tender mercies of the caretaker, and walked over to the car. He took out the car rug from the back seat. Normally used to protect the covers from the destructive tendencies of his myriad nephews and nieces, he now had a more urgent use for it.

'Noblesse oblige', he murmured softly as he laid the red tartan over Lady Evelyn. Its bright colours made the pooled blood seem less gory. In an odd contrast to Linda Wilks's death, although Lady Evelyn's body was a mess, her face hadn't been touched. It looked as composed in death as it had in life. He thought she'd have been glad about that.

Unlike her late husband, Lady Evelyn accepted that all privilege had its penalties. She had tried to protect her family— the honour of its glorious past and her hopes for its future. But she had failed and had realised that her continued existence would be a liability to her line. Predictably, she had done the honourable thing.

Llewellyn returned. 'The ambulance is on its way.'

Rafferty nodded and settled the rug more cosily around the body, tucking it in so no draught could touch her.

'Messy method to choose,' Llewellyn remarked mournfully.

Rafferty didn't look up from his study of the tartan-shrouded figure on the ground. 'For her it was the cleanest way, the best way. She must have guessed why we had come and didn't want a verdict of double murder and suicide – might blot the family escutcheon – whatever that is.'

'It's a shield for a coat of arms,' Llewellyn told him, dispensing information a little more solemnly than usual.

Rafferty nodded. 'It'll be labelled accidental death, of course, she knew that.'

'Here on earth, perhaps,' stated Llewellyn sombrely. 'But she was a Catholic. Whatever label is applied won't alter the fact that her God would know the truth of it.' With a shake of his head, he turned away. 'Did you ever hear of Bloody Mary, Inspector?'

Bemused, Rafferty stared at his sergeant. 'The drink?'

'No. The Queen.'

Rafferty's face cleared. 'Henry VIII's elder daughter, you mean?' He had heard of the lady. Llewellyn wasn't the only one with an interest in the past, he reflected grimly, as he guessed what his sergeant was about to say.

Llewellyn nodded. 'If you remember your history, duty ruled her life, much as it must have ruled Lady Evelyn's. She was a Catholic, too, and she felt it was her duty to rid the country of heretics. Hundreds died in the Smithfield fires. Their deaths were no less repugnant because they died from one woman's dutiful desire to glorify God. He wouldn't have condoned their deaths any more than he would condone the ones for which Lady Evelyn was guilty. Murder is murder, however high-principled the murderer.'

Llewellyn was right, as usual. Lady Evelyn had murdered two people, but Rafferty still felt more pity than righteous anger. Even if he couldn't condone her actions any more than God would, he felt he could understand why she had done it.

Poor, sad, disillusioned lady, the burden of her duty was, to her, equally heavy and equally strong—the upholding of the family honour. After all, God had looked after the Melvilles for five hundred years and countless deaths, insurrections and wars. But, even with God's help, no-one held onto their property during the dangerous years after Henry VII's death and the religious turmoil that was to come without getting plenty of blood on their hands. In comparison two murders must seem a trifling matter.

'Didn't you tell me that the Latin of her family motto translated as *"Honour above all"*?' he asked his sergeant.

Llewellyn gave a slow nod.

'She must have thought God would understand and approve,' said Rafferty softly. 'She sacrificed herself for the dynasty. The next link in the chain was her son, but from what Gilbert said, he was a weak link. Unless he married a strong woman, who shared Lady Evelyn's ideals, all that she had worked for risked being broken up.

'I imagine she pushed him into the engagement with the Huntingdon girl. She held the family purse-strings, of course, she probably used that to persuade him to agree.' Rafferty still gazed at Lady Evelyn's shrouded form. 'You'll see, first he'll postpone the wedding – out of filial respect naturally – but somehow I doubt if another date will ever be fixed. Next, he'll put the Hall on the market. Now he's got the money he can start indulging his own dreams instead of his mother's. I imagine he'll find that mechanic of his, Harry, far less demanding than all that rich blue Huntingdon blood.'

As Llewellyn nodded agreement, Rafferty realised how dreadfully lonely Lady Evelyn must have been. Perhaps it might have been different if her husband had loved her, for who would give all their love to a building – however magnificent – if they had a human being worthy of their cherishing?

In the end, her obsession had taken over her life, wrecking it, as well as the lives of several others. Such was the nature of obsessions, of course. Ultimately, they were always destructive. That was why they were so dangerous.

Rafferty knew the servants all slept in a separate annexe over the old stables of the Hall, and now he pictured Lady Evelyn in her echoing and empty home, carefully drawing up a tapestry of murder, stitch by stitch, until she had made her own shroud.

With a sigh, he stood up. Now he could hear the sirens in the distance. A few minutes' later, the ambulance drew up and the attendants gathered up Lady Evelyn's body. Rafferty found his shoulders straightening and his hands making the sign of the cross automatically, as he had been taught to do as a boy in the presence of death.

With a start, he realised that, with the case over, he no longer had a valid excuse for avoiding his mother and Maureen, the 'good catch'

His shoulders slumped. Feeling as he did, that was the last thing he needed right now. Families, he shook his head sorrowfully; they really could be bloody murder.

What he needed was to cleanse his mind and refresh his spirit in the best way he knew. Tomorrow, he promised himself, he would visit a building site, the new one at Colchester. The gaffer of the masons laid his bricks with a deft rhythm that soothed the soul and Rafferty felt sorely in need of such balm.

Epilogue

It was two days later. Llewellyn had been off work since Lady Evelyn's death, so the day of Jack and Maureen's wedding was the first chance Rafferty had had to show off how clever he'd been. He meant to make the most of it.

He volunteered Llewellyn to drive him to the reception, and it wasn't long before his sergeant asked him how he'd found out the truth. He didn't need a second invitation, and launched straight in.

'It was something that Ma said that made me realise the truth,' Rafferty told him airily, as he gestured to his sergeant to move into the passenger seat and got behind the wheel.

'Jailhouse' Jack and Deirdre's wedding was over, thank God, and he only had the reception to get through. He'd arranged for Llewellyn to pick him up around the corner from the church. Luckily, he'd been able to sneak away before the photographer was able to record the relationship for posterity, discarding his button-hole on the way.

'She mentioned a mother's pride in her first-born son. How much greater, do you think, would that pride be for an only son?'

Had he suspected all along and not let the suspicion rise above his subconscious? He hadn't wanted to believe Lady

Evelyn was the murderer; neither had Llewellyn. It was only the second time he had felt himself in sympathy with his Welsh sergeant since he had met him.

That embryonic empathy was the only good thing to come out of the case. Neither of them had thought Lady Evelyn capable of what looked like a particularly vicious crime. But of course, she hadn't killed the girl that way from choice. It had been essential. It must have sickened her as much as it had them.

'But the son wasn't even threatened. It was Sir Anthony who was being blackmailed and faced with exposure.'

Feeling smug, Rafferty told his conscience to 'shut it', turned on the ignition and nosed the car bonnet out into the traffic. 'You forget—the son was getting married. Sir Anthony chose the wrong time to confide his little difficulty to his wife. But Timothy's long-planned wedding was still four months off. Lady Evelyn must have known that anything could happen in that time.

'When Melville-Briggs revealed that Miranda Raglan was threatening him with exposure, she knew she needed to act, and fast. She wouldn't jeopardise her son's forthcoming marriage for anybody, least of all for a faithless husband. She had engineered it thus far, ignoring her son's inadequacies as a bridegroom. If she failed to bring this marriage off, she knew she might never manage to get him up the aisle. She wasn't a fool; she had eyes to see and ears to hear the rumours about her son. But she knew, too, that a homosexual is as capable of fathering a son as any other man—a son to continue the Melville line. That was of greater importance to her than even her son's happiness.'

He was, after all, only one link in the chain that went back centuries, he reflected. It would have been unthinkable to a woman like Lady Evelyn to let her son be the one who broke the chain and brought the dynasty to an end. He put his foot down, biting back the wry grin when he sensed Llewellyn wincing beside him. 'Take it easy, Taff. I'm barely doing sixty.'

'But it's a fifty mile per hour limit,' Llewellyn pointed out, a hint of reproof in his voice.

Rafferty eased his foot back from the accelerator. It wasn't as though he was in any great rush to reach his destination. 'She had been largely able to ignore her husband's womanising; her son's future in-laws wouldn't have blinked an eye at that, but what they would have blinked both eyes at was a real scandal. And Miranda threatened to blow the lid off a scandal that would bring nothing but shame. She had to be stopped.'

On the surface, his wealthy lady patients returned to him time and again out of loyalty, but in reality, they had no choice. He had got them hooked on very powerful drugs; no wonder they were so faithful, thought Rafferty. They were totally dependent on him, and them.

They'd have to wait for the PM on Sir Anthony to be sure, but Rafferty suspected that Lady Evelyn had dosed his tea with some of the tranquillisers in her husband's pill bottle. Melville-Briggs had badly misjudged three of the women in his life and had paid the ultimate price.

'By confiding his little difficulty he ensured he was a dead man. But first, she had to remove the worst threat to her son's marriage—Miranda Raglan.'

'But—' Llewellyn broke in.

'Wait. Gilbert wasn't the only one practised in forgery. According to him, Lady Evelyn acted as her husband's secretary when he first set up in practice. She wrote Miranda that note arranging to meet her at the hospital, not Sir Anthony. As she had never set eyes on Miranda, she killed the wrong girl.'

'But Lady Evelyn was at *The George* all night,' Llewellyn broke in, to Rafferty's irritation. 'How could she—?'

'She wasn't centre stage all night, in the way that her husband was. Funnily enough, Sam Dally remarked that that evening she had seemed subdued and content to stay in the background, and Sam just put it down to Sir Anthony's bad mood at their being late. I imagine she engineered the flat battery, so they'd be late and wouldn't have to park in the hotel car park under the door-man's eye. She could slip out of one of the side entrances and get the car without anyone noticing she'd gone.'

'But why on earth did she choose that particular night? Wouldn't it have been better to wait for an occasion when she wasn't so restricted by time and circumstances?'

'Because she had to be sure that her husband wouldn't be likely to disturb her. I doubt if he bothered to give her advance warning of his movements. Of course the limited time meant she had no opportunity to change her clothes. But she had the solution to that.

'You know, at the beginning of the case, I dug back into her family history – oh, not because I suspected her then,' Rafferty admitted when he sensed Llewellyn's scepticism ' – but because I was interested. Her family have always been staunch Catholics—quite a few members in the past joined religious orders. It seemed likely that the attics at the Hall would be stuffed with costumes of all kinds. A hooded monk's habit, for instance, would be ideal to protect her own clothes.'

'So the drunk wasn't merely hallucinating?'

Rafferty shook his head, pulled away from the lights and drew up to the next road junction, glad of an excuse to avert his face. Luckily, Llewellyn didn't know that Jack was the drunken witness to Lady Evelyn's arrival for her rendezvous with murder. Not that Llewellyn was likely to blab, in fact, Rafferty realised, he'd never met a more close-mouthed copper.

It was another thing in his favour. For the first time, he wondered whether the dapper little Welshman might not suit him very well after all. The bridal pair was toying with the idea of staying in England, and if they did, Llewellyn's discretion might just turn out to be an asset.

The weapon used for the murder had puzzled him for a long time; then the scattered keys in the porter's lodge had jogged his memory, reminding him of the weapons of war displayed in the great hall at Elmhurst. The mace had been amongst them, and he'd read in the guide book he'd borrowed from the public library, that it had been used at the Battle of Bosworth by Lady Evelyn's illustrious ancestor, Edward Melville. Rafferty suspected the symbolism of using so archaic a weapon to kill one of her family's enemies would mean much to her. Rafferty was sure that when they got the results from the lab they'd find that the blood-stains on the mace were not just those from ancient foes, but from a modern victim as well—Linda Wilks.

It had been a tragic coincidence that she had been where Lady Evelyn had expected to find Miranda Raglan; one of those bizarre twists of fate that had so often dogged Rafferty's own footsteps. He wondered if, in her death throes, she had recognised that she was about to be a star at last? The star victim in a murder hunt.

'Your speed's creeping up again, Sir.'

Rafferty glanced at the speedometer and eased back once more. 'I'm surprised you didn't choose to go into the traffic division,' he remarked caustically. 'Think of all those speed junkies you could collar.'

Llewellyn made an odd noise in his throat. To his astonishment, Rafferty realised that his sergeant was actually laughing. 'What's so funny,' he demanded.

'It's just that I did apply for traffic, but they turned me down.' His voice sounded deceptively innocent as he went on, 'Perhaps the superintendent thought that with the police image being so important, the division would be better served if I stayed in CID and acted as your personal speed trap, Sir.'

'Very droll.' Things were looking up, he reflected, his sergeant had actually cracked a funny. Rafferty shot him a curious glance, but although Llewellyn's face had fallen back into its normal Sphinx-like immobility, he was beginning to realise that there was a lot more to the Welshman than met the eye.

'Anyway, when I wondered if she could have done it, I worked backwards, and it all fitted. Several people have commented on her efficiency and great organisational skills. Was it likely she would forget to get her chauffeur to change his weekend off? Especially for an occasion that had been planned so long in advance.

'I finally realised it was essential to her plans that the chauffeur wasn't available; she needed to get away from *The George*, and also needed the use of a car that wasn't conspicuous—one that she could drive, and the Bentley was a manual. She could only drive automatics. It all fitted.'

Rafferty pulled into the car park of *The George* but made no attempt to open the door and get out. Instead, he looked down at his no longer quite so smart brown suit and sighed, aware that his sergeant managed to outshine him in the well-groomed stakes. Removing the girl's clothes; it was a precaution, nothing more. Miranda wouldn't wear cheap, mass-produced chain-store clothes; but would dress expensively, in clothes that would be much more easily traced. In the dark and with the need for speed, she wouldn't have stopped to examine whether the girl was wearing designer labels or not.

'She probably stuffed the mace and the clothes in a plastic rubbish bag and left them in the car overnight, but because she was rushing, she didn't have time to be as careful as she should have been. Forensic found smears of blood in the boot. The clothes she presumably burned them one of those great hearths at the Hall.

'She couldn't be traced back to Sir Anthony. That's why she removed Linda's face and smashed her teeth. She knew that the post-mortem would reveal the existence of powerful prescription drugs. She never gave a thought to fingerprints.

Of course, her intended victim didn't have a criminal record; Miranda's sort seldom do. But she'd have been careful to check up on that, and with her husband's contacts in the police force it wouldn't have been difficult. I wonder how she felt when she discovered she'd killed the wrong girl.'

'It's strange how Sir Anthony appeared so confident through all of this,' Llewellyn remarked. 'It's almost as though he knew nothing about the murder.'

'I don't believe he did,' said Rafferty. 'Think about it. Do you seriously imagine Lady Evelyn would confide her intentions to a man who had proved himself so unreliable, so untrustworthy? She probably told him she'd bought Miranda off and that he'd seen the last of her.

'You know, you were right when you said he was the type to get somebody else to do his dirty work for him. He must have felt 'Job done' when he passed his problem over to his efficient wife. Her desperation to find Miranda must have escalated when she realised she'd killed the wrong girl. For once, Miranda Raglan used her brain. She'd booked into that seedy hotel where she was unlikely to bump into anyone who knew her, and Lady Evelyn couldn't find her. I reckon that's when she brought forward the murder of her husband.'

Used, as he was, to the adoration of women; he wouldn't expect his previously accommodating wife to want him dead. Was it possible she'd felt some concern for other possible victims of her actions? She couldn't be sure that Sir Anthony would be the only victim; it might have been another car, rather than a tree that he smashed into. But Rafferty had to accept it was unlikely. She was in the grip of an obsession. Nothing was allowed to deflect her from her course, not even the lives of others.

'She probably hoped that with Melville-Briggs dead the blackmailer would back off, and everything would be as it was before. But we all know what hope did.'

Now he resolutely put the unhappy Lady Evelyn from his mind. He leaned over and picked up the package from the back seat, before getting out of the car and slamming the door. He shoved the parcel under his arm and gestured at the imposing white-stone facade of *The George*. 'We've got a bit of a family do on.'

He hadn't mentioned it to Llewellyn before, but somehow, secrecy didn't seem quite so important now. However, he kept his suspicions about how Jailhouse Jack could afford the hotel for the reception to himself.

'You've got a lot of relatives, haven't you, Sir?' Llewellyn commented.

'Too bloody many.' And all of them banes to his police career. Especially Jailhouse Jack.

'I often wondered what it would be like being one of a large family,' Llewellyn remarked wistfully. 'I was an only child.'

Rafferty glanced at him in surprise. 'Speaking as one of six, that's a subject on which I am an expert. It's heaven and hell, love and hate, but mostly it's messy, noisy and totally lacking in any privacy. You wouldn't have liked it,' he told Llewellyn decisively. 'You wouldn't have liked it at all.'

Llewellyn sighed. 'I suppose you're right.'

To Rafferty's surprise, Llewellyn's voice still sounded wistful. Was it possible that Llewellyn was just another lonely human being who secretly longed for some disorder in his neat and regimented existence, in spite of his denials?

Rafferty had fully intended getting rid of his sergeant once they had reached *The George*, reckoning on taking a taxi back. But now some instinct made him pause.

He'd already discovered a little of Llewellyn's family background and pretty bleak it sounded. How could he, with his rumbustious, but loving family, imagine what Llewellyn's only child life of nannies and boarding schools and university had been like? What did he know of anybody's life when all was said and done? Look how wrong he'd been about Lady Evelyn.

As a Methodist minister's son, had he been forced, like a lot of church kids, in order to spend half his school holidays at the services? Had he never gone fishing for newts in the nearest pond, bringing them home triumphantly in a jam-jar? Had he never kept green caterpillars in a match-box, waiting for them to change magically into butterflies? Had his youth been the joyless one Rafferty imagined it to be? Spent joining in doleful hymns shut inside a damp church while the world and the birds outside were singing sweeter songs?.

Rafferty wasn't really surprised, when he heard his voice saying, 'I don't know about you, Taff, but I, for one, am ready for a drink. I did say you were invited, didn't I?'

Llewellyn frowned. 'No Sir.'

But much to his surprise, Llewellyn accepted the belated invitation with something approaching alacrity. And as they strode together towards the brightly-lit hotel, Rafferty wondered if his second good deed in a week might not receive a suitable reward. For if Llewellyn really was lonely and looking for a mate, that was one area where he could help. He opened the door to reception with a flourish. 'After you, Taff.'

He'd always liked a wedding—as long as it wasn't his own And the discovery of his sergeant's unsuspected secret fancy for family life put new heart into him. His mother tended to collect lame dogs, and to Rafferty's mind, they didn't come any lamer than Llewellyn.

Fresh from his first triumph as Senior Investigating Officer with the 'Faceless Lady' case, and savouring Bradley's obvious disgruntlement at his success, Rafferty decided the solution to another of his other problems looked promising. God was being unusually accommodating at the moment. It wouldn't last, of course, but it would be a waste if he didn't take advantage of it. Maybe Ma would even agree that his sergeant's need for a wife was far more urgent than his own and likely to demand her single-minded attention. He certainly hoped so.

Rafferty gave Llewellyn one of his brightest smiles. Maureen would be here. Hadn't his Uncle Pat told him that she had always had a soft spot for the serious intellectual type? Like Llewellyn, for instance.

/

FREE BOOK OFFER

Would you like to download the first four novels in the
Rafferty & Llewellyn Mystery Series FOR FREE?

If you go to my website https://geraldineevansbooks.com
and click on my Newsletter Sign-Up Link, you will be able to
get THE FIRST BOXSET for FREE!

My Newsletter is sent out irregularly, and contains information
about new releases, giveaways, bargain buys, and other offers. I
will not spam you, pass your details on, or otherwise irritate
you. You can unsubscribe at any time.

AUTHOR BIO/CONTACT DETAILS

WEBSITE/BLOG: https://geraldineevansbooks.com

Geraldine Evans is the multi-published author of the popular Rafferty & Llewellyn and Casey & Catt British Mystery Series, as well as various other works. Her previous publishers include Macmillan, St Martin's Press, Worldwide, Hale and Severn House.

Dead Before Morning, her first mystery novel, and the first book in her now 18-strong Rafferty & Llewellyn series, was taken from Macmillan's slush pile in 1993, and published, both in the UK and the US. It was the beginning of a long career as a mystery author.

She is now an Indie, after taking the decision to go independent in 2010.

Geraldine Evans is a Londoner but moved to Norfolk in the UK in 2000.

NEXT BOOK IN SERIES

Down Among the Dead Men #2

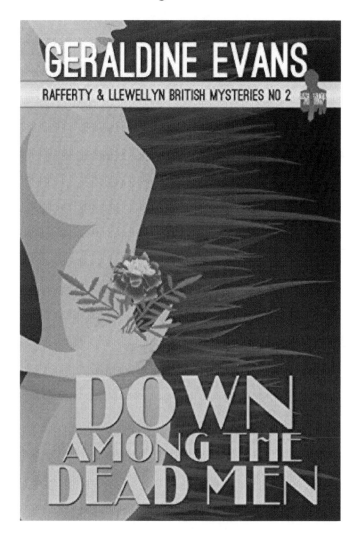

'I have fallen in love with her slow-paced but interesting books.'

Detective Joe Rafferty thinks at first that murder victim Barbara Longman has been the latest victim of the serial killer over the county border. But then he meets her family and has reason to change his mind. Everyone, it seems, had a motive: Henry the grieving widower; the victim's brother-in-law Charles Shore, the ruthless tycoon; Henry's first wife, the Bohemian Anne, who has lost the custody of her teenage son, to the saintly Barbara.

Even the long-dead patriarch, Maximillian Shore, seems, to Rafferty, to have some involvement in the murder, though how, or why, Rafferty doesn't understand until he finally grasps the truth behind the reasons for the killing. A truth sad and dreadful and which had been evident from the start, if only he had had the eyes to see.

Read the first chapter:

Down Among the Dead Men

Chapter One

*This novel uses British English spellings and slang, so please remember
that there are differences in language use. I've supplied a brief explanation
of British slang and spelling at the end of this novel.*

As though lulled by the heavy September air and the fluting
whisper of the River Tiffey half a field away, the woman lay
sprawled on the parched earth, her limbs in the abandoned
posture of a sleeping child. The sun, emerging from behind a
solitary cloud, turned her cap of flaxen hair into spangled silk
against the dry dross of the meadow. It bestowed such an
appearance of sparkling, vibrant life that Inspector Rafferty
took several steps back, his usual good sense overtaken by an
illogical fear that she would awaken and discover him looming
over her.

Feeling foolish as he sensed Llewellyn's startled glance, he
ignored his sergeant and continued to study the figure, though
more circumspectly.

Dressed in some leaf-green gauzy stuff that bunched
around her slender thighs, she had the other-worldly
appearance of a woodland nymph; in her hand a single bloom,
its crushed petals faded to an indistinguishable straw colour. A

fairy-like bower of wild meadow flowers scattered around her body completed the illusion that they had somehow stumbled into a secret, fairy-tale world where princesses slumbered, and frogs turned into princes.

Just then a faint breeze sprang up and wafted a malodorous whiff of the River Tiffey towards them. The tainted breeze brought reality back with a rush, effectively killing any lingering heat-induced fancies. The miracle was that they had sprung into being at all. For, even at 9 o'clock on a bright September morning, the Essex meadow had a desolate air. Twenty yards from the body and tumbled around a stained and long-abandoned royal blue mattress, lay a pile of worn out tyres. This was the real world, not never-never land.

Regretfully, Rafferty accepted that the woman was just another poor victim in an increasingly violent society, as mortal as the rest of humanity and as dead as it was possible to be. The tell-tale reddish-purple discoloration on the back of her limbs would have told him that sooner, if he'd bothered to look, and judging by the extent of the after death hypostasis, she'd been dead some hours. Feeling foolish again, but thankful he hadn't blurted out his nonsense to Llewellyn, Rafferty wondered how he could have forgotten that the only sleep the Sniffy Tiffey would encourage would be the permanent sort.

The smelly breeze dropped, and with the return of the dead heat, the day seemed even more stifling, almost as if some heavenly vacuum cleaner had sucked all the oxygen out of the atmosphere, starving his brain and leaving his thought processes sluggish.

But however sluggish his brain, there was no escaping the inevitable conclusions. She'd been murdered all right, smothered, he suspected, just like the other two victims over the border in Suffolk, where it was beginning to look as if a serial killer was on the loose. This latest death indicated that the serial killer might have enlarged his area of operations. The thought was a chilling one, and Rafferty made a mental note to contact the Suffolk CID as soon as they got back to the office, in order to check out the murderer's MO for any similarities to this latest killing. With a nod of his head, he drew Llewellyn away from the body for a brief consultation, leaving more room for the photographer to do his work.

After unzipping his protective overalls a few inches, Rafferty sighed with relief as he loosened his grass green tie and eased the creased shirt collar away from his clammy skin. His mouth turned down as he glanced at Llewellyn, who unlike himself, looked cool and untroubled by the heat.

Rafferty wondered how the man managed to look so spruce, so sweat-free. Swallowing his irritation, he muttered, with a dispirited attempt at his usual whimsical speculation,

'What do you reckon we have here, Dafyd? The work of the Suffolk cyclepath, as my old Ma calls him?'

Not given to either whimsy or speculation, the Welshman stated matter-of-factly, 'I've no idea, sir.' Apparently, his usual efficiency was as unaffected by the heat as the rest of him, for he continued briskly, 'I'll check out Missing Persons. See what the computer can tell us.'

Rafferty watched sourly as his bandbox fresh sergeant turned and made for the car. He was twenty yards away before Rafferty thought to stop him. 'Don't bother,' he called. 'I reckon I know who this one is.' He should, he acknowledged belatedly, as her disappearance had only been reported to him yesterday, personally—by Charles Shore, her sort of brother-in-law, and the description he had furnished fitted this woman perfectly, even down to the colour of the dress.

Liven up, Rafferty, he ordered. As he forced his mind into something approaching a policeman-like alertness, he realised that the registration number of the red hatchback behind which they'd parked in the narrow, tarmac lane, matched hers too, and he despatched two of the SOCO team to check it over.

Zipping his coveralls back up, he returned to the scene. A small shoulder bag, already dusted for prints by the scene of crime team, lay close to the body, and after checking that it was okay to touch it, he opened it. Its contents confirmed his

suspicions. 'Mrs Barbara Longman, wife of Henry Longman—
or second wife, I should say, as I gather he's divorced from the
first one. Wife number one is another member of the Shore
family. I suppose you've heard of them?'

'One of the most prominent families in the county.'

Rafferty nodded gloomily. He had a vague recollection of
an earlier tragedy involving the Shores, but as his mind refused
to be cudgelled into throwing it up, he left it to come to him of
its own accord. Just my luck, he groaned silently, as Llewellyn's
comment echoed in his brain. Why was it he seemed to get
lumbered with murders that involved important families? His
last case had been the same. For some reason, Superintendent
Bradley seemed to think this qualified Rafferty for mixing in
exalted circles. Rafferty wished he could agree with him.

Grim humour forced his lips into a semblance of a smile as
another, more likely explanation occurred to him. Shore must
have spoken to Bradley after he had reported Mrs Longman
missing and, with the early reports of the victim's appearance,
Bradley had put two and two together a bit quicker than
Rafferty had managed. With typical Yorkshire caution, old
Bradley had considered all the options. Just in case the
murderer turned out to be more intimately connected with the
Shore family than was so far indicated, he had decided Rafferty
should take the case, presumably in the belief that the Shores
would be less guarded with him than with a more sophisticated

copper. The British Columbo, thought Rafferty, with a wry grimace, that's me. He turned to Llewellyn. 'Who found her?'

Llewellyn nodded in the direction of the two teenage boys waiting at the edge of the meadow, well beyond the police cordons. Dark haired, and attractively tousled by the heat, WPC Green was with them, struggling to keep a comforting arm around each boy's shoulder, as they towered half a head above her.

'They were exercising their dogs,' Llewellyn explained, 'and one of the animals found her.'

Rafferty nodded. 'I'll just have a quick word with them.' However, the two youngsters could tell him little more than what Llewellyn had already learned and, after making sure they had a note of their names and addresses, he told WPC Green to drive them home.

He stood for a moment in mute admiration of the scene of crime team. Like a well-oiled machine, in anticipation of the many comings and goings, they had already checked and cleared a narrow path to the body, so as to ensure that the rest of the murder scene remained untouched till they could examine it. And when they did, the search would be thorough and painstaking. If the murderer had left any clues to his identity behind him, the team would find them.

Wishing he exuded a similar air of smooth competence, Rafferty's mood brightened as he watched the rounded figure of Dr Sam Dally approach the cordon. He stopped, in order to give his name to the young, clip-board clutching constable, and, after a struggle in which he finally persuaded his body into his protective gear, Dally followed the path indicated by the officer.

Like the two detectives, he'd had to leave his car a field away and walk; sweating and cursing with equal profusion, he looked ready to perform a premature post-mortem on anyone who provoked him. He bestowed a scowl on Rafferty, his unpredictable early morning temper evidently not improved by the knowledge that the usually tardy inspector had managed to beat him to the scene.

'I'm too old for all this gambolling about the countryside,' he complained, when he'd finally forced his way through nature's wonders. 'What happened to you, Rafferty?' he demanded in an irascible tone. 'Did your bed collapse? Or has Sergeant Llewellyn succeeded in recruiting you to his early morning jogging routine?'

'Neither.' Rafferty's teasing, lopsided grin earned him another scowl. 'It's not me that's early, Dilly Dally. It's you that's late. You said yourself you're getting too long in the tooth for this game.'

Sam grunted. 'And for that you can blame my dentist.' He bared gleaming dentures. 'New set—could have bought a house when my parents were young for what that bloodsucker charged me. Bloody uncomfortable they are, too. Gums are red raw.' He stopped blinding them with his magnificent new molars and put his bag down. 'Right. What have we got?'

'Been smothered like the women in Suffolk, I reckon,' Rafferty confided incautiously. 'Though it's funny—'

'Oh, Dr Rafferty now, is it?' jeered Sam. 'Sure you need me?' He elbowed Rafferty aside and, after studying the woman's body, he opened his bag and got to work.

'Reported missing last night,' Rafferty addressed Sam's bald spot. 'About nine. She'd hardly been gone any time at all, and I was going to advise them to wait and see if she turned up, but the chap who spoke to me was very insistent. I must admit, I thought it a bit odd that a grown woman should be reported missing quite so quickly.' He frowned. 'Makes you wonder if he knew something I didn't. When do you reckon she died?'

Sam muttered cryptically, 'You mean you don't know?' before adding, 'give me a chance, Rafferty. As you pointed out, I've only just got here, and a magician I'm not. Now, if you wouldn't mind getting out of my light...'

Feeling, like a spare groom at a wedding, sadly superfluous to the requirements of both Dally the virgin-clothed bride and the forensic congregation, Rafferty took the hint and left him to it. With, for the moment, nothing else to occupy him but the twin irritations of dive-bombing gnats and sweaty flesh, he sought oblivion from his torment by letting his mind wander where it would. Fortunately, it didn't need to wander far.

As his gaze rose above the bustling murder scene, Rafferty's expression visibly softened, and he almost managed to forget the gnats, the heat and this latest murder investigation, as his gaze settled on the horizon and the roof-line of Elmhurst, a mile and a half to the northwest.

He sighed happily, as he remembered the envy he'd instilled in London friends, who had escaped the rat race for a blissful June fortnight. Proudly, he'd pointed out Elmhurst's Roman remains, the small bricks they had favoured pillaged for later additions, and clearly evident in every building with any claim to historical significance.

From here, as well as the prominent ruins of the priory, in the oldest part of the town, he could see the spire – unusual in East Anglia – of St Boniface Catholic church soaring above its pygmy neighbours. Briefly, he wondered if his ma was attending morning mass.

Rafferty loved the place; the rich red blood of history seeped over its driest bones; timber-frame, flint and weatherboard jostled for space, and within a short drive he could choose between the pleasures of coast and countryside. Most of all, Elmhurst had character and he liked that. The knowledge that he had the best of all worlds, gave Rafferty a feeling of contentment he'd never experienced anywhere else.

It was a feeling that had grown on him gradually, since he and his two brothers and three sisters had been unwillingly uprooted to Essex from London by his widowed mother. That was why, although it amused him to say he earned his living from crime, he hated it when the murder of a fellow human being tarnished the place.

He sighed again, less happily this time, and wiped his sweating face on the sleeve of his disposable overalls, conscious once more of the furnace heat caused by the high pressure that had lain punishingly over the southern half of England for the past two weeks. The horizon began to shimmer in dizzying fashion, and he lowered his gaze and prayed for rain, daunted at the uncomfortable prospect of conducting a murder inquiry in a heat wave.

With a wry smile, he sacrilegiously paraphrased one of Llewellyn's more edifying quotations, murmuring, 'Oh for the return of the green and sceptred isle brought by a bloody good thunderstorm.'

The meadow was a haven for wild flowers; hazy blues, corn-ripe yellows and regal purples nestled among the dry grass. There were masses of them, and, of course, he couldn't put a name to any of them. But as his sergeant, equally at a loose end, materialised beside him, he guessed he wouldn't need to. Llewellyn, his personal oracle, would be sure to know.

He did. 'There's Spiked Speedwell, and there's Corn cockle.' The Welshman pointed them out with a long, thin finger. 'Do you know, I haven't seen those for years? The Elmhurst Echo carried an article by the local Conservation Society about these last week. Apparently, there are several rare species in this meadow.'

'Miracle they've survived then, with the tyre dumping fraternity around,' Rafferty said deflatingly. Perhaps it was an effect of the weather, but, for whatever reason, his sergeant's encyclopaedia-like knowledge irritated him more than usual this morning. Glancing back at the activity concealed behind the screens, he was thankful to see Sam Dally rise from his labours and beckon them over. 'Come on, looks like Sam's finished.'

Conscious of his sergeant's critical gaze, Rafferty was careful to avoid stepping on any of the wild flowers, but the scattering of rare meadow flowers around the body, combined with his sergeant's serious countenance, encouraged Rafferty to a moment's wild speculation. What if the woman hadn't been murdered by the Suffolk serial killer at all? Perhaps she had been killed by one of the local "Green" community, outraged at her destructive flower-gathering? He let his mind go so far as to picture screaming "Killer Conservationist" headlines, before he regretfully dismissed the idea. It was pretty unlikely.

Sam, his face shocking pink from his exertions, nodded at the corpse. 'She can be taken away now. I can't do any more here.'

The victim's head, hands and feet had already been encased in paper in order to protect any forensic evidence, and as they watched, the entire cadaver was placed in a body bag, before it was carried to the waiting mortuary van.

'I'd say she died sometime yesterday afternoon,' Sam informed them. Briskly, he began gathering up his equipment. 'I'll have to wait till I've done the post mortem to be more definite, of course.' He glanced irritably at the innocent azure sky. 'This infernal heat doesn't help matters.'

Like a true-born son of the Scottish Highlands, Sam Dally preferred his mornings crisp and even, and he had no liking for "these damned unnatural Mediterranean heat waves", as he called the current weather.

'Cheer up, Sam. The weathermen say it'll break in a day or two.' As Dally snorted his derision of the entire meteorological breed and their promises, Rafferty added hopefully, 'I'd appreciate it if you could pin the time of death a bit closer.'

Sam scowled. 'I wish you'd get it into that thick Irish skull of yours that pathology is a bit more demanding than the average old British Rail timetable. They didn't have to get up in a court of law and defend their claimed departure times; I do.'

Having vented his irritation, Sam relented a bit. 'All I'll say is that I'd plump more towards the time you're enjoying your second cup of tea of the afternoon. Satisfied?'

Rafferty nodded. It narrowed the time down nicely. If Sam was right, the time of death had probably been between three and five o'clock yesterday afternoon. According to her sort of brother-in-law, the victim had last been seen alive at 3.00 p.m. Rafferty tried his luck further. 'Can you confirm the cause of death, Sam? Was she suffocated?'

'Probably.' He picked up his bag, and smiling for the first time that morning, he added before he walked away, 'but you'll not make me commit myself till I've done the pm.'

Rafferty hadn't expected anything more, but he was satisfied. To get a "probably" out of Sam was akin to a definite confirmation from anyone else.

Before he followed Dally, Rafferty had a word with the most senior member of the SOCO team. He wasn't surprised when he was told that they had, as yet, discovered nothing of obvious interest.

But it was early days, and their painstaking work would go on for some time yet, both at the scene of the crime and back at the laboratory. Still, he was hopeful, more so because it very much looked as if she had died where she had been found. The dry grasses under her heels had been reduced to tiny, broken stalks, as if her shoes had pummelled the ground as she had struggled with her killer.

The countryside just here was sparsely populated; apart from some farm buildings several hundred yards away across the fields, there were few houses, just the tiny village of St Botolphe further along the main road, towards Elmhurst.

Rafferty headed back to the car and got in the passenger seat. Llewellyn started the car and turned its nose in the direction of the Shores' house as Rafferty got on the radio to the station. As the meadow was in such a lonely spot, he doubted much would come of the house to house. He hoped they would manage to turn up more information from a second team, arranged to question the motorists using the main road adjacent to the meadow.

Radioing done, he sat back and thought about the victim. Had she been younger, he'd have thought it likely she had arranged to meet a lover and had gathered the flowers while she waited for him. But this woman was in her late twenties, according to Charles Shore, and likely to prefer her clandestine couplings on soft sheets rather than dry grass shucks and hard-baked soil.

So what had she been doing here? Surely, in this violent age, she hadn't just come to gather flowers, no matter how rare and enticing the local flora, especially in the flimsy get-up she had on. It was asking for trouble in normal times, but with a known killer just a few miles over the county border...

***

The only route from the meadow to the Shores' house was via a road full of meandering curves. Occasionally, as the highway wound lazily eastwards, back upon itself, and the hedgerows parted, they caught a glimpse of the river to their right, straight as a Roman road, the sun making a tarnished sheet of glass of its sluggish green surface. It shadowed as a flock of black and brown Brent Geese rose from the nearby mud flats, swooped low over the water and headed north, their plaintive 'rott, rott, rott' cry echoing across the still countryside, as if mocking Rafferty and his habit of constructing theories before he had any facts to back them up.

After about ten minutes, tall grey chimneys reared up above the river's west bank. The Shores' place, Rafferty guessed. From this distance, it had a touch of Victorian workhouse Gothic. The gloomy drive, edged with dusty, dark green, graveyard yews, bearing a miserly scattering of scarlet berries, disappeared behind the house. The house itself echoed the sombre theme. It was grotesque. There was no other word to describe it. So ugly, it had a peculiar fascination of its own, like an over-the-top first prize-winner in a bad taste contest.

Constructed in grey stone, at a distance, it had looked merely drably institutional. It was only as they got nearer that the appalling decorative reminders of death – the great modern day unmentionable – became visible. The roof-line was broken up with the most fantastic gargoyles; satyrs and devils, with evil, grinning, faces, clutched three-pronged forks and stabbed, with undisguised relish, the eternally damned human wretches sharing their strange eyrie.

Of course, to the Victorians who had built the place, sex was the great unmentionable, Rafferty reminded himself. They had been only too familiar with death, in its many guises.

As he stared again at the high-rise etchings, some details of the earlier tragedy in the Shore family came filtering back. Maximillian Shore, Charles Shore's father, had been murdered years earlier, blown to bits in his booby-trapped car. The old man had been a hard bastard, by all accounts, and although the case had never been solved, there had been a suspicion that one of his business rivals had been responsible.

Maximillian Shore – or Schurr as he'd been then, before he'd anglicised it – had had a tragic beginning. His parents, his entire family, had died at the hands of the Nazis. The only survivor, he had arrived in England, with just the clothes he stood up in; penniless, parentless and homeless. Yet he had thrived. Today, the Shore family empire was international and encompassed the wide arena of newspapers, chemicals and finance. It wasn't difficult to imagine the difficulties that the traumatised orphan must have had to overcome in order to acquire the wealth that had begun it all.

The grinning devils dancing on the roof must have appealed to old Maximillian when he bought the place, Rafferty reflected, as he recalled the stories the papers had dredged up after the old man's murder. With his early experiences, he would have known more about the evil core of humanity than most. After telling Llewellyn about the earlier tragedy in the family, he remarked, 'Not a lucky family, despite their wealth.'

'Every man is the architect of his own fortune,' was Llewellyn's murmured response. 'Sallust, sir,' he explained to Rafferty's blank face. 'He was a Roman historian at the time of Julius Caesar and he—'

'Yes, yes. Thanks for another piece of useless information.'

Llewellyn lapsed into silence and Rafferty, noting the glint in the Welshman's dark eye, wondered, not for the first time, if Llewellyn paraded his erudition out of sheer mischief.

It was impossible to deduce much from that impassive poker face. 'I mightn't know much about this Sallust Johnny,' Rafferty admitted briskly, 'but, one thing I do know, is that the Super will hang me out to dry if I make a mess of the case, so perhaps we can get on?' However, before he could carry out his good intentions, as they got closer to the house, the sound of youthful voices distracted him.

'Stupid, stupid. Mini Maxie's stupid.'

'I'm not stupid.' The older boy's deeper voice broke through the piping taunts. 'I'm not stupid,' the boy repeated. 'I'll prove it, just you wait and see.' But his boasts only brought more jeering laughter.

'You?' The younger boy's voice was shrill with spite. 'You can't even get basic grades without my father paying for extra holiday tuition.' In the precocious manner of modern children, he sneered, 'I heard him telling mother that if your mother had been his sister-in-law instead of his sister, he'd suspect you were the result of some affair and had no Shore blood at all.'

The sound of a blow broke into the stillness of the morning, and the older boy's voice, its triumphant note unmistakable, echoed towards them. 'You said it! At least I can be sure I belong here, as you'll realise before you're much older, which is more than can be said for you; with *your* mother.'

'You hit me!' Rafferty wondered why the younger boy should sound so surprised. He had certainly asked for it.

'Yes, and I'll hit you again, you little rat. It's about time somebody taught you some manners. Come back here!'

The next second, a well-built and weasel-faced boy of about ten raced around the side of the house, pursued by a tall, wiry youth, of about fifteen. The smaller boy easily avoided Rafferty, but the older one, probably because his eyes had that glazed, unseeing look brought on by anger, cannoned into him. He was panting heavily and as his vision cleared, he looked wildly from Rafferty to Llewellyn, before he tore himself out of Rafferty's grasp and continued his pursuit round the far side of the house.

'They must be old Max's grandchildren,' Rafferty remarked. As he wondered what relation the dead woman was to them, he spared them a moment's pity. The years of childhood were all too brief; if the relationship was a close one, it was likely that the dark, adult passions that had brought the woman's violent death would shatter their childhood forever. The thought depressed him.

He gave the gargoyles one final glance, tightened his eye-dazzling orange tie and made for the front door. Depressing or not, you've got a job to do, Rafferty, he reminded himself. Just climb out of the slough of despond and get on with it.

End of Extract

Down Among the Dead Men
This book is available at all good on line retailers.

BOOKS BY GERALDINE EVANS

Rafferty & Llewellyn British Mystery
Series

Game of Bones #18

The Spanish Connection #17

Asking For It #16

Kith & Kill #15

Deadly Reunion #14

Death Dance #13

All the Lonely People #12

Death Dues #11

A Thrust to the Vitals #10

Blood on the Bones #9

Love Lies Bleeding #8

Bad Blood #7

Dying for You #6

Absolute Poison #5

The Hanging Tree #4

Death Line #3

Down Among the Dead Men #2

Dead Before Morning #1

Casey & Catt British Mystery Series

A Killing Karma #2

Up in Flames #1

Biographical Historical Fiction

Reluctant Queen: The Story of Mary Rose Tudor, the Little Sister of Infamous English king, Henry VIII

Romantic Suspense/Thriller

The Egg Factory

Romantic Novels

Land of Dreams (Not yet in digital)

The Wishing Fountain*

Strangers on the Shore*

(*Writing as Maria Meredith)

Short Stories

A Mix of Six: Six Short-Short Stories

The Monarch's Gift: A Rafferty & Llewellyn Short-Short

The Station Thief: A Rafferty & Llewellyn Short-Short

Pond Life: A Rafferty & Llewellyn Short Story

Non-Fiction

How to Format Your Novel for Amazon's Kindle

Lovers' Life Guide: Palmistry dating guide (Life Guides Series)

**Writing Woes: How to Avoid them and Get it Right Next Time!

(New Age: Palmistry) **Written as Gennifer Dooley-Hart

BRITISH ENGLISH USAGE AND

SPELLING

This novel uses British English spellings and slang, some of which I've listed below so you can check any with which you are unfamiliar.

BRITISH SLANG: MEANING

A
(A suspect's) Brief: Lawyer
Autumn: Fall

B
Backhander: Bribe or To Smack Someone
Balked: Done out of
Bike: Woman of Loose Morals
Bits on the side: sexual partners
Bloke: Man
Box-clever: Use your brain
Bollocking: Stern reprimand
Born the wrong side of the blanket: Illegitimate child
Brief: A suspect's lawyer
Bright spark: Clever person
Builder's bum: Bottom cleavage
Buttie: Sandwich
By-blow: Illegitimate child

C

Chippie: Carpenter / Fish and Chip Shop / A person
inclined to be snappish (Chippy)
Cock-a-hoop: Delighted
Cock-a-snook: A derisive gesture
Come clean: Tell the truth
Coughed for: Admitted to crimes
Cracking up: Having a nervous breakdown
Cup of builder's: Strong tea
Cup of Rosie Lee (Cockney Rhyming Slang): Tea
Cut him much slack: Accept excuses

D
Daft: Foolish
Divvy up: Share out
Do a (moonlight) flit: Disappear suspiciously suddenly
Dodgy: Illegal
Dodgy person: A person of suspect morals (in a legal
sense)
Do/Doing a Bunk: Disappear (usually before the law or
creditors catch up with you)
Done a bunk: Ditto
Dosh: Money

EF
Easy: Morally lax (in a sexual sense)
'I'm easy': Happy to go along with everyone else
Fit up: Put the blame on a likely criminal
Flabbergasted: Astonished
Full wack: Full price

G
Geezer: Man
Get your marching orders: To be sacked, dismissed
Give someone a bell: Telephone someone

Give something the once-over: Check something out
Gnashers: Teeth
Gobsmacked: Astonished, shocked
God-botherer: Religious
Gormless: Lacking intelligence, stupid
(Got) Form: Got a criminal record
Grass up: Inform on someone to the police
Grotty: Horrible

HI
Hacked off: Far from pleased
Half-inch=Pinch (Cockney Rhyming Slang): Steal
Have it out: Brisk exchange of views
High-falluting: Fancy, posh
Iffy Whistle (Whistle and Flute=Suit (Cockney Rhyming Slang): Stolen suit of male clothing
In a jiff/jiffy: Quickly / Soon

JKL
Jammy git: Lucky man
Jiffy bag: Padded envelope
'Let's get cracking: 'Let's get on with it'

M
Measly: Very Little
Moolah: Money
More front than Brighton / 'You've Got Some Front: Plenty of chutzpah

NO
Old lags: Prison inmates
On someone's watch: While responsible for

PQR
Pikey: Traveller, Gypsy
Pillock: Idiot
Porkie pie (Cockney Rhyming Slang): Lie
Put the kibosh: Ended any hope
Rat-arsed/pissed: Drunk
Right Pillock: Total Idiot
Right plonker: Total idiot
Ruddy health: Very well

S
Scarper: Run away
Scrote: Insult, short for 'scrotum'
Scumbag=Slag (Cockney Rhyming Slang): Insult (low-life male character)
Short and curlies: Pubic hair
Short shrift: Abrupt and unsympathetic treatment
Shtum: Don't Tell Anyone, keep quiet
Slag: Toe-rag=Slag (Cockney Rhyming Slang): Insult (Low-life male character)
Slag: Insult (Female character of low morals)
Skedaddle: Make oneself scarce / Escape
Skive/skive off: Pretend to work/Take off, when supposed to be working
Smarties: Similar to M & M's
Snout: Police informer
Sparks: Electrician
Sparks'll fly: A situation will become inflamed
Spondulicks: Money
Sticky Situation: Difficult
Stroppy: Answer back (like a smartarse)

T
Taff, Taffy: Nickname for a Welshman

Take down a peg or two: Humiliate
Take the Mick/Mickey/Michael: Make fun of
Taradiddle: Petty lie/A fib
Tea-leaf (Cockney Rhyming Slang): Thief
Tetchy: Irritable, touchy, snappish
Toe-Rag=Slag (Cockney Rhyming Slang): Insult (Low-Life male character)
Tosh: Rubbish, garbage
Tosser: Insult (male given to personal sexual abuse)
Trick-cyclist: Psychiatrist
Trouble and strife (Cockney Rhyming Slang): Wife
Turn a girl's head: Make her smitten/keen on someone

UV
Up to one's eyeballs: Very busy

WXYZ
Wasted: Very Drunk
Welly: Wellington boot
(Give it some) welly: Give encouragement to do one's best
Whistle and flute (Cockney Rhyming Slang): Suit of male clothing
Wuss: Weakling
'You make me crack up': 'You make me laugh' (sometimes used in a sarcastic manner)
'You've Got Some Front': Plenty of chutzpah

BRITISH SPELLING v US SPELLING

Alternative-v-Alternate
Colour-v-Color
Grey-v-Gray
Labour-v-Labor
Neighbour-v-Neighbor

Organise-v-Organize
Practice (Doctor's Practice)-v-Practice
Practise (as in to practise doing something)-v-Practice
Queue-v-Line of people
Rationalise-v-Rationalize
Realise-v-Realize
Recognise: Recognize

There are lots more, I'll add them to my list as I think of them.

Printed in Great Britain
by Amazon